"WE

Barbara Price [...] h to do trying to keep [...] ss and the anthrax plague."

"I know," Aaron Kurtzman replied. "But I don't think we can pick our battles this time. Don't forget that Pakistan has also been a hotbed of millennium prophecies. If they've decided to twist them to include the Indians as legitimate targets for God's wrath, we might have more of a problem than we've had in the past."

"This is it, isn't it?" Price asked, her voice weary. "The Apocalypse? We have the crazies here in the States and the plague already, and now we have a nuclear war brewing. All we need now is a catalyst to set things in motion."

Other titles in this series:

STONY MAN II
STONY MAN III
STONY MAN IV
STONY MAN V
STONY MAN VI
STONY MAN VII
STONY MAN VIII
#9 STRIKEPOINT
#10 SECRET ARSENAL
#11 TARGET AMERICA
#12 BLIND EAGLE
#13 WARHEAD
#14 DEADLY AGENT
#15 BLOOD DEBT
#16 DEEP ALERT
#17 VORTEX
#18 STINGER
#19 NUCLEAR NIGHTMARE
#20 TERMS OF SURVIVAL
#21 SATAN'S THRUST
#22 SUNFLASH
#23 THE PERISHING GAME
#24 BIRD OF PREY
#25 SKYLANCE
#26 FLASHBACK
#27 ASIAN STORM
#28 BLOOD STAR
#29 EYE OF THE RUBY
#30 VIRTUAL PERIL
#31 NIGHT OF THE JAGUAR
#32 LAW OF LAST RESORT
#33 PUNITIVE MEASURES
#34 REPRISAL

#35 MESSAGE TO AMERICA
#36 STRANGLEHOLD
#37 TRIPLE STRIKE
#38 ENEMY WITHIN
#39 BREACH OF TRUST
#40 BETRAYAL
#41 SILENT INVADER

DON PENDLETON'S
MACK BOLAN®
STONY MAN™

Fall of the West Book I

EDGE OF NIGHT

A GOLD EAGLE BOOK FROM
WORLDWIDE®

TORONTO • NEW YORK • LONDON
AMSTERDAM • PARIS • SYDNEY • HAMBURG
STOCKHOLM • ATHENS • TOKYO • MILAN
MADRID • WARSAW • BUDAPEST • AUCKLAND

First edition September 1999

ISBN 0-373-61926-X

Special thanks and acknowledgment to
Michael Kasner for his contribution to this work.

EDGE OF NIGHT

Printed in U.S.A.

EDGE OF NIGHT

CHAPTER ONE

Oakland, California, July 3, 1999

Mack Bolan watched the video monitor in Able Team's surveillance van. The picture was black and white and of low quality, but it was coming from a hidden video pickup not much bigger than a quarter. Eight of the subminiature devices covered the deserted Oakland parking garage that still hadn't been repaired after the big earthquake. Even so, the Executioner could clearly make out the players.

Inside the garage, two members of Able Team were posing as New Age cultists in the market for some heavy-duty firepower. Rosario Blancanales was playing the cult's leader, with Hermann Schwarz acting as his assistant. The third Able Team warrior, Carl Lyons, was too obviously a hardman to carry off a role in this, so he was providing security for his teammates.

Bolan had to admit that Blancanales looked good in his part. With his hair slicked back, wire-rimmed glasses, a burgundy blazer over a banded-collar silk shirt, a solid gold Rolex watch on his wrist and Gucci loafers with no socks, he was the picture of New Age chic. It was the expensive briefcase in his left hand, though, that established his credentials.

The leather case contained a million dollars in hundred-dollar bills still bound with bank bands, a down payment on what was supposed to be a three-million-dollar deal for a shipload of ex-Soviet weapons. The balance would be due when the vessel docked at San Diego and the cargo was off-loaded.

The tiny video pickups weren't big enough to incorporate sound as well as picture, so Bolan was relying on subtle hand signals from Blancanales and Schwarz to let him know how the meeting was going. If something interrupted the game plan, Lyons had a radio to alert Bolan. But, until that happened, it was switched off so it wouldn't show up on a scanner.

The weapons dealers were Cubans and exiled Sandinista Nicaraguans, nine of them. Schwarz had signaled that only six men appeared to be armed, but even so, the odds weren't in Able Team's favor. Lyons was packing heavily, though, and his semiauto SPAS shotgun was loaded with frangible buckshot rounds. If the exchange went down wrong, he should be able to give his teammates those critical few seconds to reach cover before all hell broke loose.

When the Cuban counting the bills nodded, one of the Nicaraguans brought a microphone to his mouth and spoke into it. When he received a reply, he said something in Spanish to the Cuban, who nodded again.

When Blancanales rubbed the back of his neck in

the ''go'' signal, Bolan was ready. He clicked onto the satcom radio and keyed his microphone. ''Phoenix, this is Base. The exchange has been made and the signal has been sent to the ship. You're go to take them down, over.''

''Phoenix One, roger,'' David McCarter answered. ''We're moving now, over.''

''Good luck. Out.''

Off the Coast of Baja, California

A HUNDRED MILES off the western coast of Baja, California, the sixty-foot hydrofoil cabin cruiser carrying Phoenix Force accelerated and went up on her foils. At the helm, Calvin James, Phoenix Force's expert on all things marine, thrilled at the sudden rush of speed. Spinning the wheel, he banked his craft on a new heading to intercept the SS *Bonaventure,* steaming some twenty miles away in international waters. The Panamanian-registered freighter was a known cocaine runner, but this time her hold was full of ex-Soviet firepower, including several crates of Strella antiaircraft missiles.

''Take it easy up there, dammit!'' a voice shouted from the hydrofoil's afterdeck. T. J. Hawkins was trying to manhandle an M-2 .50-caliber machine gun onto its pintel mount, and the sudden maneuver had almost sent him and the gun over the side of the boat.

''I got it.'' Gary Manning jumped to assist his teammate with the heavy gun. There were lighter fifties in service now, but none of them had the range and dependability of the old Ma Deuce. The action they were headed for might require a little heavy fire support, and few guns were better suited to provide it.

"I sure wish I could have scored us a Vulcan cannon for this gig," Hawkins grunted as he shouldered the fifty onto the mount while Manning slipped the lock pin in place.

"The 20 mm's nice," Manning agreed, "but with its rate of fire, we wouldn't be able to carry enough ammunition for it. The fifty should do almost as much damage if we need it."

"What I'm worried about is the range," Hawkins explained, as he brought the .50-caliber ammo belt up to the breech. "If the bad guys are packing those Russian 14.5 mms as advertised, they'll be bringing fire on us long before I can get this old Ma Deuce on target."

Manning grinned. "That's why we have Calvin driving this bucket. He'll keep them from getting us in their sights."

Hawkins pulled back on the heavy machine gun's charging handle twice to chamber the first round. "He'd better, man. I won't look too good with big 14.5 mm holes in my T-shirt. I sunburn too easily."

"The Chicken Plate should keep them out."

Hawkins picked the twenty-five pound ceramic armored vest from the deck and shrugged into it. The door-gunner armor was supposed to be able to withstand up to 20 mm hits, but he wasn't interested in personally testing it.

"Are you lads ready?" David McCarter asked as he stepped out of the cabin.

Like the rest of the team, the ex-British SAS commando and leader of Phoenix Force was wearing deck shoes, chino trousers and a safari jacket instead of his usual work clothes. Showing up alongside of the *Bonaventure* wearing combat boots, camouflage battle dress, assault harness and automatic weapons would be a dead giveaway that they weren't the peace-loving, incense-burning New Agers they were supposed to be.

Rafael Encizo was dressed the same, but he sported one of those snappy little yachting caps with the crossed anchors embroidered on the peak and gold braid on the bill.

"Nice hat, Rafe." Hawkins grinned. "Last time I saw a guy with one of those things, he was also wearing women's panties."

"I'm glad you like it," Encizo said, grinning back. "I'll be sure to save it for you when this gig is over."

For once in his life, Hawkins was caught without a snappy comeback.

BACK IN OAKLAND, Bolan locked Able Team's van and reset the alarm before hurrying down the alley to the parking structure. It was about to hit the fan, and he had to plug the back door before the rats could get away.

The way these things usually went, the seller chose the meeting place so he wouldn't be walking into a trap, and that had been the case this time. But, as soon as the site had been picked, Able Team had prepared it for the meeting. Not only had they been able to install the video pickups, they had also moved a couple of forklift loads of concrete blocks to barricade the side entrances. When they were done, the garage had become a trap with only one way out.

Bolan's job was to make sure that the only way the Cubans and Nicaraguans could get out of the trap was either with their hands up, or in body bags.

As he entered the garage, he hit the electronic clicker in his pocket to arm the two Claymore mines Schwarz had hidden on each side of the entrance. They had been fitted with electronic sensor fuzes that would automatically detonate the mines if a vehicle tried to go either in or out.

With the door locked behind him, he headed up the ramp, his rubber-soled boots making little noise as he ran. As he approached the corner into the parking area, he heard the detonation of a flash-bang grenade echoing off of the concrete walls. The explosion was closely followed by the authoritative roar of Carl Lyons's SPAS assault shotgun, and the high-pitched chatter of the mini-Uzis both Blancanales and Schwarz had slung inside their jackets.

The party was starting without him.

WHEN IT WAS UP on the foils, Phoenix's hydrofoil was a steady gun platform. But when James cut the power to maneuver alongside the *Bonaventure*, the hull lowered into the water and the boat started tossing on the waves. Hawkins was crouched under the tarp, covering his fifty and holding tightly to the gun mount.

The plan was to get three of the Phoenix Force commandos on board, then try to take over the ship. If that failed, James would back off and they would try to sink the vessel by blowing holes in the hull with RPG launchers. There were more modern antitank rockets than the old Russian RPGs, but for this kind of general-purpose work, they were hard to beat.

As James maneuvered the hydrofoil alongside the freighter, a dozen men packing AKs appeared on her deck. The crew was accustomed to the inspection-at-sea drill, but they weren't taking chances, not even with customers who were supposed to be opposed to violence. A rope ladder was thrown over the side, and, as the Spanish speaker on the team, Encizo started up hand over hand, with Manning and McCarter close on his heels. No matter what happened afterward, if they could reach the deck, they'd have a fighting chance.

Hands reached down to help Encizo on board, and he started talking before his feet hit the deck to distract the welcoming committee. Manning was next on board, and he moved far enough away from Encizo's side to get a clear field of fire.

As McCarter climbed over the ship's side rail, his jacket caught on a stanchion and was pulled back far enough to reveal the H&K MP-5 SD slung at his side.

One of the sailors spotted the subgun and shouted.

Oakland

BY THE TIME Bolan rounded the corner of the parking garage, his 9 mm Beretta 93-R in his hand switched to 3-round-burst mode, the battle was well underway. Two of the gunrunners were facedown on the concrete, but the rest had taken cover behind the pillars and were returning fire at Able Team.

Before moving into the line of fire, Bolan keyed his throat mike. "Ironman," he called to Lyons, "I'm coming in behind them."

"Take your time, Striker," Lyons replied. "There's only three of them to every one of us."

"I'm on the way."

Blancanales hadn't managed to score any hits on his three yet. He crouched behind the trunk of their Mercedes four-door sedan, sending snap shots at three different targets, but the heavy return fire kept him from scoring.

Bolan's Beretta stuttered briefly, drilling a short burst of 9 mm slugs into the upper torso of the gunman working his way around Blancanales's left flank. The man spun from the impact of the slugs and fell face first onto the concrete.

"Your left's cleared, Pol," Bolan radioed.

"Thanks, Striker," Blancanales sent back. "I can handle the other two."

Bolan's arrival caused the gunmen to shift positions to try to cover him as well. As one of them broke cover, he crossed Lyons's line of sight and took the full force of one of the SPAS's frangible buckshot rounds. Eight of the ten pellets slammed into his upper left side. Upon penetration, each of the balls broke into four projectiles that tore their own pathways through his chest cavity. The effect was like running into a long burst of machine-gun fire, and he was dead before he hit the ground.

As that was the last of the SPAS's 8-round magazine, rather than stopping to fill up again, Lyons pulled his .357 Colt Python to finish the job. It roared and another man went down.

Seeing the odds shrink, the Cuban who had been giving the orders broke for one of the Cadillacs that had been driven to the meeting.

"Watch that one!" Blancanales shouted as he slapped a fresh magazine in the butt of his mini-Uzi.

"Let him go," Schwarz answered. "I want to see if my new gadget works."

Tires smoking, the Cadillac leaped forward, the Cuban crouching behind the wheel to present as small a target as possible. As it screeched out of sight around the corner, the detonation of the first Claymore echoed over the roar of small-arms fire. The explosion was followed by the sound of the car slamming into the wall.

With their leader gone, the three gunmen still on their feet had had enough, but they still weren't ready to give it up. They tried to fight their way to the pedestrian exit.

Blancanales stitched one man across the chest with his mini-Uzi, Lyons drilled one with a head shot and Bolan put three rounds into the heart of the third.

In the sudden silence, the air in the enclosed structure was thick with the hot smells of burned cordite and spilled blood. In the distance, the faint sound of a siren could be heard over the noise of the city.

"Don't forget your briefcase," Lyons reminded Blancanales. "We're out of here."

Off the Coast of Baja, California

THE SHOUTS FROM THE *Bonaventure*'s deck were the signal for Calvin James to hit his throttles and get clear of the ship so the fifty would have a good line of sight. For the next few minutes, the three Phoenix Force warriors on deck would be on their own. Hawkins whipped the cover off his fifty and laid on the butterfly trigger. The mix of tracers and armor-piercing .50-caliber rounds hammered the enemy's 14.5 mm gun in the bow of the ship.

The crew of the Russian heavy weapon hadn't been at their stations, and Hawkins's first burst was right on target. The .50-calibre slugs nearly tore the 14.5 mm gun off its mount. From there, he swept his fire along the deck.

On deck, McCarter, Encizo and Manning were holding their own. The hammering of Hawkins's fifty had done more than take out the 14.5 mm gun crew—it had sent everyone else diving for the deck to escape the heavy slugs. Being flat on their faces, however, made them perfect targets for the Phoenix Force trio. The battle didn't last another minute.

"You two do the cargo hold," McCarter ordered

after he radioed for James to return. "I'll search the cabins."

The olive brown crates in the ship's hold were marked in both Spanish and Russian. The Soviets had always been good about providing instructions in the intended user's language. Encizo quickly went over the crates and found that not only was everything Blancanales had ordered present, there were more crates obviously destined for another buyer.

"Everything's here," he reported to McCarter. "Strellas, RPG launchers, grenades and ammunition."

"Rig it for demo and let's get the hell out of here before the Coast Guard shows up. I don't want to have to try to explain this."

With Encizo's assistance, Manning quickly went to work rigging the crates for demolition. With all of the explosives contained in the weapon's warheads, all it took was a few blocks of C-4 plastic explosive, two rolls of detonation cord and a radio detonator to wire it all to go off at the same time. The explosion would blow the ship's bottom out and send it and the bodies of the crew deep into the Pacific Ocean.

When the job was done, they went back up on deck to discover McCarter with a slightly battered crewman in one hand and a duffel bag in the other. "Keep track of this," he said, handing the bag to Encizo. "It's the logbook and papers from the captain's cabin."

When the commandos were back on board the hydrofoil with their prisoner, James hit the throttle and headed the boat away from the *Bonaventure.* A mile distant, he came down off the foils and steered to parallel the freighter's path.

"Fire in the hole!" Manning called out the traditional blaster's warning as he hit the firing button. The crump of the explosion echoed over the water and gouts of black smoke shot through with flame billowed from the two cargo hatch covers as the bottom was torn out of the freighter. Almost immediately, she started settling in the water.

They stayed on station until the sea closed over the *Bonaventure*. "Let's head back," McCarter said. "We're finished here."

CHAPTER TWO

The Emirate of Oman

CIA Agent J. R. Rust stood in front of the window of his office in the U.S. Consulate building and looked out over the city of Muscat, the capital of Oman. The emirate wasn't large enough to rate having an official CIA station chief, so he was carried on the books as the consulate's security officer. A rose by another name, though, made him the chief spook.

The sun had just come up over the Gulf of Oman, and the low light angle gave the muted sand and earth colors of the crowded buildings the look of something from another age. A tourist to Oman might think that he had fallen into a location set for an *Arabian Nights* movie. But Oman in general, and Muscat in particular, had long since lost its fabled charm for him. He'd enjoyed about all of it that he could stand.

It wasn't just the normal discomforts of a Middle East posting that had gotten to him this time. He was an old hand in the Middle East and had spent most of the past twenty-five years there, and he had a permanent Clint Eastwood squint from peering into the sun. He was well inured to sand fleas, water rationing, Stone Age sanitation, having to smuggle in booze and 101 other inconveniences that faced any Westerner living in this part of the world. To complete his résumé, he spoke several dialects of Arabic, as well as Iranian Farsi, so he knew these people. He knew them cold.

Even with all of that going for him, Rust had a sinking feeling that he was going to end his career in this place, and it wasn't going be pretty. Something was going on down there in the narrow streets and crowded bazaars of Muscat, something serious. And try as he could, he just couldn't get a grip on it. For the past several months, the mood in both the mosques and the back alleys had been tense and expectant, and it had his hackles up. It reminded him entirely too much of Tehran before the return of Ayatollah Khomeini in 1979. That had been a textbook State Department rat-screw, and he'd been damned lucky to have gotten out with his balls intact.

With his linguistic abilities, Rust spent a lot of time in the town soaking up random intelligence. Because of his north Texas-German heritage, there was no way that his fair eyes and light brown hair were going to allow him to pass for a local, and he didn't even try. But knowing the language allowed him to eavesdrop anywhere he went, and he was hearing a lot. The problem was that it wasn't making much sense to him. For some completely unknown reason, the Muslims were talking about the coming millennium in the way that they usually talked about the return of the Mahdi.

Rust was well aware of the effect the millennium was having on most of the Christian world. But the "Millennium Madness," as the stateside media had started calling it, was supposed to be a purely Christian phenomenon. It was based on an inaccurate calculation of the year of the birth of Jesus, and medieval prophecies about his Second Coming.

It made a certain amount of sense for Christians with overactive imaginations to get excited about the year A.D. 2000, but the Omanis were Muslim. And like all Muslims, they didn't use the Christian calendar. To them, the year A.D. 2000 was going to be the year A.H. 1378, in the Year of the Hegira, counted from the prophet Mohammad's flight from Mecca. In the Muslim mythology of saviors and prophecies, 1378 shouldn't be a significant year, but that wasn't what he was hearing.

In particular, he was hearing the imams, the Muslim teachers, preach that the days of the West were numbered and that God was going to loose his vengeance on the unbelievers of the world. It was the usual message that Islam would sweep the world to proclaim God's glory that cropped up every few years or so. But this was the first time he had heard it tied into the Christian millennium.

Usually, he heard that kind of talk when the imams spoke of the Mahdi, the Shiite Muslim savior whose return was to usher in the Islamic triumph. The problem was that the Mahdi wasn't expected to come for another sixty years or so. Maybe with all the media coverage about the millennium, the imams had gotten their dates screwed up.

The biggest problem Rust had to deal with in Oman, however, wasn't the imams preaching doom, it wasn't Langley's indifference to his reports and it wasn't even the feeling that he was sitting on some kind of time bomb. The biggest problem Rust had to deal with was the American consul to Oman herself, Cynthia P. Blackworth. And the problem was coming to a head this day, the Fourth of July.

The silly Beltway bitch simply wouldn't take his advice on anything about the locals. She still thought that she was living in some ritzy suburb of Washington and insisted on acting as if she were. Worse than that, she treated the Omanis as if they were recent immigrants to her exclusive neighborhood. It was bad enough to have a female consul in a Muslim nation, but to have one who had her carefully coiffured head firmly planted in her overly broad fundament was a disaster in the making.

As a general rule, Rust didn't have trouble working with women. He was a man of the times and wasn't threatened by women in high places. Nor was he threatened by the third-rate political hacks who usually headed most American embassies and consulates as long as they took him seriously and utilized him as was intended. Not only did Cynthia Blackworth not take his advice on how to deal with the locals, she

"And may it be upon you and yours," Ali replied in the same tongue.

"Your father is well?" Rust asked.

"A merciful God has blessed him with health and wisdom."

"May he live long in God's grace. Can I get you something to drink, a punch?" Rust switched to English.

"Only a fruit juice, J.R.," Ali replied.

"Do you want something extra in it?"

Ali frowned. "No."

As Rust went to fetch the prince a glass of freshly squeezed orange juice, he realized that the situation was worse than he had thought. If Ali was passing up a chance for a little Jack Daniel's whiskey in his juice, something was wrong. As soon as this was over, he would get on the fax and update both Langley and the State Department.

Now that the prince was present, the ceremonies could begin. Once again, Blackworth hadn't invited any of the high-ranking military American officers stationed in Oman to her gala. The woman was decidedly antimilitary and refused to have "her" consulate darkened by warmongers. Rust had pointed out that the Fourth of July was a military holiday because it had taken guns and soldiers to make good the piece of paper that had declared the United States to be free of Great Britain, but she had refused to budge.

So, the ceremonies were purely political with no military pomp and dignity. Blackworth had followed his advice, though, and had cut most of the school-children's program. But she insisted on having the younger children sing an off-key version of "God Bless America." In the suburbs of Washington, it would have been considered cute. In Oman, it was considered a minor sacrilege, particularly for those Omanis who spoke English. The United States was a nation of unbelievers and God didn't bless infidels.

When Blackworth's poorly written and haltingly delivered speech was over, the crowd was released to mingle and eat. Rust noticed that the buffet offering American-style foods wasn't being sampled by many Omanis. And those who did were putting little more than fruits on their plates. On the other side of the court, though, the Arab-style buffet was doing well, but all the takers were Omani.

To give his trained ears something to do, as well as to get away from Blackworth, Rust ambled over to find his dinner. For a kid from a small Texas town, he had developed a real taste for roast lamb and couscous.

As soon as the last of the guests were gone, Rust retreated to his office to write up a report for Langley. Opening the cabinet of his private bar, he poured himself a tall glass of whiskey and dropped in a couple of ice cubes. Normally, he restricted himself to one drink a day, but after knocking that first one down, he went back for a refill. He had earned it.

Parking the glass to one side on his desk, he booted his computer and started composing his report. He started with a summary of the latest millennium rumors he had picked up in the bazaar and again asked if similar intelligence had been picked up in any of the other Middle Eastern stations. He had asked the same question before but had received no answer. If this was just something that was originating in Oman, that was one thing. If these prophecies were being repeated in other Arab nations, someone needed to start taking them seriously and find out what in the hell was going on.

Then he started reporting on the guests at the party, particularly young Prince Ali. His abrupt mending of his ways had to be significant. If nothing else, it could mean that he was starting to suck up to the conservative religious element in Oman, which could only spell trouble. Unlike his father in his younger years, Ali wasn't a man of inner strength, one who would go his own way and shape the nation to his own vision. He was a weak man and would do whatever the most powerful element of Omani society at the moment told him to do.

Rust hoped that the old emir held on long enough for him either to be transferred out or to retire. He had gone through the 1979 debacle in Iran, and he had no desire to have to go through something like that again.

He was just getting ready to send his report when the intercom buzzed. "Rust, this is Chambers in the dispensary. You might want to come down here."

The consulate didn't have its own doctor. The military hospital at the Muscat air base provided them on call. It did, though, have a two man in-house medical team, and Chambers was the chief medic.

"What's going on?"

"I think we've been hit with some kind of virus. I've got half a dozen really sick people, and two more are waiting for bed space. I've got a call into the air base for a doctor, but you might want to take a look at this as well."

Chambers had an irrational fear that the Arabs were going to take them out with a biological attack someday, and he could get a little tiresome on the topic. But if that many people had suddenly gotten sick, he needed to check it.

By the time Rust got down to the dispensary, the Air Force doctor and two medics were there. Chambers met him at the door and handed him a surgical mask. "Put this on. I don't want you catching whatever this is."

Rust nodded in the direction of the doctor who was bending over a patient on the examination table. It was Sara Harpen, Blackworth's social secretary. "Has he figured out what it is yet?"

As if he had heard the question, the doctor straightened. "Do you have a satcom radio here?"

"We do," Rust answered.

"I need to call Germany and get a medevac flight in here. You've got some real sick people, and they need to get to a fully staffed medical facility ASAP."

"Follow me, please."

BY THE TIME Rust and the Air Force doctor got back to the dispensary, Cynthia P. Blackworth was in residence, so to speak. She was sitting on the examination table, puking into a bucket Chambers was holding. If this was a foodborne illness, Rust would have expected to see her first in line. The way she had been wolfing down the double cheeseburgers and shrimp salad, a batch of mayo gone bad in the heat could have done her in. Maybe God would be good to him and make her sick enough to be sent back to the States.

"Doctor!" one of the Air Force medics called out. "We have a code over here!"

Not waiting to see the outcome of the medical emergency, Rust made his way past two more victims waiting in the hall to make a radio call of his own. The shit had hit the fan, and he needed to borrow an umbrella.

CHAPTER THREE

Stony Man Farm, Virginia

Summer in Virginia's Shenandoah Valley was pleasant in the last year of the twentieth century. Enough rain had fallen to keep the foliage and crops green and the heat close to something tolerable. The farm hands who worked at Stony Man Farm were thankful for the unexpected mild weather, as it made their day jobs a lot easier. At this time of the year, the crops needed a lot of attention so they'd survive to be harvested and preserve the Farm's cover as a viable agricultural enterprise.

In the Farm's computer room, however, Aaron Kurtzman wasn't paying much attention to the weather. Rain or shine, hot or cold, it didn't matter to him as long as he had a mission to track. With the Farm's tactical adviser, Yakov Katzenelenbogen, back in Israel for the funeral of an old friend, he was holding down both chairs for the duration. And with both Able Team and Phoenix Force in the field, he had his hands full. At least, though, having both of them working in the same part of the country made it easier. He didn't have to sweat keeping track of different time zones.

"McCarter says that they've secured the shipment and sent it to the bottom of the Pacific," he announced to the blond woman standing beside his wheelchair.

"Thank God." The relief in Barbara Price's voice was real. "The last thing in the world we needed right now was for a shipment of Strellas to hit the West Coast."

"We don't really need that stuff anywhere in the country," Kurtzman said amending her statement. "Not with the millennium turning out the way it is."

She shook her head. "I wonder what's going to be next?"

Kurtzman knew that was a rhetorical question on one hand, but deadly serious on the other. The Millennium Madness was bringing the least-stable elements of American society out of the woodwork in droves. There was still half a year to go before the year 2000 arrived, and already every law enforcement and intelligence agency in the country was working overtime trying to keep New Year's Day 2000 from being a bloodbath. They had their hands full, and the President had asked the Stony Man action teams to give them a hand.

"So far, at least, these cases we've been given haven't been all that difficult to work," he said. "The people involved aren't the nation's best and brightest by far. But the lunatic fringe rarely is."

"What I'm afraid of, though," Price said, "is that

we're picking off all the easy cases up front and the difficult ones will surface later. And all at the same time.''

So far, Stony Man Farm had been tasked only with taking care of the situations that raised immediate national security concerns or required the swift application of deadly force to be brought to a successful conclusion. These were the same guidelines they followed for their more usual covert counter-terrorist operations, so they were well accustomed to the routine.

What made their missions different was that instead of going up against terrorists bent on destroying America for political or ideological reasons, their targets were mostly people who really believed in the myths of the coming millennium. That didn't, however, make them any less of a threat to the safety and security of the nation. As the Stony Man team knew only too well, a man who believed too much could be a serious danger no matter what those beliefs were. And since these people sincerely believed that Western civilization was headed for a total collapse, they were arming themselves for the Armageddon they believed was sure to follow.

Arming for self-protection was one thing. There were few households in the United States now that didn't own at least one self-defense weapon. In mid-1999, the best way for a politician to suddenly find himself out of work was to start lobbying for gun control. With the millennium crazies out there, no one wanted to hear about someone taking away their guns.

The real problem, though, wasn't with individual gun owners. It was with fringe groups that were arming themselves to take out their neighbors.

Everyone from New Age cults to Christian fundamentalist militia groups was buying weaponry like someone was holding a fire sale. With such a ready market in the United States, everyone from ex-socialist governments to terrorist groups was dumping their excess hardware for top dollar. And not all of the weaponry being smuggled into the country was high tech or even that modern. A shipment of British Number 5 Mills grenades left over from World War I had been intercepted and confiscated.

"Maybe with all the arms shipments that have been intercepted, the word will get out that it's not worth taking the risk," Kurtzman suggested.

"Fat chance of it ever being that easy," Price snorted. "We're going to be up to our belt buckles in this for several more months, six to be exact, before this even starts to clear up."

"Then there will be the aftermath of Armageddon."

"Don't remind me."

"In the meantime, though," Kurtzman said as his hands danced over his keyboard, "until Hal calls us again, I'm going to use this time to get caught up on what's been happening in the rest of the world."

"While you're doing that," Price replied, "I have to go back to my office and work on the semiannual budget. I really wish that Hal would get us someone to take care of the paperwork, so I could devote all of my time to the operations.''

"It'll never happen," Kurtzman grinned.

"Don't rub it in."

Now THAT THE LATEST millenium mission was concluded, Kurtzman was happy to go back to what he really liked to spend his time doing—cruising through cyberspace looking for the early signs of a developing crisis. The information was out there and he had access to it.

All over the world, the summer of 1999 was producing a bumper crop of intelligence, but not a lot was going on militarily. There were no major wars in the offing and only a few local squabbles, all of them in Africa. Nonetheless, he kept updated on them in case they started getting out of hand. No one wanted to see another Rwanda or Zaire pop up while everyone's attention was focused on other things.

The biggest producer of intelligence information this year, both foreign and domestic, was the approach of the third millennium. Like any man of science, Kurtzman knew that the new millennium wouldn't really start until New Year's Day 2001. But he also knew that for most people, including those who really should know better, the countdown to the year 2000 was on.

For some Americans, all-night celebrations had been planned, the hotels were booked solid and they were waiting for the biggest party of the century. Others, however, were in a blind panic expecting the end of the world to occur.

The list of who fell into which camp was long and complicated. For instance, Hispanic-American Catholics tended to expect Armageddon, while most Irish Catholics didn't. Many of the New Age groups expected the dawn of a Golden Age, while others were building bunkers to ride out the storm. Even the more fundamentalist Protestant groups were divided between those who expected the world to end in flame and those who expected the Second Coming.

Considering the diversity of culture and belief in the United States, that wasn't unexpected. The big surprise, though, was the effect the millennium was having on the rest of the world.

Kurtzman had been amazed when he had learned how many nonwestern countries had gotten involved in the Millennium Madness as it was being called in the media. The millennium was Christian mythology, but it was being taken to heart by the non-Christian world. For every Westerner who was gearing up for either the Apocalypse or the biggest party of the century, there were dozens if not hundreds of Asians, Africans, Middle Easterners and others, who also waited. Most of them didn't know what they were waiting for, but they were convinced that change was coming and that change wasn't necessarily a good thing.

This was specifically true in the Muslim nations. The Muslims were not seeing the Virgin Mary in every road sign or water seep, but they still believed in the power of the millennium. They believed in it so much that imams had popped up all over the Islamic world preaching prophecies that the millennium would ring in the destruction of the West and the triumph of Islam all over the world.

It was difficult, though, for Kurtzman to accurately gauge how widespread these rumors were. Most of the Western embassies in the Muslim world were not reporting on this phenomenon. His best information had come from the CIA security officer at the U.S. Consulate in Oman, a J. R. Rust.

Apparently the man was a talented Arabic linguist and had gone to great lengths to go outside the consulate's walls to take the pulse of the local population. That was the job of the CIA staff at foreign embassies, but this guy was working overtime at it. He had filed several detailed reports with the CIA headquarters at Langley on the prophecies.

According to Rust's reports, the imams were saying that a cache of ancient writings from the time of the prophet had recently been uncovered in the holy city of Mecca. These writings weren't being credited to Mohammad's hand. That would be blasphemy and the punishment for that crime was death. But claiming that they were from the prophet's era and that they had been found in Mecca gave them great credibility to the Islamic faithful.

These prophecies spoke of God taking vengeance on the unbelievers of the world and bringing death to them so that Islam would become the single, undisputed ruler of every nation on earth. The concept was so outlandish and unrealistic that no one seemed to be taking it seriously. For instance, there were no State Department comments on it at all. But that wasn't unusual. State was often the very last ones to notice something that was happening right under their noses.

Kurtzman had put marker programs on all of his feeds to tag all incoming messages about problems in the Middle East, and when the icon told him that he had a hot one, he clicked on it.

According to the report that flashed up on his screen, almost the entire staff of the U.S. Consulate in the Emirate of Oman had come down with some kind of disease. An emergency call had gone out for them to be medevaced to a military hospital in Germany, and the Air Force was rushing in a couple of C-141 hospital planes to fly them out.

That in itself wasn't alarming. According to the report, the staff had started falling ill after a midday Fourth of July party. Potato salad or caviar that sat too long in the sun was notorious for felling party-goers with the age-old malady commonly known as the outhouse quick step. What was different about this epidemic was that only the American personnel had been affected. And whatever they had gotten was serious.

Two of the Oman staff, including the consul, Cynthia Blackworth, had died before they could be evacuated. Several more had died during the flight to Germany, and the survivors were all in critical condition. But the fact that the Omani help at the consulate hadn't been affected would make it easier to track down what had been contaminated, something that only the U.S. personnel had eaten. The hospital in Germany should be able to get this sorted out quickly, and he would go back to it then.

Tagging the Omani report for instant retrieval, Kurtzman continued his cruise through cyberspace. There was so much information and so little time.

Oman

CIA AGENT J. R. RUST worked feverishly to shred and burn all of the classified documents in the Oman consulate. He was the only member of the U.S. staff who had still been on his feet when the medevac planes took off, and he had volunteered to stay behind to do what had to be done. He had a government-issue 9 mm Beretta 92 pistol strapped to his waist and an M-16 leaning against the wall, but he knew that the weapons weren't going to do him a hell of a lot of good if the mob outside the walls decided to storm the compound.

He still had three of the Omani local contract security guards on the gate, but he knew they were more symbol than substance. Even if he still had the full contingent of the twenty-four guards that he'd had on contract before the Fourth of July party, it wouldn't help. Not with that crowd out there. As he fed documents into the shredder, he had the windows open so he could hear what the imam was telling the crowd. Since the imam was using a battery-powered megaphone to harangue his listeners, every word was coming through loud and clear.

If he heard him tell his followers to storm the compound and kill the infidels, Rust intended to go up to the roof and sell his life as expensively as he could. He didn't have a death wish, but he also had no intention of going through a repeat of what the embassy people in Tehran had suffered in 1979.

But so far the imam wasn't howling for his blood. In fact, he was being rather calm for a fundamentalist rabble-rouser. He kept catching bits and pieces of the harangue where the imam was giving praise to God for having struck down the unbelievers. That was the usual take on an incident like this—give God the credit. But this time, the imam wasn't extolling the crowd to take advantage of the divine intervention and take out their frustrations on the survivors. In fact, he was urging his listeners not to take righteous vengeance on the infidels. He was telling them to leave it all in the hands of God.

Rust knew that approach raised his chances of getting out of this thing alive, but it just didn't sound right to him. Now that the imam had the infidels on the run, as it were, why was he letting them off the hook? Usually an incident like this ended with howling fanatics burning the building to the ground and dancing in the ashes. As long as he had worked in the Middle East, Rust still couldn't predict what the locals were going to do.

Whatever the reason was, though, he wasn't going

to argue with the man. If the imam could keep the crowd under control for another half hour, he'd be finished and could call for the evacuation bird. Maybe he'd live to collect his pension after all.

THE SYRIAN WATCHED the helicopter touch down on the roof of the U.S. Consulate just long enough for the last American to scramble on board. The compound was empty of the unbelievers now and was guarded by only the last handful of the faithful who still took the foreigner's gold. It would be easy enough to drive them off, but there was no reason for him to go inside the compound now. There was nothing of value he could learn there because the prophecies had come true just as they had been foretold.

The curse of God had struck a blow at the great Satan of the United States, and there was nothing the Americans might be plotting that would be of any importance now. From this point on, no matter what they tried to do, they wouldn't escape the righteous wrath of God.

They had been struck down in Oman as they would soon be struck anywhere that they polluted the lands of Islam. And the Yankees weren't the only infidels who would feel God's wrath. The British and French would also suffer for their sins against the faithful. The millennium was coming. It would usher in the triumph of Islam all over the world.

God had foretold that this would come to pass, and

he had been privileged to witness the start of it with his very own eyes.

The Syrian gathered his few belongings and left his observation post. The Air Omani flight to Damascus was leaving in a few hours, and he would be back in Syria tonight. From there, he would make his way to the mountain on the Turkish-Syrian border and make his report to his master.

There, too, he would be rewarded for his work as was always the case with those who hadn't failed the master. Once more he would taste the delights of paradise with his own lips and would know the bliss that awaited the faithful who did well in God's eyes.

CHAPTER FOUR

Cairo, Egypt

The uncontrollable sprawl that was called Cairo was an unmitigated urban disaster on the Nile, an Islamic version of Mexico City. Less than a thousand years ago, the city had been the capital of the Fatimid Dynasty, which had ruled an Islamic empire stretching from the Atlantic to the Persian Gulf. Even when Cairo's Arab rulers fell to the Turks, it had long remained a powerful city, the jewel of the Nile.

Today, Cairo was a study in contrasts that spanned the centuries. On one side of a six-lane boulevard stood a tattered Victorian grand hotel built during British rule. To one side of it were several hundred-year-old two-story shops with apartments on the top floor. On the other side, a modern glass-fronted office building with satellite dishes and a helicopter landing pad on the roof had been built. Across the boulevard, crowded with everything from donkey carts to air-conditioned Mercedes tour buses, was a small, newly restored Turkish palace that served as district office of the

Egyptian National Police. It was a jumble that delighted tourists from all over the world.

As one left the center of Cairo and headed south, however, the startling mix of today and days long past ended. In this part of the city, everything had been built in the past twenty years or so, but it looked like a neglected ancient slum. The small mud-brick structures, huddled together along narrow, unpaved alleys, were interspaced only by brushwood pens holding malnourished goats. Since modern sanitation in these slums was nonexistent and water was too precious to waste on bathing, the reek of unwashed humanity mixed with rancid cooking oil and the stench of animal droppings to create an atmosphere that only someone who lived there could endure.

Needless to say, Cairo's growing affluent classes and foreigners didn't often visit that part of town. But it was there that Egyptians who had nowhere else to go went to live, and they went in droves. Some of them were farmers who had lost their lands to development, unpaid taxes or bad luck. Others were herders, small shopkeepers, craftsmen, orphans or other dispossessed people who had found an emergent, increasingly modern Egypt incompatible with their ancient ways of life.

The only thing that these marginal peoples had in common was that they were uneducated in the ways of the modern world and they all had large families. The median age in these slums was well under twenty. An entire generation of young men was growing up who would have no chance of making a living in the modernized Egypt of the coming millennium. They had little to look forward to except unremitting poverty and a life of poorly paid physical labor.

Often, a population of this kind became a hotbed of political radicalism in an attempt to equalize the inequities all around it. In Egypt, however, the underclass had turned to religious radicalism instead, and fundamentalist Islam ruled in Cairo's slums. The imams of the small mosques scattered through this area reminded the faithful of the Muslim glories of ages past and preached a future when those glories would again return.

The imam of one of these mosques looked out over his congregation as he proclaimed the greatness of God. From his accented Arabic, the worshipers knew him to be a foreigner, but a man of God had no nationality. It was enough that he had wisdom and the word of God. That this imam brought word of the newly discovered ancient prophecies coming true had packed the small building to overflowing.

The whispers about the ancient writings that promised a better life for all of God's faithful had swept through the narrow alleys and crowded huts of Cairo's slums like a desert storm. Anything that promised the people hope of escaping a life of hand-to-mouth poverty and uncertainty was welcomed. None of these people would think to question how and why God had suddenly decided to become involved in their lives. It was only important that he had.

"As the prophecies foretold," the imam shouted so

all could hear him, "God the merciful has struck the first blow to free the lands of the believers from the contamination of the infidel. The great Satan of America has been driven from the lands of Oman, never to return."

A gasp passed through the crowd of worshipers. In their minds, all of the troubles of the world could be laid at the feet of the Americans, and anything that dealt a blow to the great Satan was miraculous.

"In this glorious time," the imam continued, "watch in wonder as God brings forth his vengeance. His hand is upon the infidels and they cannot escape it. But, beware his wrath because his eyes are on all of us and his reach is wide. Do not contaminate yourself or allow your family members to become contaminated with the things of the West. Remain pure in God's eyes. Eat and drink only that which is permitted. Avoid contact with the unclean and God will pass you over. If you ape the ways of the unclean, however, you too will pay the price that God is extracting from those who do not follow his law."

When the worshipers left the mosque, they hurried home to tell their families what they had heard. Those men whose children had found jobs in the foreign tourist trade forbid them to go back to work lest they be contaminated and fall to God's wrath. In many cases, this would cut the family's already marginal income to nothing and reduce them to begging. But it was more important to obey the imams than it was to eat.

Stony Man Farm, Virginia

"AARON," HUNT WETHERS CALLED across the computer room, "the hospital in Germany has identified the disease that took out the Omani consulate. They got hit with a mutant strain of anthrax."

Kurtzman wasn't too surprised to hear that. It would have taken something that serious to have caused the deaths that it had. At the latest count, almost half of the Omani victims had died and none of the rest were out of danger yet.

"And that can only mean that it wasn't an accident. Someone has declared biological war on us."

Kurtzman nodded his agreement. Anthrax was one of history's oldest diseases. The name itself came from the ancient Greeks who had written about it attacking their sheep and cattle. In its natural state, it could cross over to human populations, but it required specific conditions for that to happen, so it was rare. In a mutated form, however, all bets were off.

Because of the genetic makeup of the *Bacillus anthracis* that caused the infection, it was relatively easy to mutate in a laboratory. For that reason it had been among the first natural disease-causing pathogens that had been tried out as a possible weapon of war. As with all the other biological war agents, the anthrax bacillus had been modified to make it more deadly by enhancing its ability to attack humans.

"Didn't the British have an accidental release of mutated anthrax at one of their bio-war facilities back in the fifties or sixties?" Wethers asked.

Kurtzman thought back. "That's right, on that little island in the Channel they were using as an experiment station. If I remember correctly, it killed a couple of the researchers and they had to abandon the lab. I think they even considered nuking the place to sterilize it and keep it from spreading. Anyway, that accident pretty much put an end to anthrax experimentation in the West."

"So, the question is who's been messing around with that nasty little bug now?"

"I think we'd better start by looking at the usual list of suspects," Kurtzman stated.

"The so-called terrorist states?"

"Them as well as the remaining Communist regimes and any of the narco nations."

"How about the Eastern Europeans?"

"Them too," Kurtzman agreed, smiling slightly. "We don't want to be accused of being biased. We're an equal-opportunity agency here and we abide by all of the pertinent federal EEOC regulations on finding the scumbags who are behind this latest crime against humanity."

"I'll get right on it."

"Make sure that you check in with our contact at the CDC. Their Brush Fire teams will be on top of this, too, and we might save each other some time that way."

The federal Center for Disease Control in Atlanta was the world's top chaser of dangerous diseases. It had its Brush Fire teams and equipment on standby ready to be rushed to anyplace on earth where a new disease cropped up. Mostly the teams ended up going to Africa and South America where Mother Nature was always busy cooking up new pathogens to rid herself of the humans who plagued her. HIV, Ebola and hemorrhagic fever were only a few of her most popular ways to kill off humankind.

"Will do."

"And while you're doing that," Kurtzman stated, backing his wheelchair from behind his work station, "I'll go give Barbara the good news."

California

THE HYDROFOIL CRUISER Aaron Kurtzman had arranged for Phoenix Force's use was moored in a San Diego marina where it was doing double duty as team house and barracks. The boat slept six in the cabin, and there was room for overflow on the deck.

Rather than recall the Phoenix Force commandos to the East Coast after the S.S. *Bonaventure* raid, Barbara Price had left them in California, anticipating their going into action in that area again soon. While there was no shortage of millennium nutcases anywhere in the nation, there seemed to be more of them in California than in any five other states combined. Part of that was simply because California was by far the most populous state, but most of it was that the Sunshine State had long been a magnet for the disaffected and the lunatic fringe.

Now that the third millenium was being rung in, it seemed that every maniac with the price of an Amtrak ticket in their jeans or backpack was headed for California and not just for the major cities. From Yreka to the Mexican border, the police and the social service agencies were working overtime to try to control the mob. But it wasn't working, and San Diego was as good a place as any to see that it wasn't.

As Phoenix Force enjoyed its stand-down in San Diego, the men couldn't avoid seeing what was happening in the city. The hydrofoil's mooring slip was on the southern side of the marina, and they had a commanding view of the beachfront chaos outside. With the threat it represented, David McCarter had ordered around-the-clock deck watches, and the craft was ready to put to sea at a moment's notice.

The marina was surrounded by a chain-link fence topped with razor wire and patrolled by a private guard force, so it was more or less secure. Each night, though, several unauthorized visitors had to be extracted from the wire. The public beach on both sides of the marina looked like a combination of the Woodstock Nation, a homeless convention and the world's biggest beach party.

Too many people to count had simply moved onto the beach and staked out a claim. Everything from camping tents, to makeshift lean-tos, sleeping bags and tattered blankets marked someone's home away from home. The dress code was optional as well as behavior. When the city's police force hadn't been able to clear the beaches, they stopped even trying. The best they could do was to station a couple of ambulances and squad cars at a nearby fire station to carry off the bodies.

Each morning, the medics and the cops swept the beach to pick up the ODs, the stoned swimmers who had gone into the surf and washed up drowned, the slashed and shot from drunken brawls and those who had simply died. Little effort was made to do more than tag them and bag them before delivering them to the coroner's office.

Even there, most of the bodies were given only a cursory medical examination and had their photos and prints taken before going into cold storage. With the death rate in San Diego having soared to three times its normal rate, space was at a premium. The bodies that remained unclaimed after two weeks were cremated and the ashes put in another storage facility.

The millenium dead were being treated as if they were victims of a war, which in a way, they were. As in all too many American cities, San Diego was at war with the forces of irrationality, and the outcome was seriously in doubt. Civilization could only exist when the majority of the people agreed to conduct themselves by certain rules and standards. The opposite of civilization is anarchy, and anarchy isn't kind to cities.

If San Diego survived the millenium, then an effort would be made to figure out who the stored dead had been. Until then, they would rest in cheap cardboard boxes with their case number scrawled on the top with a black felt-tip pen.

"You know," T. J. Hawkins mused as he stood the afternoon radio watch in the pilothouse with Gary

Manning, "I've been to a couple of all-night beach parties and a few family picnics in my time, but I'll be damned if I've ever seen such a rat screw in all my life. It's a good thing that my aunt Matilda isn't here to see this. She'd come down with a terminal case of the vapors. We'd have to give her a whole bottle of her medicine just to revive her."

Manning chuckled. Though he was a Canadian, he'd been working with the American version of English for a long time now. But being around Hawkins and his down-home Southernisms was a continuing education.

"What kind of medicine did she take?"

"Sour mash."

WHILE PHOENIX FORCE enjoyed its stand-down, Able Team was hard at work. They were base-camped in a motel where they were working with the prisoner Phoenix Force had recovered from the *Bonaventure*. Carl Lyons was an old hand at prisoner interrogation. That didn't mean that he liked it, because he didn't, but he also didn't shrink from it. It was just part of his job, and he always did his job well. He had to admit, though, that the way he did it with Able Team made a hell of a lot more sense than how he'd had to do it when he'd been wearing an LAPD badge.

For one thing, there were no lawyers involved, and he didn't have to play stupid mind games with the perp to try to sneak something past some public defender. Calvin James had provided them with an interrogation cocktail. Plug it into the guy's arm, and he'd be eager to tell you everything he had ever known.

"Our man is about ready to go," Gadgets Schwarz said as he monitored a brain-wave scanner and adjusted the IV drip.

Though Able Team hadn't been able to take a prisoner in the Oakland parking garage shootout, Phoenix had been kind enough to capture the S.S. *Bonaventure*'s first mate when they took the ship down on the high seas. Having the captain might have been better, but since the first mate usually saw to the handling of the ship's cargo, he could prove even more useful in the long run.

Now that their man was ready, Rosario Blancanales stepped up to the plate to do his thing—talk to the guy. Even with the drugs coursing through his system, chemically removing his inhibition and fears, having Lyons on his case would likely cause him to go into cardiac arrest. Lyons wasn't called the Ironman for nothing.

"Your name is Ramon, right?" Blancanales asked in Spanish.

"Ramon Garcia, yes."

"And you are the first mate on the *Bonaventure*?"

"Yes."

"Okay, Ramon, I'd like to know…"

CHAPTER FIVE

Washington, D.C.

Hal Brognola sat in his Washington, D.C., Justice Department office quietly crunching a pair of Maalox antacid tablets as he went over the notes he had taken at the emergency meeting in the Oval Office.

Besides the President and himself, only the secretary of state, the national security adviser and the director of the CIA had been invited to the meeting. The topic had been the anthrax terrorist attack on the consulate in Oman, and that information had to be kept locked up tight. With the millennium coming, there would be blind panic on a national scale if word of it got out.

A carefully worded State Department press release had blamed the mass malady in Oman on food poisoning. The fact that so many people had died and the others were still hospitalized had been glossed over. Millennium Madness was causing enough panic in the country as it was without adding to it by announcing that an unknown enemy had used a biological weapon against the United States. A mysterious disease would fit right in with the fears of too many of the population. One of the Four Horsemen of the Apocalypse was named Pestilence.

At the beginning of the meeting, the President had informed the others that Brognola was to head the investigation and that they were to cooperate with him to the fullest extent. The Man also imposed executive classification on all information about the incident and required that the access list be personally vetted by himself. He emphasized that under no circumstances was anyone to be informed without his consent, and that included the vice president as well as the congressional leaders. No matter how it turned out, there would be hell to pay on Capitol Hill when this was over, but it had to be that way for now.

Brognola was used to working within these tight guidelines, they were standard operating procedure for almost all of the Stony Man operations. Though he was still carried on the federal register as a Justice Department official, his real job was that of special liaison to the President, and the leader of the Stony Man Sensitive Operations Group. It was a long way from his earlier days as an organized-crime buster, and at times like this, he wished that all he had to worry about were Mafia punks wearing flashy pinky rings and white ties. Looking back on those days, he realized how uncomplicated life had been then.

With this kind of executive branch security lock on the investigation, he couldn't risk even using the secure phone to alert the Farm team. He would present this situation to them in person. Before he flew down, though, he had a couple of calls to make.

During the briefing, he had noted that the CIA security officer in Oman, J. R. Rust, hadn't been affected by the anthrax attack that had felled everyone else. This same agent, he also learned, had been the author of a series of well-detailed field reports on the Islamic prophecies about the Western world being destroyed during the dawn of the millennium. Several other station chiefs at U.S. embassies in the Muslim world had made passing comments about these vague threats to the United States, but no one except Rust had taken the time to look into them in any detail.

The man was either a psychic or he was damned lucky. Either way, Brognola wanted to bring him in on this, and the fact that he was CIA meant that he wouldn't have to be taught about security.

Reaching for the secure phone on his desk, he hit the speed dial for the private line for the director of Central Intelligence.

"Jim?" he said when the line was picked up. "Hal Brognola here. Look, I have a favor to ask regarding our recent meeting with the Man. I need to borrow one of your field agents for a while."

Virginia

J. R. RUST WAS IN THE MIDDLE of a lengthy debriefing at the Langley, Virginia, CIA headquarters when he got a message to report to the director immediately. It wasn't often that an agent of his rank got to meet the director and even rarer yet for him to be invited to go to his penthouse office. As he headed for the special express elevator that went to the director's suite on the seventh floor, he wished that he had worn a cleaner shirt and his other suit. On the trip up, he vainly tried to polish the tips of his shoes by rubbing them against the backs of his pant legs.

The director didn't waste time with social pleasantries. "Rust, your debriefing has been canceled and you are to report immediately to Andrews Air Force Base. You are being assigned to work with a Justice Department man, a Hal Brognola, and you will consider his authority to be the same as mine."

Rust was stunned. Even though the Company and Justice were both federal agencies, they weren't on the best of terms and never had been. The whys and wherefores of that were long and complicated and had more to do with political turf wars than anything else, but they were real. For him to have been picked for this particular assignment meant that he was deep in the shitter with someone.

"May I ask what this is about, sir?"

The director fixed his eyes on him. "It has to do with your expertise in the Middle East. Mr. Brognola will brief you as necessary."

Rust knew better than to ask more questions at this point. "Yes, sir."

"And, Rust..."

"Yes, sir."

"You are not to mention this assignment to anyone without my specific permission. No one."

"Yes, sir."

"The car is waiting for you."

Stony Man Farm

BARBARA PRICE LEANED BACK in her chair when Aaron Kurtzman finished telling her about the mutated anthrax. "If this is the first shot in a new terrorist war," she mused, "I wonder why they tried it out first in Oman? In the grand scheme of things in that part of the world, it's a nothing place. What is it anyway, maybe a million and a half people? There's only one airport in the whole place and that's in Muscat, the capital city. As soon as the oil runs out, those people are going to take a great leap back into the Middle Ages. I don't think running us out of there makes much sense."

"But in one way it does," Kurtzman replied. "Which is probably why they chose it as the opening shot. The operative point is that the Omanis are living in 1999 with a Middle Ages mentality. They might have laptops, watch satellite TV and drive Toyota pickups, but they don't realize how long it takes to go from breeding racing camels to manufacturing internal combustion engines and silicon microchips."

She frowned. "But what does that have to do with making our consulate there a target?"

"With their mindset, the Omanis can believe in ancient prophecies about the millennium wiping out their traditional enemies without thinking that if it does, it will destroy the standard of living they now enjoy. They also won't be looking for a scientific explanation as to why this took place in their small country, much less how. They'll just see it as being the hand of God at work, and they'll tell all their neighbors that the prophecies are coming true.

"In fact," he said with a smile, "I'll bet you a week off that when I check with our news clipping service I'll find the story has already reached every Muslim population in the world from Bosnia to Pakistan. Whoever was responsible for the attack will have insured that."

"I know better than to take a bet like that, Aaron," she replied. "But if you're right about the attack being keyed into those prophecies, this won't be an isolated incident. If the President doesn't want to see more embassy people die, Hal had better get us involved in this ASAP."

"We already are," he replied. "I've got Hunt and Akira working on a list of likely suspects already."

"I'll let Hal know."

HUNT WETHERS'S PRELIMINARY investigation of legitimate anthrax researchers went quickly, and with the exception of one man, everyone who was known to have worked with the bacteria was where he should be and their research was being properly monitored and published.

The only anthrax researcher who wasn't properly accounted for was a Bosnian Muslim named Insmir Vedik. Dr. Vedik had been on the staff of the Sarajevo medical university specializing in livestock diseases, including anthrax. He had last been seen in Sarajevo in 1991 at the outbreak of the Baltic war when he had joined the Bosnian army as a medical doctor, and has not reappeared. It was thought that he had died in the fighting. Since there was no way to confirm that, he was scratched off the list of possible suspects.

With the legitimate anthrax researchers all accounted for, that left the outlaws. These were the scientists, all too often products of the defunct European Communist regimes, who sold their expertise to the highest bidder. Most often, that meant that they hired out to one of the terrorist states of the Middle East or to a narco cartel in Latin America. In this case, though, since the attacks seemed to coincide with the Muslim prophecies, the possible South American connections would be looked at later. That didn't mean that the work would be lessened.

International concern about the terrorist nations building chemical weapons was well-known. Iraq's use of chemical agents against the Kurds had drawn worldwide condemnation and calls for stricter controls on chemical weapons. Of even greater concern, although not as well publicized, was outlaw research on biological weapons. Such research had been banned by UN treaty and international conventions, but such legal niceties didn't mean much to men who were paid well to create evil for their masters.

Under UN control, an international effort was already in place to track down outlaw research on biological weapons development. The problem with policing these weapons, however, was that they were so simple to make. Compared to the massive facilities needed to produce most chemical weapons, it required very little equipment to grow germs and the labs could be hidden anywhere. In fact, all it took to do this deadly work was a small room that could be converted into a sterile lab. Any well-equipped hospital would do nicely.

The first step in Stony Man's search would be to plug in to the UN inspection teams' reports and see what they had found, or not found, recently. From there, it would get more difficult. But the clock was ticking, maybe more loudly than it had ever ticked before. Compared to mutated anthrax getting out of control, a nuclear weapon going off was hardly worth noticing.

California

ABLE TEAM'S INTERROGATION of the *Bonaventure*'s first mate had gone well. After telling Rosario Blancanales more than he really wanted to know, the man was sleeping off the effect of the drugs. When he came to, he would be turned over to federal authorities for deportation.

"Who the hell is this Zion guy, anyway?" Lyons asked as he listened to Blancanales translate the interrogation tapes. "I've never heard of him."

The most interesting thing that had come out of the chemically assisted interview was that the same men who had arranged the weapons shipment for Able Team were working to put together a major deal for a cult leader who went by the name Immanuel Zion.

"You need to keep more abreast of current affairs, Ironman," Schwarz said. "He's been on all the talk shows, and he even makes it on *American Update* at least once a week. He's red-hot right now. He runs one of the largest apocalyptic cult groups in all of California. And considering everything else that's going on down here, that's saying a lot."

"But what does he do besides take money from the millennium whackos?"

"The Seekers of Truth," Schwarz corrected him. "His followers call themselves the Seekers of Truth."

Lyons snorted. "The truth is that he's shaking those poor bastards down for everything they own."

"Don't forget that he's offering them something as well," Blancanales said. "He's using their money to buy military hardware in the name of protecting them with it when the end times come. According to the line he's peddling, it's really going to hit the fan when the millennium arrives and the faithful have to be able to defend themselves from the forces of evil, and that translates to all of the rest of us.

"He can also use his private army to make sure that no one demands their money back," Blancanales continued.

"There is that," Schwarz admitted.

"That's only when he isn't using it to convince property owners to sell at Armageddon-is-coming prices," Schwarz added. "According to last night's *American Update,* he just acquired a surplus Titan III launch complex. The previous owner had bought it a couple of years ago to use it as an underground bio-tech facility. But when he died in an unexplained car crash, the property was willed to his son, who just happened to be a member of Zion's group, and it was immediately deeded to the cult."

Lyons shook his head. "How in the hell do you know all that crap, Gadgets?"

Schwarz shrugged. "I have to keep abreast of what's happenin', my man. If you're going to be in the know, you have to know what's going down. I call it my 'Know Your Enemy' classes."

Lyons had a look of complete puzzlement on his face. "I can't believe that you waste your time watching that bullshit."

"The question isn't Gadgets's viewing habits," Blancanales commented, "as much as it is why this Zion guy thinks he needs a surplus missile complex."

"He says," Schwarz stated, putting the vacant, unfocused smile of a dedicated cult follower on his face, "that he will turn this one-time symbol of the evil that is nuclear war into what he calls a temple of the Coming Kingdom. It will become a place where all that is good about America will be preserved so that after the evil time has run its course, civilization can be started anew."

"Bullshit!" Lyons snorted.

"But you have to admit," Blancanales said, "that if the *Bonaventure* had been able to deliver his order to him, he could have turned a missile silo into a fortress. Not only did he want the run-of-the-mill, ex-Soviet small arms, he had also ordered several U.S.-made Phalanx air defense systems and TOW antitank missiles. If what our canary said is true, he was looking to create a serious threat."

"But why?"

"Maybe he really thinks that civilization is going to collapse," Blancanales pointed out. "You have to remember that not all of these cult leaders are scam artists. Some of them really believe the bullshit they're pumping out."

"All it means to me," Lyons said, "is that he's looking to make himself a place to hide while his people freak out and do their best to trash southern California. When it's all over, he can come out of the ground and be a hero."

"Either way," Blancanales said, "I think that someone needs to make sure that he doesn't get his hands on that launch complex. We ought to be able to do something to queer that deal."

"I'll have a talk with Barbara," Lyons said.

CHAPTER SIX

Over the Shenandoah Valley

The unmarked Bell JetRanger helicopter ferrying Hal Brognola from Washington to the Farm had an additional passenger this time. J. R. Rust, CIA field agent and late the security officer of the Oman Consulate, was on board and blindfolded for the ninety-mile flight. After reading Rust's initial debriefing on the Oman incident, Brognola had decided to borrow him from the Company for the duration to have the benefit of his expertise on both Middle East affairs and embassy security as well as his having been an eyewitness to the Omani incident.

For his part, Rust was still a little dazed and not sure who he had angered to have been picked for this assignment. But his initial briefing by Brognola when he met him at Andrews Air Force Base had piqued his interest.

"We're coming up on the facility now," Brognola said as he removed Rust's blindfold.

"That little farm?" Rust asked.

"That's it."

To the CIA man's eyes, the farm the Justice Department official pointed to looked no different than any of the other gentlemen's hobby farms. There was the main house, a cluster of barns, equipment sheds and outbuildings, crops growing in the sun and orchards bearing ripening fruit. It was all very rural and ordinary looking. It was true that the fences and gates looked to be in good shape, maybe a little too good, but that was it. There was nothing to indicate that this was the home of the nation's most top secret covert operations center.

Over the years, Rust had heard the occasional hushed rumor about this place, but he had never believed them. Even among experienced CIA field agents who should have known better, rumors and myths about everything from UFO crashes to who really shot JFK abounded.

"You realize," Brognola said, breaking in on the agent's thoughts, "that you'll never be able to say a single word about this to anyone, not even your director, unless you have prior White House clearance."

"I'm good at keeping secrets, Mr. Brognola." Rust sounded offended. "I've been with the Company for over twenty years now, and I can recite the national security statutes backward and forward."

Brognola smiled thinly. "The difference here, Mr. Rust, is that unlike with Company secrets, those who slip up about this place don't go on trial. No one will ever go before a Senate Intelligence Committee hearing with their TV cameras and say a single word about Stony Man Farm. We simply can't allow that to happen.''

Rust heard the subtle, but matter-of-fact threat and was shocked. Back in the good old days, the Company had used a "kill before betrayal" policy on occasion, but it had been rare even then. Now, with the massive media coverage and close congressional oversight, the CIA operated strictly under the law, and the current laws didn't allow that kind of proactive mission protection.

"I understand that part of it," Rust replied. "What I still don't understand, though, is why you brought me into this."

"Like I told you at Andrews, there're several reasons why I asked your director to put you on indefinite loan to us. To start with, you're the only one of the Oman staff who's not in a hospital bed or dead. And you were the only station chief in the entire Middle East who bothered to pay attention to the millennium prophesies and to properly record them. We picked up the odd report from some of the other stations, but your reports and eyewitness account gave us a complete record of what happened in Oman.

"Mostly, though," Brognola said, shrugging, "I wanted to have someone helping us who has a good nose for the region. For the past twenty-five years, you've been through many of the more serious incidents that have occurred in the Middle East and you've survived. Iran, Lebanon, Kuwait, you've been through it all and that makes you the kind of man I want to have working with me.''

"But there are a lot of men who have far more expertise on the region than I do.''

"The so-called Middle East experts are fine,'' Brognola said. "But you're a survivor, and I like to work with men who are either damned good or damned lucky. No matter which one you are, I need you.''

Rust laughed at the backhanded compliment. "I like to think that I'm a little bit of both.''

The chopper pilot banked the JetRanger to turn into the wind for landing on the Farm's helipad. No sooner had the ship flared out and skids touched down than four men surrounded it. Although they were dressed in farm clothing—well-worn jeans, work shirts, boots and baseball caps—Rust saw that they were armed. All four carried large-caliber automatic pistols in shoulder rigs and two had MP-5 machine pistols slung at their sides.

Brognola stepped out first and flashed a hand signal to let the blacksuits know that he wasn't under duress from his passenger. Even so, two of them stepped up to pat Rust down. The CIA man stood stock-still for the procedure and wasn't offended. Had he not been searched, everything he had been told about this supersecret organization that no one knew about would have been pure bullshit. He was still reserving judgment, but so far it looked right to him.

When the security team was done, Brognola led Rust up the porch to the front door of the farmhouse. Up close, the agent could see the subtle signs of the armor in the walls, the Lexan windows with the flat-screen projector units showing peaceful interior scenes and the miniature video security units covering the approaches. The place might look like an eighty-year-old farmhouse in need of a fresh coat of paint, but it was a fortress.

Brognola keyed the electronic door lock and waved Rust through. Inside, the CIA man found a woman waiting for him. She was tall, blond, well built and looked like a fashion model dressed for the shooting of a Purina Hog Chow commercial. Her well-washed jeans were formfitting, revealing slim hips and long shapely legs terminating in scuffed cowboy boots. The faded man's shirt had never looked that good when a man had worn it. Her honey-blond hair flowed down her back and her makeup was photo-shoot prefect.

She smiled and stuck out her hand. "Welcome to the Farm, Mr. Rust," she said, a Lauren Bacall-Demi Moore voice that stopped him like a hammer blow. "I'm Barbara, the mission controller around here."

Rust instantly realized that he had been working for the wrong branch of the government. Mission controllers didn't look like her in any organization he'd ever worked with, but he managed to keep his eyes off her breasts as he shook her hand.

"I'm glad to be here, I think, ma'am. And please, just call me J.R."

"Okay, J.R. If you'll please follow me, we have a briefing ready for you in the war room."

The interior of the farmhouse showed its earlier, more peaceful personality, but the security measures that had been added were like what he would have expected at a nuclear weapons facility, not a spook shop. Every door was armored and had an electronic lock. Every inch of the rooms and hallways were covered by video cameras. The elevator's control panel wasn't marked with floor numbers and he noticed that while Barbara punched the top button, the elevator went down.

The war room he was led into was dominated by a huge conference table and banks of video screens along one wall. A rather motley-looking crew was seated around the table, including a burly, older man in a wheelchair, a young Oriental wearing a ponytail and a middle-aged redheaded woman. Whoever had chosen this team hadn't been the same guy who had picked the unit's mission controller. But he was willing to take it on faith that they were more than capable.

Price made the introductions, and Rust tried to remember each one and the part they played.

As soon as Brognola took his place at the head of the table, the briefing got underway. The dignified black man who had been introduced as Dr. Hunt Wethers led off with a nod to the CIA man. "Thanks in large part to Mr. Rust's reports from Oman, we have a fairly good idea of the content of the Muslim millennium prophecies."

He smiled at Rust. "So, if you will bear with us, I'd

like to fill everyone in and, if I leave anything out, feel free to break in.''

Wethers proceeded to recap Rust's reports as well as add what little had been reported from other stations in the Islamic world. ''Have I left anything out?'' he asked at the end.

''No,'' Rust replied. ''That about covers everything I picked up.''

Next, Aaron Kurtzman, the man in the wheelchair, ran through the facts of the attack. ''As you all know, we got deliberately hit by a mutated war agent. We have to find out who did it and put them out of business before they do it again. To that end, we have already eliminated all the legitimate anthrax researchers and have started looking into the outlaw bioresearch operations.''

He looked at Brognola. ''We're going balls-out, but how long it will take us to get a lead is anyone's guess.''

''I don't need to tell you,'' Brognola replied, ''that the President wants this information last week. He can keep a lid on the Omani incident. But if this is tied to the prophecies and isn't an isolated event, the next time one of our embassies is hit, someone is going to start figuring it out and we'll have a panic on our hands.''

Kurtzman nodded his understanding.

''Now,'' Brognola said, reaching into his briefcase and pulling out another folder marked with the diagonal red stripe, ''what's the status of Phoenix Force and Able Team?''

Price quickly recounted the action teams' activities for the past two days, briefing him on the new lead regarding the Immanuel Zion operation.

"Put Phoenix on standby for deployment and turn the California operation completely over to Carl. I want David and his people ready to move out the moment we can find a target to launch them against."

"I can recall them now," Price said, "and start them on a premission briefing here and load out."

"Do that.

"Next," Brognola said, "I need to talk to Katz. Do you have a secure line to him?"

"I have a secure e-Mail in place," Kurtzman spoke up.

"Good, I want to recall him, too. Or at least see if I can get him working on this from Tel Aviv."

WHEN THE BRIEFING BROKE UP, Price approached Rust. "I've had a room set up for you on the third floor, so you can get cleaned up if you want. Hunt wants to talk to you as soon as he can."

"Let's do it now."

Price took him to the computer room and, when Rust spied the coffeemaker prominently parked on top of the filing case, he headed toward it. "May I?"

"I'd better warn you about that stuff, J.R. That's likely to be a little different than what you're accustomed to."

"You mean the coffee?"

"You might want to call it that." Wethers grinned.

"Most of us around here refer to it as dirty battery acid with a touch of motor oil drained from a Mexican taxi for texture. And that's on a good day."

"I was raised on a ranch in Texas," Rust said, grinning. "So it sounds good to me."

"Good man," Kurtzman called out from his workstation. "I have put a lot of effort into perfecting the gentle art of the bean, and I like to see my work appreciated."

"At least let me find you a clean cup," Wethers offered. "It'll take a little longer to kill you that way."

After getting his coffee, Rust followed Wethers to his workstation and took a seat.

"The first thing I'd like you to help us with," Wethers said, "is the exact wording of what you heard being said about the millennium and its effects on the West. We have copies of the so-called prophecies, but exactly what the imams have had to say about it might make a difference."

He called up a text in Arabic script on the monitor. "For instance, we have translated this word as meaning inevitable. How would you read it?"

Rust looked at the word for a moment. "That text came from Jordan?"

Wethers nodded.

"Then I'd say that it means forthcoming."

"Good." Wethers typed in a correction. "That clarifies that a little. Now, what's your reading of this?"

The breadth and depth of information Wethers had available at his fingertips stunned Rust. He had spent a little time in the Company's computer rooms, but Langley had nothing on these guys. As fast as he mentioned something, Wethers had it up on the screen, cross-checking it with every source in cyberspace.

As soon as they had gone over all the translations, Wethers had him go over his own reports to try to remember the exact wording he had heard. Rust was still trying to remember the Arabic words he had heard in Oman when lunch was delivered to the computer room's workstations. Like everyone else, he ate where he sat and he was still there when Kurtzman called time-out for dinner.

CHAPTER SEVEN

Amman, Jordan

The French embassy in Amman, Jordan, was the next nest of unbelievers to feel the wrath of the so-called ancient Muslim prophecies. As had happened in Oman, the entire European staff fell ill to a virulent disease that struck from out of nowhere. Within a day and a half of its appearance, almost everyone was comatose and, despite medical care, several had died. Unlike with the Americans in Oman, however, the French evacuated their staff with the utmost secrecy.

The casualties were driven to the airport in unmarked vans and secreted on board Air France charter flights. It was nighttime when the planes landed at Charles de Gaul International Airport outside Paris and were directed to taxi to a terminal that had been temporarily closed to civilian traffic. There, the patients were loaded into waiting army ambulances and driven to a military hospital.

Stony Man Farm, Virginia

HUNT WETHERS turned in his swivel chair to face Aaron Kurtzman's workstation on the opposite side of the Computer Room. "Aaron, I think the French embassy in Jordan might have been hit with an anthrax attack. There's been a flurry of encrypted messages flying back and forth to Paris and a company of the legion has been flown in to take over security of the compound."

As part of the Farm's ongoing intelligence-gathering activities, Stony Man routinely kept track of foreign embassy communications. The fact that the messages were encrypted only made the job more fun for Kurtzman. Breaking communication codes was one of his favorite pastimes. He had to admit, however, that the French never presented him with much of a challenge. They were at least two generations behind the United States in their security codes. Nonetheless, since the French were still caught up in their old cold war envy of American power, they had to be watched closely.

"Stay on it," Kurtzman advised. "If it is another biological attack, we need to know ASAP."

A DIA electronic intercept satellite had been parked in a permanent stationary orbit over the Middle East, and Wethers used its input to follow the next chapter in the French-Jordanian episode.

ALONG WITH THE REST of America's allies, the French government had been warned about the anthrax attack in Oman. As a result, the company of French foreign legionnaires that had been flown into Amman to secure the empty embassy compound had been ordered to eat and drink only the army rations they had brought with them. Because of professional paranoia, however, no one in the French government bothered to tell the legion why the order had been given.

Soldiers being soldiers, even in the iron-disciplined legion, the men quickly tired of their regulation diet of canned bread, stew, blood sausages, smoked fish and sour wine. Particularly when the local street vendors showed up offering savory, hot roast beef sandwiches stacked high with cooked onions. The beef was a little tough, but between the thick loaves of fresh Western-style bread, it was a welcome change.

No one thought to wonder why, in a land where the meats of choice were mutton and goat, beef of any kind was suddenly available. Most of the legionnaires simply figured that it was horse meat, but that wasn't a problem for them. Horse meat was considered a delicacy in much of Europe, and it was a favorite in the legion.

A day after the vendors appeared, half a dozen of the legionnaires reported to the medic with symptoms of a virulent flu combined with internal bleeding and skin lesions. Figuring that they had picked up a local bug, the medic gave them the standard army antibiotic treatments for Middle Eastern maladies and returned them to duty. Twelve hours after that, the 120-man company of battle-hardened legionnaires had been rendered combat ineffective. In a word, almost every man was sick or dead.

Again, the evacuation was carried out in greatest secrecy. The French were never ones to admit to a disaster. This time, however, the embassy compound was simply locked and left unguarded.

FOLLOWING CLOSE ON THE HEELS of the French embassy attack, several British, German and Russian embassies in the Middle East were also hit. Putting safety before national face, the Germans and Russians quickly abandoned all of their locations in the region. The British, however, decided to stick it out, vowing to hold on until the bloody end. They did send all of their dependents and nonessential personnel home and flew in their food and drink, but they stayed at their posts.

The British Empire might be on its last legs, but its spirit would live on.

THE INABILITY to get a handle on whoever was behind the millennium plague was starting to have an effect on everyone in the Executive Branch, and that included the Stony Man Farm crew. Kurtzman and his team had done everything they could and still hadn't been able to get even a hint as to who was behind the attacks. Not surprisingly, the DIA, CIA, ONI, NRO, NSC, FBI, ATF, CDC and every other alphabet soup federal agency involved had also come up empty-handed.

Outside the United States, the same went for the UN, Interpol, the British MI-6, the Russian SVR, the French SDECE and almost every other intelligence agency on the planet.

The consensus, however, was that the attacks were the product of an outlaw Islamic terrorist organization. Most of the so-called Islamic terrorist groups were actually state sponsored, directed and financed. Libya, Syria, Iraq and Iran were famous for backing terrorist operations as an alternative way to make war on their enemies. In the long run, it was cheaper and they could usually escape retaliation by saying that they didn't know anything about the groups and had no control over them.

With the exception of a few UN delegates who were paid to promote the Islamic fundamentalist party line, absolutely no one had ever believed that the well-known terrorist groups were independent. However, that fiction was held to be the truth in the make-believe world of international diplomacy. This time, though, the risk was so great that even the Islamic UN delegates were calling for retaliation. The problem was no one knew who to strike back against.

In an unexpected and unprecedented move, some of the Islamic nations started investigations of their own into the source of the plague. Their reasons for offering their help were completely understandable. Of major importance was their fear that the Western powers would let their frustration get out of hand and start retaliating against them in a Christian version of a jihad.

The second concern was that anyone who would risk attacking the embassies of the major powers wouldn't hesitate to attack their other enemies such as the rulers of certain Islamic states. Regardless of how they appeared to the West, the Islamic nations weren't monolithic. In most of them, a thin veneer of society held all the power and the people had very little say about their lives. While a nominal form of democracy was practiced in a few nations such as Turkey and Egypt, most of the Islamic countries were outright dictatorships or, at best, absolute monarchies.

The men in power stayed where they were only because they could successfully oppress their own people. Saddam Hussein wasn't the first, nor would he be the last, Arab leader to rule with ruthless terror over his own people. But if there was an independent group powerful enough to drive the Western nations out of the Middle East, no one in the region was safe.

So, for the first time since the end of World War II, the Islamic nations were actively spying on one another, trying to discover which of their neighbors and allies was responsible for these acts of bioterrorism. And, to clear their own names from the list of possible suspects, they were inviting in UN inspectors to freely look around.

Washington, D.C.

IN THE OVAL OFFICE, the President had called in the secretary of state for a classified briefing. He had just received the first reports of the plague having reached the general population in France. The medical personnel treating the Amman embassy casualties hadn't taken adequate precautions and had taken the plague home with them.

"I want you to start an orderly evacuation of all of our embassies in the Islamic nations immediately," the President told a startled secretary of state. "I have alerted the Air Force and the Marine Corps, and they'll support the operation with airlift and ground security forces. How long will it take your people to accomplish this?"

"To be honest with you, Mr. President," the secretary said, "I really don't know. This is a completely unprecedented act, and we simply don't have an experience factor to work from here.

"In fact—" he paused for effect "—I would like to ask you to reconsider this idea. I think that its premature for us to take this step. After all, it will make us look weak in the eyes of the host nations and create an—"

"The order stands," the President said, cutting him off. "And I don't want to hear any more about it. I also want your plan on my desk before the day is out."

"Yes, sir."

Stony Man Farm, Virginia

WHILE HE WOULDN'T have called himself a man of direct action anymore, Rust quickly tired of being cooped up in the farmhouse. While he was computer literate, he wasn't in the same league with Kurtzman, Wethers and the others in the computer room, and there was nothing he could do to help with the data search that was going on. After he had been thoroughly debriefed, there was little for him to do between the times he was called in for a consultation on some specific point or other.

When he asked Barbara if he could go outside, she had him draw farmhand clothing from the stores, apprised him of the danger areas to stay out of and added his photo to the authorized access list and gave him the door code. That done, he was on his own.

Now that he was out on the grounds, he started seeing the extent of the Farm's defenses. Several of the smaller outbuildings weren't actually buildings at all, but hardened bunkers. Heavy weapons were positioned and camouflaged to keep them from being spotted by aerial or ground observation.

After a ten-minute stroll, he stopped for his midday smoke next to one of the bigger buildings. Leaning against the wall, he lit up.

"I wouldn't be doing that around here," he heard a voice behind him say.

"I'm sorry," Rust automatically replied as he crushed the tip of his smoke against the bottom of his shoe and turned. "I didn't see any No Smoking signs."

The man in jeans, boots and a work shirt had a smile on his face. "You're that CIA guy who's helping us, aren't you?"

"J. R. Rust." He stuck out his hand.

"I'm John Kissinger," the man said, taking his hand. "But they call me Cowboy around here. I'm the resident gun nut, and I run the armory."

It figured that the Farm would have to have a man like him on the payroll, but as with everything else, the armory wasn't marked.

Kissinger caught the look on Rust's face. "We aren't much on signs or name tags around here, so you need to ask if you want to get somewhere you've never been before. But if you're interested, I'll be glad to give you the two-bit tour of my end of it."

"Sure."

Rounding the corner, Kissinger opened a door and led him into a large work area. The men working on their weapons behind a long table were dressed casually, but there was something about the intensity of their work that told Rust he had finally bumped into the Farm's muscle. Plus, they all had that unmistakable look of bad news that all professional warriors carried like a second skin.

It wasn't anything obvious like having Death Before Dishonor tattoos on bulging biceps. It was in the way they moved, the fact that they had all noted his entry, saw Kissinger with him and went back to what they were doing without missing a beat. Had he been an intruder, he didn't think he would have lasted very long.

"I'd better introduce you to the guys," the weaponsmith said as he steered Rust to the table.

The first man could only have been British, he had the unmistakable look of the islands as well as the bearing of a guardsman or the SAS. "David," he said with a British accent. "Pleased to meet you."

"J. R. Rust."

"I know."

"Calvin." A muscular black guy stripped down to shorts and a Navy SEAL T-shirt stepped forward. "Welcome aboard."

"Thanks, I think."

James grinned. "You'll go far around here with that attitude. It pays to be skeptical in this place."

"Gary," a man with the look of a professional engineer waved from where he was using an electronic test set on what looked like antipersonnel mines.

Rust waved back.

An older Hispanic man looked up and nodded. "Rafael."

Rust nodded in return.

The younger man working with him wiped his hands on his fatigue pants and walked forward to greet him. "T. J.," he said. "Pleased to meet ya."

"I'm J. R."

"From Texas?"

Rust grinned. "Guilty."

"Good. As the only redneck around here, I've been feeling like a whore at a church social. It'll be nice to have someone to talk to."

Rust laughed.

"I don't think I've ever seen that particular combination," Rust remarked as he looked at the weapon Hawkins had been working on. It looked like an H&K MP-5 SD with a 38 mm grenade launcher fitted under the silenced barrel.

"That's one of our home-built items," Kissinger said as Hawkins handed over the piece. "We put together special-purpose weapons, depending on our mission requirements. That launcher can accommodate a full range of 38 mm rounds, but it was designed for a special incendiary round I cooked up. Dragon's Breath, I called it."

"You guys roll your own ammunition too?"

"Only when we can't get it off the shelf. Some of our targets require that we carry specially designed ordnance to take them out."

This operation was looking better and better with everything he saw. He was beginning to understand why the President had formed this small, self-contained private strike force. With the intelligence-gathering, mission-planning, supply and command-and-control functions all in one place, these people could plan, outfit and launch a mission with minimum delay and maximum flexibility. That was a hell of a lot more than he could say for the Company.

"Do you guys have a code name or something?"

"We five are Phoenix Force," McCarter said. "The other action unit is Able Team, and they're working in California right now."

Rust hadn't realized that the Farm's operations were conducted inside the United States. Executive actions were supposed to be confined to foreign nations. Covert operations against American citizens was one of the biggest no-nos on the books. "What are they doing there?"

"They're trying to keep the Apocalypse from breaking out," Hawkins explained. "Some real crazy people out there are getting crazier every day."

Rust could only agree, but he wasn't sure what a commando team could do to stop that. California had been replete with fruits, nuts and flakes for as long as it had been a state.

CHAPTER EIGHT

Dakar, Senegal

The evacuation of the U.S. Embassy personnel in Senegal started off well, more or less, for a good idea gone bad. Ambassador George Wilson had argued with his bosses at the State Department about the President's order sending Marines to secure the evacuation. He felt that it was an unnecessary provocation and would only further humiliate his office. Being ordered to evacuate was bad enough, but to do it under the guns of Marines was unthinkable.

The secretary of state, one of Wilson's old Georgetown frat brothers, agreed with him, but he knew that he didn't dare openly cross the Man on this one. He did, however, order the Marine unit commander to keep his troops confined to the airfield instead of sending them into Dakar itself.

The Marine major in charge of the evacuation protested the change in plan, saying that his men couldn't adequately guard their charges unless they were actually with them, but the State Department order stood.

When the ambassador tried to send his own Marine embassy guards to the airport early so the Senegalese wouldn't see them with the ground convoy, the gunnery sergeant in charge of the detachment flat-out refused to leave.

"But I order you and your people to go," Ambassador Wilson thundered.

Gunnery Sergeant Wilmo Barnes stood firm. "I can't do that, Mr. Ambassador, sir. It's an illegal order and under the terms of the Nuremberg Laws, sir, I cannot obey an illegal order."

The ambassador stormed away to yell at someone else, and Sergeant Barnes went to check the crowd outside the embassy fence again. The imam with the bullhorn was still haranguing a crowd that seemed to grow larger even as he watched. So far, though, none of the listeners were digging up the curb stones, and he saw few weapons. That didn't mean that the AKs weren't there, however. It only meant that they would be saved for later.

After checking the nervous young Marines by the front gate, the sergeant keyed the mike of his radio to report in with the Marine Tactical Operations Center at the Dakar airfield. When the shit hit the fan, he wanted them on-line for an evac.

WHEN EVERYTHING WAS finally ready, Ambassador Wilson gave the signal for the convoy to pull out of the embassy compound. Sergeant Barnes hadn't been able to talk Wilson out of leading the convoy in his flashy black Mercedes stretch limo with the U.S. flags on the front fenders. The ambassador had insisted on leading the parade, and he was welcome to it.

Barnes did, however, have a two-and-a-half-ton truck as the second vehicle in line. His best driver was in the cab, and his shotgun was packing an M-249 SAW, the 5.56 mm light machine gun. Another SAW and several M-203 grenade launchers were with the troops in the back of the truck.

The sergeant had far less firepower than he would have liked for this job, but the embassy guard detachments were woefully short on heavy firepower. The higher-ups at the State Department had proclaimed that showing weapons was provocative so the detachments were lucky even to have what they did. Barnes vowed that if they got out of the situation alive, he was going to make a trip to Washington specifically to tell the State Department brass exactly what he thought of their policy.

When the gates opened, the crowd moved back of its own accord, creating a narrow gauntlet for the convoy to pass through. In the back of the limo, Ambassador Wilson felt vindicated. A display of military strength would only have incited the demonstrators. He had no way of knowing that the imam with the loudspeaker had ordered his listeners to let the unbelievers go free and to leave vengeance in the hands of God.

Two blocks away from the embassy, however, the people lining the streets hadn't been able to hear the imam's words to let the Americans leave unmolested.

All they saw was the agents of the great Satan running away, and they saw a good opportunity to gain entrance to paradise by killing the unbelievers.

In a flash, the crowd surged into the street, blocking the path of Wilson's limo. Another group got between the limo and the truck. "Steady," Barnes told his men. "Don't shoot until I give the order. And when I do, clear a path to that alley on the right front."

After the mandatory shouting and fist waving at Wilson's limo, the first rock smashed against the armored glass in front of the driver, but didn't punch through. Neither did the second rock, although it did splatter broken glass on the ambassador and his wife. Her screams were drowned by the chanting from the crowd and her husband screaming at the driver.

When the first bursts of AK fire didn't penetrate the armored doors of the limo, a shout went up for something that was sure to work, an RPG.

Though every instinct told Barnes to return fire, he couldn't. He had been commanded not to fire on the locals without a direct order from the ambassador. As long as Wilson was alive, he was required to obey the order.

"Steady," the sergeant repeated. "Wait for it."

The RPG rocket was fired from such a close range that the warhead didn't have time to arm before it punched through the limo's rear side window and struck the ambassador at the base of his neck. With the full thrust of the still-burning rocket motor behind it, it tore off his head and continued to pass through

Mrs. Wilson's upper body before lodging halfway through the armored door on her side of the car. Then it detonated.

The fact that the core of the explosion of the shaped-charge warhead blew into the closely packed crowd, sending a dozen of them to God wasn't of much concern. A blow had been struck against the Yankees. The survivors chanted slogans and fired their AKs into the air.

Sergeant Barnes smiled grimly. He had just been released from his orders. "Do it to 'em!" he shouted.

With a storm of Marine fire sounding in the background, he keyed his mike. "Bold Tower," he radioed the Marines at the Dakar airfield, "this is Tango Alpha Six. We are under fire. Prime's vehicle is lost, and I am taking evasive action. Key on my beacon and bring everything you can ASAP, over."

"Tango Alpha Six," the Marine com center replied. "This is Bold Tower, we have your beacon and are on the way."

AT THE AIRFIELD, Major Alan Cunningham jumped into his Hummer command vehicle. He would have liked to have been riding in a LAV-25 scout car with the 25 mm Bushmaster autocannon in the turret, but the heavy armored car wasn't part of the standard equipment load for a mission like this. He did, however, have an M-19 40 mm automatic grenade launcher on his Hummer, and it would have to do.

"Move out!" he ordered the Ready Reaction Force, and the eight Hummers rolled as one.

NOW THAT WILSON HAD GONE UP in flames with his limo, Sergeant Barnes was also free to implement plan B. The fact that the late ambassador hadn't known of this plan B wasn't an accident. Running a gauntlet of screaming killers along the main roads of Dakar wasn't Barnes's idea of good tactical thinking. He was an old Mud Marine and knew that there was more than one way to get from point A to point B.

The sudden hail of fire from the Marines in the truck had cleared an area in front of them, or mostly cleared it. Barnes had given orders to shoot to kill, and the road was covered with still-twitching bodies. But the guys who had been packing AKs and the RPG gunner were either down or fleeing the kill zone. No one had told them anything about the Americans fighting back.

"Run over those bastards," he ordered his driver, "and turn right at the next alley!"

The drivers of the other vehicles had been ordered to follow the lead truck no matter what, and they kept close on Barnes's tail. The alley was narrow and obstructed with sellers' stalls, but the heavy vehicle plowed its way through them without slowing. The mere sight of the Marines in the back of the truck kept anyone from objecting.

Rounding a bend, Barnes saw that the alley terminated in a cluster of shacks and lean-tos that had been built across the way. "Keep going!" he yelled. "Plow through it!"

The driver sent the truck crashing through the shacks, sending pots, pans, sticks of furniture, ragged clothing and everything else in the way flying. It was rough on the occupants of the place, whoever they had been, but it cleared a pathway to the next paved street.

"Hang a right!" Barnes shouted to the driver as he looked over his shoulder to make sure that the rest of the vehicles were still behind him. The other drivers had been instructed not to stop for anything, even flat tires or casualties. As long as their engines were running, they were to keep up any way they could.

So far, so good, Barnes thought as the driver sped up. But they were still several miles from the airport. "Bold Tower," he radioed, "this is Tango Alpha Six. We are on the Candy Stripe heading east."

"Bold Tower, roger. Help is on the way."

MAJOR CUNNINGHAM'S Ready Reaction Force was less than a mile from the airfield when it ran into an enemy convoy traveling toward them. Several dozen trucks and cars packed to overflowing with armed men came to a stop, blocking the road. Brandishing their weapons, the gunmen jumped to the ground and clustered in front of their vehicles, shouting insults and firing into the air.

The major halted his vehicles and radioed a warning to the rear detachment before approaching alone. When the linguist in his Hummer ordered the mob to let them pass, an RPG rocket flashed out of the crowd and hit the unarmored side of the vehicle. The shaped-charge warhead ripped through the thin steel and detonated the fuel tank.

Cunningham and his crew were dead.

When he saw the major's Hummer go up in a fire-ball, Gunnery Sergeant Ray de Silvo laid on the trigger of his 40 mm grenade launcher.

"Free fire!" he shouted over the radio. "Take all the bastards!"

Rather than picking out the armed men and firing only on them, the Marines cut loose on everyone blocking their way. The concentrated storm of fire cut through the crowd like a buzz saw. A few of the gun-men tried to fight, but with no cover, they didn't last long. In moments, no one was left standing. If the Sen-egalese weren't able to run away, they were simply cut down.

Those who had been close enough to the rear to make their escape were very confused by the turn of events. It wasn't supposed to have turned out this way. Their leaders had told them that the Yankees never fought back. They had always run away like dogs or stood like stupid sheep and allowed themselves to be slaughtered. Something was dreadfully wrong when Americans fought back.

A quick report showed that except for the crew of the major's Hummer, they had taken few casualties. Three men had taken minor hits and they were given first aid. The bodies were recovered from the Hummer, wrapped in ponchos and laid out in the back of one of the vehicles. The United States Marines didn't leave behind their dead.

"Okay people," the sergeant called out over the tactical radio net, "let's go find Gunny Barnes, round up his folks and kiss this fucking place goodbye."

He was answered with cheers.

When the Ready Reaction Force moved out again, no one tried to oppose them. As a matter of fact, the sound of their engines alone sent the locals scrambling for cover.

WHEN THE MARINE Ready Reaction Force returned to the airfield a little less than an hour later, they were herding what was left of the embassy convoy. They were also carrying the bodies of all the American dead except for those of Ambassador Wilson, his wife and his driver. CNN wouldn't show videotapes of U.S. servicemen's bodies being dragged through the streets by howling mobs this time. What was done with the ambassador was no concern to the Marines. He hadn't wanted their help when it had been offered, so he wasn't going to get it now.

While the Marines guarded their perimeter, the evacuees were quickly loaded into the choppers and flown to the waiting Navy ships offshore.

Washington, D.C.

THE DEBACLE IN SENEGAL had immediate and serious repercussions. For one, the President accepted the on-the-spot resignation of the secretary of state. He didn't, however, grant the man immunity from federal prosecution for having violated a Presidential directive. He had done the crime and he could damned well do the time.

As soon as the ex-secretary left the Oval Office, the President called the second man in the State Department and told him that he was now the acting secretary of state. He then told him that effective immediately, all American embassies and consulates were being put under the command and control of the Defense Department and that he was to so advise all ambassadors and consuls of the change immediately.

When the new acting secretary protested that this was a violation of accepted diplomatic protocol, he was relieved on the spot, as well. Another call to the next man in line in the vast State Department hierarchy made him the newest acting secretary.

When he heard the fate of his two predecessors, the man wisely said, "Yes, Mr. President. Whatever you want."

Next, the President called Hal Brognola. It was time to put a stop to this.

CHAPTER NINE

San Diego, California

When Phoenix Force pulled out to return to the Farm, Able Team had taken up residence in the hydrofoil moored in the marina. The boat was on a prepaid, long-term lease, and there was no point in leaving it unoccupied. This arrangement suited Gadgets Schwarz just fine; he liked fast boats with comfortable accommodations.

"You know," he said as he reached into the minifridge on the bridge to pour a cold beer, "if we keep this thing stocked well enough, we can escape to sea when this place self-implodes and be okay for weeks."

"Or explodes," Rosario Blancanales replied as he looked at the crowded beach outside the fence. Even though the marina's private security force had been reinforced, they were still keeping an around-the-clock watch on the boat.

The situation on the beach hadn't gotten any better, but it was getting a little more organized. Even in the midst of utter chaos, humans were prone to try to bring order to their surroundings. It appeared that the ever-growing population had split into three contingents. The Christians who were waiting for Armageddon, or the Second Coming, were clustered on the end of the beach closest to the marina. The far end was occupied by New Agers who chanted, danced and drummed far into the night waiting for only they knew what.

In between those two camps was a loose confederation of druggies, dealers, drunks, the homeless, petty criminals, gangbangers and other marginal members of society. They weren't as much waiting for the millennium to come as they were looking for targets and opportunities to practice their particular crimes. And they were finding good targets. People who were concentrating on the millennium weren't watching their backs.

Now that the beach scene had somewhat sorted itself out, the police were making more of a presence in the area, but the body collection was still the high point of the day. While the raw numbers of bodies to be carried away each morning seemed to have tapered off, the nature of the deaths had changed. Before, a dozen or so bodies would be laid out for collection every day mostly ODs, drownings and other self-inflicted deaths. Now, homicides were starting to show up as the unaffiliated group preyed on the hapless Christians and New Agers. Assaults and rapes were also becoming a daily occurrence.

Most of these people had come to the sea to try to escape the city, but the city had followed them.

Watching a group of believers walk into the surf for their daily ablutions, Schwarz was reminded of their new mission. Now that Phoenix Force had been recalled, Able Team was working the new lead on their own. And as always when it came to making that critical person-to-person contact, Blancanales, also known as the Politician, was their pointman.

"What have you found out about our new bunch of crazies and their leader?"

"Zion's outfit is a textbook cult organization," Blancanales replied. "Like that commune David Koresh set up in Waco, it's real short on scriptural authority and long on charisma. Our man Immanuel doesn't exactly claim that he talks to God, but he doesn't deny it, either. When asked about it, he just smiles and makes another holy pronouncement."

"How long before you think you'll be able to get inside?" Schwarz asked.

"I've already joined the tribe, so to speak. All it required was a five-hundred-dollar show of faith. But like with most cults, the good stuff is only revealed to a select chosen few."

"Let me guess, those fortunate few are chosen on the basis of the size of their bank accounts."

Blancanales smiled. "You'd have made a good cult leader."

"Con man, you mean."

"It's the same thing.

"Anyway," Blancanales said, "I've expressed my

desire to get closer to the 'truth,' as it's said with them, and they're going over my application right now.''

''Running your bank account numbers.''

''That and my association with undesirable elements like the police or the FBI.''

''You'll come up clean there.''

Blancanales nodded. ''Aaron and the gang worked up a good background for me. This time, I'm a wealthy Mexican-American businessman who's a failed Catholic with two ex-wives and no kids. The kind of guy with no future and nothing to spend his money on.''

''That should work.''

''I hope so,'' Blancanales said seriously. ''Because if they get all of the hardware the first mate said they were on the market for, they'll be better armed than the police around here.''

''Who isn't nowadays?''

Blancanales glanced over at the chronometer. ''When's Carl due back?''

''He didn't say,'' Schwarz replied. ''He's working on a lead Aaron came up with about a shipment of Phalanx air defense weapons that went missing from the Coronado Naval Yard.''

''That's the kind of thing we really want to see out there in the hands of these folks.''

''They can use them to shoot down avenging angels when Armageddon comes.''

''Right.''

THE END OF THE COLD WAR had left the American government with a lot of military property that Congress felt was no longer necessary. With Soviet Russia's military might down the drain, the last thing any politician wanted to do was to pay for a military that was no longer needed. Some of this excess material was boxed and put away in case a need for it ever arose again. Some was destroyed or sold for scrap, some of it was loaned out to friendly nations and some was put into boneyards to become spare parts.

Even so, a lot of government property couldn't be so readily disposed of, particularly real estate. In a base closing frenzy, Congress put everything from naval yards to SAC bomber bases on the auction block. For pennies on the dollar, anyone could own a deactivated military base. All it took was money and not very much at that.

Among the properties being auctioned off were several Titan III missile launch complexes. While they had cost taxpayers millions to construct, they were being sold for a fraction of the cost. But even so, the General Services Administration that conducted the auctions felt lucky to get even that much.

The problem with missile complexes was that they were of little use to anyone except for launching missiles. And to make the situation worse, they were always in very remote locations. For people who were used to driving to the corner store for a six-pack, living in a missile silo would be a hardship.

Yet several surplus missile silos had been sold to people who liked living in the middle of nowhere. One was being used as a manufacturing facility for light aircraft and another for solar energy panels. The original buyer of the Titan III complex Immanuel Zion had just acquired had intended to use it as an underground greenhouse to grow exotic plants. With the climate controls that were built into such structures, any growing conditions on earth could be artificially reproduced. Zion, however, had no interest in growing anything in it except his power base.

What made this particular Titan III complex so interesting to him was partially its location, miles from nowhere. Mostly, though, it was the fact that its decommissioning hadn't been carried out exactly to specification. When the Department of Defense turned over the missile launch sites to the GSA for further disposal, they had given the civilian bureaucrats a lengthy list of things that needed to be done at each site to render them useless as military facilities.

This list had included such obvious things as taking out the missiles, draining the fuel tanks, taking down the radar, removing the computers and deactivating the minefields—simple tasks that only required following directions.

Zion's Titan site had been originally designated 438AH. Somewhere in the paperwork process for deactivation, a typo or photocopying glitch had turned the designation into 436AH. That was just two numbers off, but a world apart as far as the configuration of the two sites went. Thirty-eight Alpha Hotel, as the site had been called, had been the first of a series of

Titan III sites that had been slated for remodeling. This work had included installing a semiautomatic ground and air defense system that was linked to, but separate from, the launch control room.

When the decommissioning crew arrived in the desert, they thought they were working on 36 Alpha Hotel, an unimproved site, not 38, because that's what it said in their paperwork. Therefore, they didn't bother to even look for the site's defense complex because it shouldn't have been there. And since they were paid by the job, they didn't bother to look for anything that wasn't on the list. Time was money, and they got nice bonuses when they finished a decommissioning before scheduled.

It was a simple enough mistake, but it gave 438AH the potential to become the most heavily defended piece of property in civilian hands anywhere in the world. It was the perfect place for the headquarters of an organization that wanted to survive the coming collapse of civilization. And Immanuel Zion planned to do exactly that.

IMMANUEL ZION HAD BEEN born Vincent Gorman, but that hadn't been a name that would attract fanatic followers. Back when he had been running a TV evangelism scam, he had been known as Brother Billy Faithful. Like his birth name, that moniker, too, had been abandoned when the Texas State Attorney General's office had started sniffing around his bankbooks. He didn't mind the change to Immanuel Zion, though.

His current organization was making him money so fast that he couldn't count it.

Unlike so many of those who were preying on the fearful and the gullible, Zion really believed that the world as he knew it was going to come to an end with the new millennium. He didn't know what was going to happen after that, Armageddon or the Second Coming, but he wanted to be ready for whatever it was. And the way he was going to do that was to be strong enough to deal with anything that came his way.

The books were showing that he had almost twenty thousand believers of his brand of the end-of-the-world scenario. Of that number, about eight thousand were men of what could be called military age, and almost half of them were organized into the paramilitary units called the Eyes of Zion. Most of them, though, would be cannon fodder if it came down to serious fighting. A smaller group, some five hundred, were the Chosen, his personal SS as it were. Along with religion, Zion had always been interested in the lives of powerful men, and he knew the role that dedicated, loyal cadres always played in their rise to power. If it was good enough for Hitler and Stalin, it was good enough for him.

While he had no military background himself, Zion had advisers and subordinate leaders with sound military backgrounds in charge of his troops. Normally, trained veterans weren't attracted to apocalyptic cults; pie in the sky didn't appeal to them. But Zion had been smart enough to create incentives to aid in recruiting the kind of men he needed. His version of heaven-on-earth didn't exclude enjoying sex.

As was always the case with cults, more women than men were attracted to Zion's teachings. Of the women who flocked to hear him, only the young and the attractive were invited to join the ranks of the Chosen. And once recruited, their primary function was to service the men of the elite units.

This wasn't done in a German-army-whorehouse fashion, though. The women were bonded to their men in a ceremony conducted by Zion himself. Women liked to have their sexual activities sanctioned by authority, any authority. Outsiders might have negative things to say about the lives these women were living, but their activities had been blessed by Zion, and he was blessed by God.

But even with well-organized and well-satisfied troops, Zion needed more weapons if he and his people were to ride out the coming storm. Small arms weren't a problem, particularly paramilitary assault guns like the AK-47 look-alikes, and handguns. His shortfall was in heavy weaponry to defend his stake in the new millennium.

The machine guns, rocket launchers, mortars and antiaircraft defenses he wanted weren't available at every gun show like small arms were. To get them, he had sent his most trusted Chosen to make contacts in the black market. After buying some heavy weapons stolen from National Guard armories and the like, they stumbled onto the cartel arms merchants and hit the jackpot.

Knowing that anything that caused friction within the United States was good for business, the Latin American drug cartels were using the millennium fears as a way to increase their profits. With their access to surplus weapons from the defunct Soviet states and terrorist organizations, they were running the biggest arms smuggling operation in history. If you had the money to buy, there was no limit on what they could deliver.

Zion's first big cartel buy, however, had gone missing. The S.S. *Bonaventure* had failed to reach San Diego and was reported as having been lost at sea. With it had gone his several-million-dollar order. Much of the order had been simply standardized small arms and ammunition. But he had ordered almost a hundred Russian-built, shoulder-fired, antiaircraft missiles and a stock of RPGs, grenades, land mines and mortars.

These could all be readily replaced. The *Bonaventure* wasn't the only cargo ship smuggling weapons into the country. And the loss of his two-million-dollar down payment could be made up on any weekend of the year. But it would take time to replace them, and he was in a hurry to start turning Launch Complex 438AH into a sanctuary for the Chosen of Zion.

Stony Man Farm, Virginia

EVEN WITH ALL THE EFFORT that was going into tracking the source of the millennium plague, Aaron Kurtzman and crew were still keeping track of Able Team's California operation. To update Hal Brognola, Barbara Price went to get the latest reports.

"Carl says that they're closing in on Immanuel Zion's operation," Kurtzman said, "but it's tough going. The Eyes of Zion boys aren't taking anything at face value. Anyone who seeks admittance to the ranks of the Chosen of Zion is being very thoroughly vetted. Unlike with most of these religious scams, the money isn't enough to get you through the door of the inner temple. Rosario says that his cover is being investigated all the way back to high school."

"Will it hold?"

"I think so," Kurtzman replied. "I had both Hunt and Akira make sure that he's covered in depth. It helps that he's operating under a Mexican ID. It makes checking his earlier years more difficult."

"Why do you think that they're going to those lengths to do a background check on these people if all they want is the money?"

"I'll be damned if I know," he admitted. "All I can think is that it keeps out the wolves in sheeps' clothing. Plus, it gives this God-on-earth an edge when he deals with these folks. Knowing someone's high school girlfriend's name and address, as well as her hair color and bra size, gives you an aura of real omnipotence."

She shook her head. "There must be easier ways to make a living."

"There are, but playing God has perks that few jobs

can match. As long as there are gullible people in this country, guys like Immanuel Zion won't ever have to worry about going on food stamps.''

''You've got a point there.''

CHAPTER TEN

San Diego, California

The antechamber to the sanctuary of the temple of Zion was paneled in dark wood, and the floor was covered in thick carpet. Indirectly lighted, the effect was rich and warm. At the far end of the room, a massive desk and leather chair sat bathed in light as if they were a heavenly throne. The effect had been carefully crafted, and it worked. It would be easy to see an enlightened man living in such a place. The four guards, though, even without showing their weapons, were a bit off-putting.

Rosario Blancanales had welcomed Immanuel Zion's summons to the temple and reported for his interview well before his appointment. His eagerness wasn't all pretense, however. He really did want to join the club as soon as possible. The vetting process had taken longer than he liked, and it would be even longer before he could gain enough trust with these people to learn anything of real interest.

"Remember," the escorting bodyguard said, his

voice low as if not to disturb the aura of the room, "you are to address the Light of Zion as Master. If he offers his hand, you are to take it in both of yours and touch your forehead to it. Once that is done, you are to step back at least six feet. If you get closer to the master than that, you will be removed."

The guard caught a signal and motioned Blancanales to go forward. At that exact moment, Immanuel Zion appeared as if from a shadow. More good theater.

Zion looked like a combination of TV preacher and talk-show host. Blancanales knew that the man was forty-six, but his thick mane of gray hair made him look older and wiser. Combined with unwrinkled skin and deep-blue eyes, it gave him the aura of someone who has beaten time and knows all the answers. It was a trick that hucksters, both religious and political, commonly used to dress up their scams.

He was dressed in what most people had come to expect from a cult leader—a silk suit, banded-collar silk shirt, expensive shoes and enough gold and diamonds on his wrist and fingers to be noticed. On him, though, it looked almost tasteful.

"Master," the guard standing by the dais announced, "may I present Arthur Corona, one who yearns to join us as a seeker of truth?"

Zion smiled and stepped down to greet him. Blancanales took the proffered hand in both of his, brought it to his forehead and stepped back as he had been told. The steady eyes of Zion's guards never left him as he went through the motions.

"I'm happy to tell you, that your application to become a seeker of the truth of Zion has been accepted."

Blancanales let tears form in the corners of his eyes. "I am honored, Master."

Zion gave him a few moments to compose himself. Some of his followers had passed out upon hearing of their exulted change in status. "You have earned the honor and are welcome in our midst," he said. "Tell me a little about your life in the mundane world and what you hope to find in your new life with the Chosen."

Blancanales quickly ran through his cover résumé, hitting the high spots before plunging into New Age babble about the quest for truth and spiritual enlightenment. It was all very typical, but Zion listened as if it were the first time he had heard this particular line of drivel.

When Blancanales's spiel ran down, Zion struck a pose that was supposed to give the impression of a man listening to his inner voices.

"I know your search is true," he said solemnly, "but the time hasn't yet come for all of the seekers to be gathered together for the revealing of the truth. Until that time comes, you must continue your mundane life. But take heart, it will not be long now and there are things you can do until then that will help all of us in our quest."

"But how can I help, Master?" Blancanales asked, his voice full of emotion. "I'm only a small businessman."

"Many of the seekers," Zion said, starting his pitch, "aren't as fortunate as you have been in the mundane world. You can share your good fortune with them to help make their transition easier."

"Just tell me how, Master."

"And," Zion continued, "to make your own transition to our ways easier, I will send you a helpmate. She is an experienced seeker and can guide you to greater understanding."

Blancanales was shocked, but he managed to keep his face neutral as Zion extended his hand again to signal the end of the interview.

As he walked down the faux marble steps of the temple of Zion, Blancanales felt the need to take a long, hot shower. Zion wasn't the first con man he had ever worked, but he was one of the slimiest bastards he had ever encountered. Sending a woman to live with him as a reward for his financial contribution was a little too much like prostitution for his taste. To say nothing of the fact that having a woman living with him was going to make this gig a little more complicated than he really needed.

But there was no way that he could have refused his helpmate without ruining the whole deal and setting them back to square one. Lyons was going to blow a fuse, but it couldn't be helped. He had to be on the inside to work this one and if that meant taking a woman into his life, he would just have to be careful, very careful.

WHEN BLANCANALES ANSWERED the knock at his door that evening, he was stunned. The woman standing in the hallway was in her late twenties, tall with long dark-blond hair and well built, wearing a clinging white dress. He hadn't expected Zion to send a dog, but he had certainly not expected someone like this, either.

"My name is Sarah Carter," the woman said simply. "The Master sent me."

"I'm Arthur Corona," he said as he stood aside. "Please come in."

The apartment the Farm had set up for him looked well lived-in, a place where a man had lived alone for some time. It wasn't run-down, merely plain and lacking a woman's touch. He caught her scoping it out as he led her into the living room and invited her to take a seat.

He offered refreshment, but she declined and instead launched into what would be a self-confession in a Communist nation. "I know that the Master has sent me to help you become a seeker," she started, "but I'm unworthy of this and you may refuse me if you want."

He hadn't expected her to take this tack and frowned. "Why would I want to do that?"

She cast her eyes down. "In my mundane life, I was a failure. I lived every day for myself without giving any thought to seeking the truth or to helping others find it."

"But what did you do for a living?"

She met his eyes. "I was a dancer. I taunted men with my body so they would pay me money."

Bingo, Blancanales thought, and from what he could see, she would have made a bundle at the world's second-oldest profession. Recruiting hookers and exotic dancers was a good way for Zion to make sure that he had the bait he needed to keep his minions happy. Whether this woman was a true believer or just hired help didn't really matter. Once she was in his bed, she was a spy that would be difficult to get rid of. But, if he sent her away, Zion would simply replace her with another one.

"I know that my mundane history troubles some men," she said, "so I wanted you to know about it. If it bothers you, I'll leave now."

"No, Sarah, stay." Blancanales shook his head. "I, too, have things in my past that I'm not very proud of. We all do, and only the truth will set us free."

"Are you sure?" she asked.

"I'm sure." He smiled.

"But—" she stood and walked over to where he sat "—you must be more than sure, Arthur. You must know it in your heart."

Her hands went to the top of the sheath dress, released something and the dress slithered down her body to her feet. Under it she wore only a pair of white bikini panties and a great tan. Blancanales couldn't help but look in wonder at what she was offering. She held out her hand and he rose to take it.

The things he had to do for his country, he thought as she led him to his bedroom.

"YOU HAVE A WHAT living with you?" Carl Lyons roared, his eyes bulging with disbelief.

After an interesting evening and night, Blancanales had "gone to work," leaving Carter alone in the apartment while he reported the latest. There was nothing there that would blow his cover, so he had invited her to make herself at home. Now, he was reporting that he had finally made it inside as one of the Chosen of Zion.

"An exotic dancer," Blancanales replied, working hard to keep a straight face. "She was my prize for joining the club and giving them all of my money." He shrugged. "It's just like opening a new bank account, but it beats the hell out of getting a fondue pot."

"Blonde, brunette or redhead?" Schwarz grinned.

"A dark blonde with brown eyes, long legs and a great tan. Our boy Zion really knows how to pick 'em."

"I understand," Schwarz said, snickering, "that if you get tired of her, you can trade her in for a new model."

Blancanales lifted one eyebrow. "It may be some time before I'm ready to see how that part of the system works."

"Enough of this Punch-of-the-Month-Club crap." Lyons wasn't at all amused at the turn of events. "What does the wonder boy want you to do next?"

"I'm supposed to keep working in case he needs me to do something for the cause."

"For how long?" Lyons asked. "When is the great moment of truth to come?"

"He didn't say, but he indicated that it wouldn't be too long now."

"You shacking up isn't getting us any closer to those damned weapons," Lyons said. The lack of action since Phoenix Force had been recalled was starting to get to him.

"Seeking the truth takes time," Blancanales said, quoting one of Zion's pronouncements.

Lyons didn't even bother to answer that one.

THE MOUNTAINOUS BORDER region of north-eastern Syria adjoins both Turkey and Iraq. This critical terrain overlooking the Tigris River is the classic invasion route into the fertile land of Mesopotamia, and control of this region had been fought over for millennia. Today, though, with national boundaries firmly drawn and well guarded, it is a region rarely visited by anyone who doesn't have business there. And few did.

Deep inside the area's highest peak was an abandoned copper mine that was first dug back in the early Bronze Age when the red metal was the basis for civilization. Nearly two thousand years later, when iron became the metal of choice for both tools and weapons, the mine was abandoned and quickly disappeared from memory.

But those things that were lost from the mind of man

could be found again. Three thousand years after the last copper ore was brought out of it, the network of narrow shafts and tunnels in the core of the mountain was discovered again. But, even with the value of copper in the modern world, the mine wasn't reopened by its finder for the remaining ore. A place that had been forgotten for so long had a much better use as the millennium approached.

With the greatest of secrecy, the network of forgotten tunnels was enlarged to create an extensive underground fortress hidden from the sight of both men and electrons. This place was the home of a man who was known only as the Old Man of the Mountain. The nom de guerre wasn't original with him, but it did have a long history.

During the Crusades, the original Old Man of the Mountain had been the Hasan, the leader of a group of drug-using killers known as the Hashshashin, from which came the English word *assassin*. The first Old Man of the Mountain had been a Muslim, but he had targeted both Christians and his fellow Muslims for apparently random deaths. No one knew what the goal of his many attacks had been, but he had been feared and his wishes had been obeyed. To do otherwise invited certain death.

This modern Old Man of the Mountain didn't have to resort to getting his followers stoned on hashish to insure their loyalty to him and his plan. Every one of his operatives had proved his loyalty to the pan-Islamic dream of a world ruled by the Koran many times over.

They had been recruited from the most experienced men of every Islamic terrorist organization in the Middle East, and he had been very careful about who he invited to join his band. Of the fifty men who were in his cadre, only two of them had failed him so far. The manner of their deaths had gone a long way to insure that no one else wanted to fail.

One of the Old Man's most important partners in his plans was a Dr. Insmir Vedik, a Bosnian refugee and scientist seeking revenge for the destruction of his country and his family. When the Christian Serbs and Croatians descended on Muslim Bosnia, the great powers of the West, the United States included, stood by and refused to stop the slaughter. They had even refused to let other Islamic states go to the aid of the outnumbered and outgunned Bosnians. Three generations of Vedik's family had died in the holocaust of the nineties, and he wanted payment for their blood.

Since his thirst for revenge on the West fit nicely into the Old Man's plans, he had been brought into the mountain complex to do what he had done before, bioresearch on animal pathogens. There, Vedik developed a strain of anthrax that was specific to people who ate bovine products. Cow's milk, cheese and beef all contained an enzyme that wasn't found in other meats, milks or cheeses and the mutated bacteria zeroed in on that enzyme.

This bioweapon was finalized by late 1997, but the Old Man wasn't ready to use it then. There was no point in killing millions of Westerners simply to kill them. Any butcher could do that, and the Old Man wasn't a butcher, he was a dreamer. It was true that his dreams encompassed the deaths of millions, but they would die for a dream. And for the dream to come true, the stage had to be set. That took another year and culminated in the appearance of the millennium prophecies throughout the Islamic world. Six months after that, people started to die.

Even though Dr. Vedik's mutated anthrax had successfully driven most of the infidels from the lands of Islam, the Old Man of the Mountain wasn't satisfied. The dream still wasn't complete. The ultimate conquest by Islam would require more than a plague. The dream would also require fire and blood. The fire would come from the destruction of atoms and the blood from the unbelievers.

Stony Man Farm, Virginia

AS HARD AS THEY HAD TRIED, Aaron Kurtzman and his computer room staff hadn't been able to find a target to send Phoenix Force against to solve the problem of the millennium plague. Neither had the rest of the American intelligence community, but that didn't matter. Both the President and Hal Brognola were so used to Stony Man pulling a rabbit out of a hat on command that they couldn't take no for an answer.

To give himself a break from the pressure, Aaron Kurtzman started clearing his cyber in-box of more routine information. On his first look, though, he reached out for the intercom button. "Barbara," he said, "I think you should get down here."

"What is it?"

"We've got a shit storm brewing again in Pakistan. We have an intercepted military transmission that looks like there's a coup in the offing."

"That's not exactly news, Aaron. Ever since the country was formed, it's either been run by a dictator or a military junta. Another coup in Pakistan is just business as usual."

"The problem this time," Kurtzman explained, "is that the military has been listening to the Islamic prophecies. One of their generals went on the air saying that the time has come to finally rid themselves of their enemies once and for all."

"But their generals always say that," she countered. "If they don't, they don't get to be generals. The Indians have heard it time and time again, and they know that the Pakistanis can't pull it off."

"This time they might be able to."

"What's changed?"

"In all the millennium fuss, you must have missed seeing a report that the Red Chinese delivered a dozen Red Dragon missiles to the Pakistani military a couple of months ago. Even with everything else that's on our plate right now, we've been keeping a close eye on those rockets, and I think that they're in operational status."

"But they're short-ranged, aren't they?"

"They're intermediates and have enough range to

hit Calcutta and Bombay from anywhere in Pakistan, but that's not the problem. These Chinese firecrackers can be fitted with nuclear warheads.''

"Not that one again."

"I'm afraid so."

Price's sigh was clear over the intercom. "I'll be right down."

"Bring Hal, too, if he's around."

CHAPTER ELEVEN

When Barbara Price reached the computer room, Aaron Kurtzman had the maps and recon photos up on the monitors and the translations of the radio intercepts printed out. It took only a few minutes for her to come to the same conclusion that he had.

"Damn it anyway," Price said, shaking her head. "We really don't need this right now. We have enough to do trying to keep a lid on the Millennium Madness and the anthrax plague."

"I know," he replied. "But I don't think that we're going to be able to pick our battles this time. Don't forget that Pakistan has also been a hotbed of millennium prophecies. If they've decided to twist them around to include Indians as legitimate targets for God's wrath, we may have more of a problem with them than we've had in the past."

He clicked up a map of the Indian subcontinent. "We're riding a tiger, and all we can do is try to hold on until the end of the ride or we're going to end up being someone's lunch."

"This is it, isn't it?" she asked, her voice weary.

"The Apocalypse? We already have the crazies here in the States and the plague, and now we have a nuclear war brewing. All we need to add is famine and we'll be there."

"You mean like what's going on in what used to be called Zaire? In case you missed it, the UN sounded an alert for emergency food supplies in the region last week. The Belgians tried to fly a cargo plane into Kinshasa this morning and it got blown out of the sky."

He clicked to change screens. "I'm working up the spot report for Hal right now, and Hunt has set up an intercept lock on the Pakistani military communications. We'll be able to listen in on everything they put on the air. Hopefully, this coup will just be business as usual for those guys, but we need to keep an eye on it. Even with everything else we're tracking, this has got to be given a high priority."

"Do it."

Kurtzman refrained from telling that he already had.

The Pakistani-Indian situation had been a problem for the Western world ever since the partition of British India in 1947 created the two nations. The partition itself had cost almost a million lives, and the Muslim Pakistanis and the Hindu Indians had fought several wars since then. Though these wars had been very costly in human lives, none of them had spread beyond the Indian subcontinent. More important, though, was that the great powers hadn't gotten involved beyond supplying arms to the warring nations. However, that aid had been turned into a catastrophe waiting in the wings.

By an odd twist of cold war politics, the United States had ended up supporting the Islamic Pakistanis while the Russians had worked with the English-speaking Indians. Even so, everything might have worked itself out if nuclear power plants hadn't been given to the two combatants. In spite of their being of different designs, the waste of both nations' supposedly peaceful power stations was what was called bomb grade material. Within months of commencing electrical power generation, both nations started collecting the waste material. Within a few years, the waste had been refined and the weapons built, tested and stockpiled for future use.

So far, the primary thing that had kept the two nations from starting the world's first real nuclear war with weapon exchanges on both sides had been the delivery problems. Neither nation had missile systems capable of launching a successful nuclear attack. The delivery of the Chinese missiles to Pakistan had now changed that.

So far, India hadn't been stricken with the millennium plague. They weren't a Christian nation as such, but considering that they were the traditional religious as well as political enemies of the Muslim Pakistanis, it would follow that the prophecies about the enemies of Islam would affect them as well. Not being willing to wait for God to strike down their Hindu enemies, the Pakistanis had apparently decided to speed things up a bit.

As Kurtzman had predicted, the moderate civilian government in Karachi was overthrown and replaced by a military junta with strong Islamic fundamentalist overtones. One of their first official acts was to declare a state of hostility against India, and the situation instantly went critical.

Even though India had been spared the plague, a Hindu form of Millennium Madness had hit them too, and religious fundamentalism was on the rise there as well. Immediately after the Pakistani coup, the moderate Indian prime minister stepped down and was replaced by a man from the radical Rama party. His instant response to the Pakistani declaration was to put the Indian armed forces on war alert and to move reinforcements into the long-disputed Kashmir region along the Pakistani-Indian border.

Since the United States had played such a strong role in the military development of Pakistan, the President tried to dissuade the new junta from making good their threats against India. This time, though, diplomacy didn't work. The Pakistanis were seeing the prophecies as their salvation and the junta leaders threatened to use some of their nukes on any U.S military forces that tried to interfere in what they were calling the will of God.

With his overtures ignored, the President had no choice but to turn to the chairman of the joint chiefs of staff and order him to prepare a military response to the situation. However, if there was any way to avert a nuclear war, he wanted to try that first.

The DIA and CIA had determined that the Pakistanis had only two means of delivering their nuclear warheads. One squadron of their U.S.-supplied F-16 Falcons had been secretly equipped with the special launch racks necessary for delivering nukes. In addition, they now had the recently delivered Red Dragon intermediate-range ballistic missiles. If these delivery systems could be taken out, it wouldn't really matter if the bombs remained. A nuclear war might not break out.

With the help of the spy satellites provided by their new allies, the Chinese, the Pakistanis were keeping close tabs on the American forces in the region, and their threats to react to any deployment had to be taken seriously.

So, with only one place left to turn, the President called upon America's premier covert action force to take care of the problem for him.

AT THE PRESIDENT'S ORDERS, Hal Brognola moved to the Farm to oversee the operation.

"The Man's pushing me for the plan, Aaron," he said to Kurtzman via telephone. "The joint chiefs aren't happy about being put on hold, and he has to have something to keep them from going for an immediate preemptive strike."

Ever since the United States had been caught with its pants down on a bright Sunday morning in a place called Pearl Harbor, "shoot first" had played a prominent role in American military thinking. And if there had ever been an occasion that cried out for a preemptive strike, this was it. The President, though, wasn't anxious to go down in history as the man who ordered the attack that could well turn into the next world war. Ringing in the new millennium with mushroom-shaped clouds wasn't going to look good, no mater what spin was put on it.

"We're about done," a weary Kurtzman replied. "All I need is the printout from the NRO on the satellite run they did for us. Meet us in the war room in half an hour and we'll be ready to make our presentation."

"Thirty minutes then," Brognola conceded.

"More or less."

"Not a minute more, Aaron!"

UNLIKE MOST of the Stony Man operations, this mission would be undertaken with the full knowledge and cooperation of the American military, at least at the highest level. To preserve the necessary plausible deniability scenario, however, the information was being released on a strict need-to-know basis, and the access list had been vetted by the President himself. Only the chief of staff of each service and his operations officer would be briefed when Brognola went over the mission in the Oval Office.

With Kurtzman's wheelchair parked next to her, Barbara Price launched into her presentation. With

Brognola's permission, J. R. Rust was being allowed to sit in.

"Because the Pakistanis have hooked up with the Red Chinese," Price said, "and are using their recon satellites to warn them of U.S. movements, this will be a little trickier than we would like. For instance, we won't be able to make a normal insertion, whatever passes for normal around here."

There were chuckles from almost everyone seated at the conference table. In the past, everything from tramp steamers to hang gliders had been used to get the Stony Man action teams in place so they could do their thing. If this insertion was going to be out of the ordinary, it had to be something really off the wall.

"This time, Phoenix Force will go in via stealth bomber by way of Diego Garcia."

Diego Garcia was a small island in the middle of the Indian Ocean that the United States had turned into a large parking lot and service station for the bombers and strike aircraft tasked to keep an eye on the Persian Gulf and Middle East. During the Gulf War, the fleets of B-52 bombers that had hammered Saddam Hussein's Republican Guard units to a bloody pulp had been stationed there. This long after the war, a few B-52 cruise missile carriers were still stationed there. But America's main punch in the region was now a small force of B-2 stealth bombers that rotated in and out on a thirty-day basis.

"The pressurized, paradrop pods have already been flown to Diego and are being installed in one of the stealth bombers along with long-range tanks for flight.''

''Why the extra fuel?'' Jack Grimaldi asked. Along with McCarter and Bolan, the Farm's resident pilot was attending the briefing because he was going in with Phoenix Force this time.

''With the Red Chinese satellites dogging us,'' Kurtzman answered, ''we can't risk them spotting an air-to-air refueling. They might not be able to track the stealth bomber, but they'll sure as hell be able to pick up the KC-10 tanker and know that we're up to something.''

''What's the targeting plan?'' Brognola asked.

Kurtzman keyed his laptop and one of the big-screen monitors flashed to life, showing a satellite photo of a military base in a desert location. Four truck-mounted missile launch platforms were clearly visible, and two of them had their missiles in place.

''The drop will be made on the missile launch complex at Gandara,'' Price said. ''We feel that that's the top-priority target this time. Once we take out the Red Dragons, we'll have removed the most dangerous threat to India. Then, if we're not able to take out the F-16s in the second phase, it won't be as critical. The Falcons are vulnerable to Indian fighters and antiaircraft missiles if it comes down to that.''

''After they take out the missiles.'' Kurtzman flashed up a map as Price continued. ''Phoenix will go overland to the Pakistani air force base at Palimiro and attempt to destroy the nuclear weapons racks, which will render the F-16s impotent. We won't have to hit the jets themselves if we can destroy the delivery systems. That way, we won't disturb the balance of power and maybe encourage India to try an air attack of her own.''

Brognola could read a map as well as the next man and saw the distance Phoenix Force would have to cover. The two targets were nearly on the opposite ends of the country. "What's the transportation from the missile site to the air base?"

Bolan answered that one. "The satellite photos of the missile facility show that they have a large motor pool, and I thought we'd just help ourselves to what we'll need. Since they'll be military vehicles, it should make it easier for us to blend into the landscape."

"You haven't mentioned an extraction plan," Brognola said. "How are they getting out?"

"That's the sticky point," Price admitted. "At this point in time, we don't have an answer for that."

"Which doesn't mean," Bolan spoke up, "that we're not going in. We're taking Jack with us, and we plan to hijack a Pakistani aircraft at the secondary target to use for our extraction.

"Or," he said, shrugging, "we'll walk to the coast and flag down the first passing ship."

Brognola winced when he saw the distance from Palimiro to the coast. Phoenix Force had better be able to snatch a ride out of there because it would be a long hike. "The Man isn't going to like our not having a viable extraction plan."

"We've gone in without one before," Bolan pointed out. "And I'm not sure that we can afford to wait to work something out. If you can get us a sub stationed somewhere offshore, we'll make our way to it.''

Brognola made a note and looked at Price. "What's the projected outcome?"

"The Pakistanis will have to know," she said, "that we were responsible for foiling their plans, but there will be no proof of American involvement. Maybe with the delivery systems destroyed, the State Department boys will be able to go in and calm things down."

She shrugged. "If, however, Phoenix isn't able to do the job, then it will be up to the joint chiefs to do their thing. But at least we'll have tried."

Brognola knew that scenario could mean the death of Phoenix Force, but the President didn't call on Stony Man unless the good of the many greatly outweighed the good of the few. The preemptive strike scenario would put many more American lives at risk. There was no way that it could be done without taking some casualties.

The big Fed nodded. "That's all the President really wants, a chance."

"This will give it to him without blocking anything the joint chiefs want to do as a backup in case we fail."

Brognola looked across the table at David McCarter. "Are your people ready for this, David?"

"Piece of cake," the Briton answered sardonically. "We jump out of an airplane no one can see, blow up some nuclear missile warheads, walk across half of Pakistan, blow up some bomb racks, then swim home."

EDGE OF FURY

CHAPTER TWELVE

Hal Brognola turned to J. R. Rust to get his input. Throughout the briefing, the CIA man had sat quietly like a visitor on strange turf should, taking it all in. But the big Fed could see that his mind had been hard at work. And, as his résumé showed, he was no stranger to their target area.

"Mr. Rust, what do you think of the plan?"

Rust risked a slight smile. "If I hadn't been hanging around here for the past couple of days, sir, I'd think that I'd stumbled into a James Bond movie. This is well out of my range of expertise, but it sounds plausible."

He paused. "If everything goes exactly as planned and if Phoenix Force gets real lucky."

"What do you mean?"

"Well, you're dropping your men into an Urdu-speaking country and, as far as I know, no one on the team speaks the language."

"And?"

"And in a Muslim nation, it's easy to get yourself in deep doo-doo if you don't know what's going on around you. And if you don't speak the local language, you're not going to know diddly. But since I just happen to speak Urdu as well as Arabic, I think you should consider letting me go along.''

Brognola turned to McCarter. "David?"

"Are you parachute-qualified, J.R.?" McCarter asked bluntly.

The CIA man shook his head. "No, but I've watched all the movies."

"You know that we'll be jumping at night from thirty-five thousand feet and if you break something going down, we'll have to leave you there."

Rust met his eyes. "I know."

McCarter looked at Bolan, who nodded and said, "We can give him to T. J. Hawkins to bird-dog."

"A HALO buddy jump at night?" McCarter's voice revealed his skepticism. "Not too bloody likely."

"Just to guide him down to the pull point," Bolan elaborated. "Then they can separate. Once his chute's deployed, he should be able to make it the rest of the way on his own."

McCarter shrugged. "Not quite my cup of tea, but we can try it. If he prangs, we won't be out much."

Rust could have been insulted by McCarter's brutal assessment of his value to the mission, but he knew that it was accurate. He wasn't a trained commando. He also knew, though, that if the team got into trouble and needed him, their survival could well hinge on his being with them.

"Mr. Rust?" Brognola asked.

Rust took a deep breath. "I'm in."

THE NEXT FEW HOURS WENT BY in a blur for Rust. Volunteering to join Phoenix Force on the mission had moved him into a zone he had never visited before, the carefully controlled chaos known as mission prep. When he'd met Phoenix Force's T. J. Hawkins earlier, he'd thought that the ex-Ranger was just another easygoing good old boy, the military was full of them. Now, however, he was finding out that the jovial Southerner could also be the drill sergeant from hell.

"You want to do what?" Hawkins's voice rose to a shout when Rust told him that he was supposed to be outfitted for the jump. "You're completely out of your rabbit-assed mind, son. No one goes on a night HALO drop unless he's fully qualified, and you don't know a T-10 from a T-shirt. A cherry jumper might make it if he was lucky, but you're not even that. You're just a goddamned Company spook."

Rust had expected some version of this reaction, but, as one good old boy to another, he knew how to deal with it.

"I may be a Company man, T.J.," he said quietly, his eyes locked on Hawkins's, "but I'm not just some candy-ass Langley desk jockey. I've done my time in the field. As a matter of fact, I made it all the way out of Iran when the Ayatollah's thugs stormed the Tehran embassy without having to call on a commando team to bail my ass out.

"And," he added, "that was with an AK slug in

my shoulder.'' Before Hawkins could answer, Kissinger came up to them with his arms full of weaponry. ''I got you a Beretta 92 and an H-K MP-5 like you wanted, J.R.''

Hawkins looked at the weaponsmith as if he had two heads. ''You're in on this, too?''

''What's wrong?'' Kissinger asked. ''Striker told me to issue these pieces to J.R.''

''Okay, okay.'' Hawkins put a beatific smile on his face. ''I give up. As they say in Zen, it's simply mind over matter. I don't fucking mind and you don't fucking matter. If you want to get your sorry ass killed, I'll be glad to show you how it's done.

''But,'' he added, sticking a finger under Rust's nose, ''don't come pissing to me, son, if you crash and burn.''

Rust kept a straight face. ''I won't. I'll be dead.''

Hawkins shook his head.

BROGNOLA HADN'T FELT confident when he'd entered the Oval Office to deliver the Pakistan assault plan to the President. No matter how many times he briefed the Man on Stony Man operations, it was always an ordeal, and this time had been no different. But after the President had gone over the hard copies in the packet and had listened to the brief, he'd approved, as he usually did.

Once more the men who made the Sensitive Operations Group work would fly off to do America's dirty work. Brognola clearly saw the need for the operation, but the logistics of it still bothered him. He had glossed over that issue with the Man and had put a double coat of gloss on the nonexistent exit plan. Bolan and Phoenix Force were going in because they had to, and they would take out the targets because they were simply the best at what they did.

But sometimes even the best needed more than skill. Sometimes they needed a break to go along with it. Bolan had been his usual confident self when he had talked about walking out of Pakistan if they had to, and he knew that the Executioner had meant every word of it. But he didn't even want to think about the circumstances that would lead up to making that ordeal necessary.

Damn, he wished that he had been able to talk to Katz about this one before he had to present it. The Israeli had a real way of planning contingencies for suicide missions.

ON THE DRIVE BACK to Andrews, Brognola stopped off at his favorite deli along the way. In a city like Washington where people of nearly every nation on earth could be found running some kind of food establishment, this was his favorite place for lunch. It was run by an Egyptian family, but they featured cuisine from all over the world, and all of it was excellent.

"Do you want cream cheese on that, sir?" the man behind the counter asked after taking his lunch order for a loaded bagel.

He did, but since his last physical had pointed out

that his cholesterol levels had gone off the chart, he was trying to practice restraint. "Not this time, Ali, just the lox and cucumbers."

"Yes, sir."

"And, on second thought, make that two of them."

"Yes, sir."

At the cash register, he noticed a plastic container of teriyaki sticks. These grease, gristle and spice concoctions were one of Barbara Price's passions and, since they were individually wrapped, he could pocket them and not ruin a good suit. He added two of them to his tab and stuffed them in the inside pocket of his coat.

Now that he had secured his lunch, he drove on to Andrews to catch his ride back to the Farm. He'd eat on the way there.

SARAH CARTER WASN'T soothed or impressed by the rich, warm furnishings of Immanuel Zion's office in the temple. She knew a con when she saw one. But she did feel the power it represented, power that could be easily turned against her if she wasn't very careful.

"What have you learned about our new seeker, Arthur Corona?" Zion asked her.

"He appears to be exactly what he claims to be," she replied calmly. Her experience with men had left her with little awe for the male of the species, even for a man like Zion. Her reasons for joining the Temple of Zion were a bit different than most of the other women. In her case, she was running away from a man, not toward one.

"I've gone over his apartment in detail and nothing is suspicious about it. He hasn't lived there very long, and according to the neighbors, he's friendly, but pretty much keeps to himself. From the way he responded to me, though, I can tell that it had been some time since he's had a woman living with him."

Zion let his eyes drift slowly over Sarah's body. He could well imagine what Corona's response to her had been. One of the drawbacks of this job was that he had to limit himself to sampling only a few of the available women at any one time. However, the next time he had a vacancy in the special group that attended to his personal needs, she was going to be the next appointment. It was a shame to waste her on a nobody like Corona.

Reluctantly, Zion got back to the matter at hand. "What does your gut tell you about him?"

She tossed her hair in annoyance before answering. She knew damned good and well that Zion wasn't talking about her gut feelings, but something a little farther down. She had caught him looking at her, sizing her up like a steak in the meat market. It was a look she knew entirely too well, but it wasn't going to do him any good. She might be selling her ass for Zion's operation, but that didn't mean that she was going to sell any of it to him.

"He is a good man," she said sincerely. "A little battered by life maybe, but still ready to devote himself to something he can believe in. He will be a good seeker.''

''Do you think he can be trusted?''

''He seems to be an honest man,'' she replied truthfully.

Though Zion had little use for women beyond their original purpose, he had learned to trust their instincts. If she thought he was okay, that was good enough for him.

''Go back to him,'' he said. ''And continue to be his helpmate, but always be watchful of everything he does. If he's not faithful to the truth of Zion, I must know about it immediately.''

She had always wanted to live a life of adventure. But now that she was, she didn't find the Jane Bond role all that much fun. It was more of a lie than flashing her breasts and crotch in the spotlights of smoky bars had been. But for the time being, she had no choice. The Temple of Zion was the one place that Dingo would never think to look for her.

She dropped her eyes. ''Yes, Master.''

BUCK JACOBS, Zion's chief of security, waited until Sarah Carter was out of the room before making his report. But before he could start, his boss locked eyes with him. ''I want her slotted to be my next new personal attendant.''

''Can do,'' Jacobs replied. Since he always got the pick of the attendants who were cycled out of Zion's harem, he was more than ready to send her in to replace a redhead he'd had his eye on for some time now. Not only was the pay good around this place, the benefits couldn't be matched.

"I agree with her," Jacobs said. "Corona's clean. I can't find a thing to keep us from using him for the job. His company goes into Mexico all the time to make deliveries and pickups from the NAFTA companies. In fact, most of his trade goes back and forth across the border, and his trucks are well-known."

"Good," Zion said. "Because I have to get those Phalanx systems up and running as soon as I can. There's no point in starting work on the Titan site if I can't defend it."

The Phalanx was a radar-guided and -controlled 20 mm Vulcan cannon system that had been designed to take care of close-in air defense chores for Navy ships. It fired three thousand rounds of depleted uranium or tungsten ammunition per minute, and any aircraft that crossed its path ended up looking like a sieve in very short order.

A number of the Phalanx systems complete with radar and fire-control computers had been taken off decommissioned Navy ships at the Coronado Navy shipyard and packed for long-term storage. A half dozen of the crates had disappeared from the docks, and Zion had been able to secure three of them. With them guarding the skies above his planned desert stronghold, he wouldn't have to worry about anything less than an all-out military attack.

"I'll contact Corona tomorrow and get it set up."

"But," Zion said, "watch him closely until it's completely over. If it looks like he's trying to put one over on us, off him immediately. Don't even wait to talk to me about it, just do it."

"No problem."

"Now—" Zion flipped through a leatherbound notebook he kept in a locked desk drawer "—what's the situation on replacing the goods that disappeared with the *Bonaventure*?"

"Something really weird happened with that deal," Jacobs said, "and I don't like it. Not only is the ship gone, but the guys I went through to set it up are gone, too. I've had to make a new set of contacts, and they're being real cautious about taking on any new customers without checking them out thoroughly first."

"Surely they can't have any qualms about dealing with us?" Zion said in disbelief. "We're the biggest thing in the entire goddamned state."

"That may be, but they're starting to get a little shy about working with religious organizations. They're saying that we're not good risks, and they think that we have big mouths."

Zion's eyes narrowed. "You do what you have to do to convince them to play ball with us. I want those weapons as soon as possible."

Jacobs hated it when Zion got like that. He might be a big deal in the world of the lunatic fringe, southern California division. But the people he was trying to strong-arm were pros, and they didn't take kindly to threats. But they did like money, and Zion had money coming out his ass.

"I'll see what I can do."

"Don't just see," Zion snapped. "Do it!"

CHAPTER THIRTEEN

Over the Atlantic

Several hours later, a Lockheed C-141 Starlifter sped over the Atlantic, ferrying the Stony Man warriors to the Indian Ocean island of Diego Garcia. In the hold, T. J. Hawkins went over the HALO jump gear one piece at a time with J. R. Rust, yelling to be heard over the noise. A C-141 wasn't an airliner, and no weight had been wasted on soundproofing.

Even on a good day, regular parachute jumping was dangerous, but a High Altitude, Low Opening jump, particularly at night, was a good way to get an amateur killed. In the freezing cold of the high-altitude night sky, a person had to know the equipment by feel. A wrong move would kill a jumper a long time before his or her body could reach the ground.

"And while this is critical," Hawkins said as he was wrapping up his explanation of the oxygen system they needed to breathe most of the way down, "it's not the most difficult part. We're jumping at twenty-eight thousand feet. That's over five miles high, and we have to free-fall down to a thousand feet before popping the chutes so we won't show up on their radar screens.

"But to get there in one piece, you have to know how to free-fall properly. Screw that up, and you'll never be able to make a clean deployment. And deploying that low doesn't give you much time to grab a reserve if your main gets tangled. You'll just make a big hole in the ground."

Though it was far too late for him to back out, Rust was beginning to rethink his impulse to go to Pakistan with these maniacs. Everytime Hawkins mentioned something about the gear he would be using, he also mentioned that forgetting it would kill him. He had always figured that sky divers were suicidal and now he had proof of it.

"Get down on the floor, facefirst." Hawkins said. "We'll review the free-fall position again."

As Rust laid on the floor, Hawkins stood over him moving his arms and legs and explaining what that move would do while he was falling through the air.

"It's like you're being your own airplane. Your arms and legs are your control surfaces. Move them and the rest of you will move in response. Move your right arm and you turn right, left arm move left. Now, when you want to speed up, you…"

WHILE HAWKINS WAS GOING OVER the HALO procedures with Rust, Bolan and McCarter were in the front of the plane going over the latest satellite recon shots of the target area that had been faxed to them while they were in flight. The C-141 transporting them was a Special Operations Command bird and was outfitted with satellite communication and data links that gave them full interatction with the Farm.

Not much had changed at the primary target area. The third Red Dragon missile was still not on its launcher, so it looked like they would be arriving in plenty of time to take them out of the equation. After double-checking the route they would take in from the drop zone, they went over the intelligence reports for any political developments that would affect the second phase of the operation.

From the latest reports, the Pakistani military junta had turned up the heat yet another notch by demanding that the disputed Kashmir region along their border with India be turned over to them without delay. While they didn't openly mention making a nuclear strike if their demands weren't met, they did say that if they weren't, unprecedented measures would be taken.

In reply, the new Indian prime minister issued a statement saying that any aggressive acts by the illegal Pakistani junta would result in instant retaliation of the most forceful kind. The proclamation was followed up by mass mobilization of the Indian armed forces and the largest troop movement since the 1971 war. The diplomatic channels were still working overtime to try to defuse the situation, but neither government was backing off.

The commandos were going to be in time to shut down the Pakistani missile operation, but it was starting to look unlikely that they would be able to get to the secondary target before hostilities broke out. And, once the first nuke was dropped by either side, their survival would also be unlikely. Being at ground zero was a good way to ruin your day.

AS SOON AS THE STARLIFTER touched down on the tarmac at Diego Garcia, it was directed to taxi into a large hangar. As soon as the doors were closed behind it, a security cordon of Air Police in Hummers with gunmounts surrounded the building. The extra security didn't raise too much curiosity among the base personnel, however. Ever since the Gulf War, the airmen at Diego had become accustomed to seeing hush-hush flights coming in and out on a fairly regular basis.

For dealing with the military, Bolan had assumed his persona of Colonel Rance Pollock. Should anyone want to check on him, he would find that the colonel was listed as a personal liaison officer to the President and his authority wasn't to be questioned.

"We'll be here for seven hours," Bolan announced as soon as the team and their gear had been off-loaded. "The Air Force has a meal ready for us, and we have been given the use of air crew quarters so we can shower and sleep until we have to move out."

"Let me at that food," Hawkins said. "I'm a growing boy and the in-flight service on that Starlifter was less than satisfactory."

James grinned. "What's the matter, T.J., you lose

your taste for pony peter and plastic cheese sandwiches? I thought you Rangers lived on them.''

Hawkins shuddered. ''When I was in the Army, I always heard that the blue suiters ate like real people, not grunts.''

''If you wanted to join up for the cuisine, my man, you should have become a Squid, they eat real good.

''But,'' the ex-Ranger pointed out, ''they don't serve wine with their meals like we did.''

RUST WAS CAREFUL not to groan when Calvin James's cheerful voice roared in his ear, ''up and at 'em, J.R. We've got half an hour until suit-up time.''

The CIA man had to glance at his watch to make sure that he had actually slept. It seemed like it had only been moments ago that he had gotten into bed. Unfortunately, his watch gave him the bad news adjusted for the new time zone.

A light breakfast had been set out for the team, but Rust limited himself to coffee and orange juice. He had never had motion sickness before, but he had also never jumped out of an airplane in the middle of the night.

The suit-up procedure took more time than Rust had expected. After donning his night-black combat suit and assault harness, he got into a heavy, insulated, electrically heated HALO suit complete with gloves. The air was cold at twenty-eight thousand feet, and a case of frostbite was a reality he didn't want to have to deal with. The suit was topped off by a visored helmet with a built-in radio and night-vision goggles. Finally, the main chute and reserve went over all that. Their weapons, ammunition, water, food and other combat essentials were packed in equipment bags that would be hung on the front of their parachute harnesses.

As soon as they were suited up, an enclosed van took the Stony Man team to another hangar to meet their ride. The Northrop B-2 stealth bomber hunkered on its landing gear like a giant bat with its wings spread out to seventy-two feet. In the shadows, the plane's dark charcoal-gray paint looked as dark as a bat as well.

They didn't have much time to check out the plane, though. Their take-off time had been dictated by the orbits of the two Chinese satellites that were watching American forces in the area for the Pakistanis. They had to load up and be gone before the spy birds made their next pass.

The M-286 Personnel Pod, pressurized in the bomb bay of the B-2, had been developed for use in the B-1 Lancer to deliver people at supersonic speeds. The stealth bomber wasn't supersonic, but the pod worked just as well. The suited-up jumpers were cradled four to a pod like human bombs. While in flight, the pressurized pods had communications with the flight crew and with each other. Over the target, the bomb bays of the aircraft would be opened and the jumpers released like they were bombs.

The Stealth bomber's ground crew assisted the

Stony Man warriors into their pods, made sure they were hooked to the communications gear and locked them in. A few minutes later, the B-2's four 19,000 horsepower F118-GE-100 turbines spooled up, and it taxied out of the hangar to the runway. A few minutes later, the team was airborne heading east over the Indian Ocean.

Almost as soon was the bomber's wheels were up, Hawkins started running Rust through the parachute drills again. He was going over the oxygen system for the third time when Rust spoke up. "Give it a rest, T.J.," he said. "If I don't know it by now, I'm never going to and I'm starting to get confused."

"I second the motion, T.J.," James cut in. "I'm tired of hearing it, too."

"It's your ass," Hawkins replied.

"Believe me," the CIA man answered. "I know."

Stony Man Farm, Virginia

FOR SOME REASON, Barbara Price hated waiting out the initial drop the most. Once the team was on the ground, the guys would go about doing what they did best. And while that carried much greater risks, she was confident in their ability to turn even a poor suit into a winning hand. On the way there, however, they were always at the mercy of someone else's skills and luck.

"The team is feet dry," Kurtzman announced, using the old Navy flyer's term for an airplane crossing a coastline after having flown in over water.

"What's their ETA to the release point?" Price asked.

"Three twenty three," he replied. "They're right on the profile."

"I'll be in my office," she said. "Give me a call when they drop."

Over Pakistan

RUST WAS an action movie junkie. He had seen dozens of movies about people jumping out of airplanes under any number of circumstances, both realistic and fanciful. He had to admit, though, that jumping out of a B-2 stealth bomber wasn't like anything he had ever seen in a movie.

In fact, he didn't jump at all. When the time came for him to go, the pod rotated, the bottom suddenly fell out of his compartment and he dropped free of the bat-shaped plane like a human bomb. The team had been dropped in sequence, and he had been the second to the last to be released.

The last man out was Hawkins, and he swooped down to take charge of his jump buddy. Rust had tried to go into the spread-eagle, sky-diving position as Hawkins had told him to do, but it wasn't working for him. He was slowly tumbling out of control.

Hawkins flew—and there was no other word for it—right in beside him, and grabbing his left hand, pulled it away from his body. "Hold your left leg out as far as you can," he called over the com-link.

Rust did as he was told and felt Hawkins hook his boot over Rust's left ankle.

"Now," Hawkins called, "put your right arm and leg out the same way!"

The CIA agent obeyed and suddenly he was stable in the air. He knew he was falling, but he had no sensation of it beyond the rush of air past his helmeted ears.

"See," Hawkins said. "Do it right and there's nothing to it."

The time it took to fall over twenty-thousand feet went quickly. At eight thousand feet, Hawkins reminded him to take off his oxygen mask. A few seconds later, it seemed, they were at the release point.

"See you on the ground!" Hawkins shouted as he pulled the D-ring to Rust's main chute.

The canopy opened with a snap and drove the harness crotch straps up into Rust's groin with stunning force. At the same time, Hawkins disappeared from view like he had a rocket strapped to his back. A second later, he saw his black chute blossom open below him. Hawkins had swooped past him to open later so he would be on the ground first.

As Hawkins had said, the steerable chute was as easy to use as the handlebars of a bike. Pull on the left-side toggle and it went left. A tug on the right straightened it out again. The night-vision goggles allowed him to see the IR beacons on the team's canopies, and it was relatively easy to follow them down. It was only when he saw the ground rushing up to meet him that he started to feel a little uneasy. It looked like it was coming up too fast, and he tensed.

At the last possible moment, he remembered what Hawkins had said about releasing his equipment bag before he hit the ground. Releasing that extra weight to fall free would keep him from breaking his legs.

No sooner had he released the bag than he hit the ground. He had forgotten to flex his legs, so the force of the impact felt like they were being driven up into his armpits. Stunned, he fell heavily to the ground. He was fighting to get his breath when the canopy caught a gust of ground wind and started dragging him across the rocky ground.

He was dragged several yards before he remembered to pull hard on both toggles to collapse the chute. He lay on the ground, fighting to catch his breath when Hawkins ran up to him. "Are you okay?"

"I think so," Rust replied from a prone position. "I can move all my toes and nothing seems to be broken."

Hawkins shook his head. "You're the luckiest, dumb son of a bitch I ever saw," he said, his accent heavy. "If you'd of waited another half second to drop that bag, I wouldn't even have to bury you. All I'd have to do is just push dirt into that big ole hole in the ground you'd of made."

"Sorry to have disappointed you, T.J."

"That's all right, Bubba," Hawkins said. "There's still a whole bunch of ways for you to get your Company ass killed before this church social is over. I may get a chance to bury you yet.''

Rust was experienced enough to know that Hawkins didn't mean any of this abuse personally. It was just the adrenaline talking. He knew that he would feel the same way if he'd been required to take an untrained man with him on a dangerous Company operation.

''Until then,'' Rust said, holding out a hand, ''how about helping an old man get up.''

WHILE THE COMMANDOS got into their gear and checked their weapons, James and Manning gathered the chutes, HALO suits and empty equipment bags and buried them under a pile of rocks. Normally, they would have burned them to destroy the evidence, but they couldn't afford to have someone see the fire. Manning did, however, put two booby-trapped thermite grenades under the pile.

Bolan and McCarter verified their location with the GPS and found that the bomber had put them right in the middle of their planned drop zone. GPS systems made even night drops go like clockwork. Next, they activated the satcom link and sent a brief signal back to Stony Man Farm with the directional antenna. There was no reason to believe that anyone was actively watching for strange radio signals, but taking unnecessary chances would be foolhardy.

When the Farm acknowledged, McCarter keyed his com link. ''We're go.''

Silently, the commandos shrugged into their rucksacks and took up their tactical formation for the march into the missile site. Hawkins and James went up on point, T.J. for security and Calvin to navigate with the GPS unit. Bolan, McCarter, Manning and Encizo followed, with Rust and Grimaldi bringing up the rear.

The CIA man had spent many evenings under a desert moon, so marching across the sand at night wasn't a new experience for him. Neither was the pace the team was keeping. He wasn't a fitness freak, but he liked to stay in shape and walking was his workout. Nonetheless, by the time the fifth mile had passed, he realized that walking to keep the blubber at bay wasn't the same thing as walking to war.

Fortunately, though, he didn't have to disgrace himself by asking the point men to slow down. Grimaldi did it instead. "Redneck, Flyboy," he heard in his earphone, "we're not running a damned marathon are we?"

Rust heard Hawkins chuckle. "Roger. I'll try to hold it down for the lame and lazy in the rear."

CHAPTER FOURTEEN

San Diego, California

Carl Lyons was feeling a bit like a bastard child. With Phoenix Force launching into Pakistan and the millennium plague situation still unresolved, the Farm's resources were stretched to the limit and Able Team had pretty much been left on its own. He didn't really mind working alone. That was one of Able Team's strong suits. He just wished that they had something more important to do. In the grand scheme of things in the world right now, their mission was strictly a second-front operation that any decent cop could do.

Even so, it would be nice if they could stop more weapons from coming into the world's most well-armed nation. But he didn't think that they could really do anything to make a difference to the body count that was coming. The millennium was going to run red with blood no matter what they did. But if the information from the *Bonaventure*'s first mate was true, they could limit the carnage somewhat and take out a few of the scumbags who were profiting from America's fears. And if they could take down the Temple of Zion in the process, he'd be more than happy to do it.

In fact, he would take a great deal of personal pleasure in seeing this so-called Immanuel Zion go facefirst into a stone wall. The man was a first class scumbag, and he was seriously polluting the already overpolluted air of southern California. But since they hadn't been directly tasked with cult busting, it would have to be done in the context of stopping the weapons-smuggling operations.

Beyond following up any Temple of Zion leads that Blancanales could develop, the only thing of real import that they had to work on was the theft of several Phalanx close-in weapons systems from the Coronado Navy shipyard. Those 20 mm antiaircraft guns were serious hardware and, in anyone's hands, they could do an incredible amount of damage, millennium or not.

One of the best tools a police force had to work with nowadays was its aerial units. More and more, the choppers were making the critical difference between losing the war against criminals and just holding back the tide. In mass disturbances like those that were expected to ring in the millennium, police forces on the ground would be almost helpless without their air assets to back them. But even one Phalanx placed in the right spot could make the skies over a major city a very unhealthy place for police helicopters, as well as for anything else with wings.

Finding them was important, and while Blancanales

and Schwarz were concentrating on the Temple of Zion operation, he was trying to bird-dog them. The problem was that everyone from the ATF to the Navy was also looking for them and they were stumbling over one another's feet. He had another appointment with the local office of the Navy Criminal Investigation Service, but he wasn't confident that they would have anything new he could follow up. The track was so muddy now that only God knew were the Phalanxes had gone.

THE TEMPLE OF ZION looked like a high-budget, made-for-TV movie reconstruction of the temple of Solomon in ancient Jerusalem, only several times larger. It was squat, square and dominated its surroundings by its shear bulk. But what looked like gleaming white marble was merely a special kind of concrete. This theme of massiveness was continued by an entrance that looked to have been built for giants. The main doors were covered in what looked like gold, but wasn't, and they were purposefully huge, twenty-five feet high and twelve wide, so as to dwarf those who entered to worship.

Inside, the ceiling of the main hall was two stories high, which also made one feel insignificant in God's temple. No building in the ancient world could have had such a cavernous interior without needing a forest of pillars to hold up the roof. But Immanuel Zion had had one advantage over whoever had built Solomon's temple—steel rebar and concrete.

The interior of the great hall was done in the same faux marble as the exterior and gave an additional sense of openness. A few thin slabs of real marble had been mounted around the raised dais at the front of the huge room, but that was it. Zion had better places to spend his money and the people who gathered to hear his words were in no frame of mind to notice such details.

Rosario Blancanales and Sarah Carter arrived a few minutes before the second service of the day and had trouble finding a place to sit. The hall could hold some three thousand people, and it was packed to the walls. There were three main services each Sunday along with other smaller gatherings in the meeting rooms. Before the day was out more than ten thousand people would pass through the doors. With an average faith offering of fifty dollars a head, that was half a million bucks Zion's machine would take in on this one day.

The temple was also open the other six days of the week, and that was when the serious business was conducted. The Sunday services were just to satisfy the demands of the people and to recruit those who might be worthwhile to add to the ranks of the Chosen.

In Hollywood terms, the service was a high production, part rock concert, part tent revival and part New Age get-together. Thanks to the miracle of electronics, Zion's voice was as clearly audible to everyone in the room as if he were speaking to them alone. The lighting dimmed and brightened, depending on the subject being discussed. And as the topic went from the horrors of the coming millennium to the glories that would follow it for the Chosen of Zion, the crowd responded as if reading a script.

Blancanales wished he had Schwarz and one of his gadgets with him to see if Zion was using subliminal audio effects to prompt the crowd. It was either that or he was pumping some kind of hypnotic drug into the ventilation system. The effect culminated when the offering plates were passed. He'd never seen so many people grabbing for their wallets.

In concert with the rest of the temple's high-tech accessories, the collection plates had built-in credit card scanners like at a department store. Slide your card through, punch in the amount of your gift and it was electronically transferred to the temple's account.

As Blancanales and Carter were leaving, one of Zion's monitors, as the temple's guards were called, came up to him. "The Master wants to talk to you."

Blancanales had spotted the video pickups dotting the ceiling of the temple and knew that somewhere, someone was watching over the flock like a spotter watching the gamblers at the tables in Las Vegas. And for the same reason—money as much as security. That was how this thug had known where to find him in the crowd.

"Certainly," he replied before turning to Carter. "Why don't you go on home, Sarah," he told her. "I'll meet you there."

Carter didn't like Zion paying attention to Arthur

like this, but she knew better than to say anything about it. She squeezed his hand. "I'll be waiting."

Stony Man Farm, Virginia

THE COMPUTER ROOM WAS buzzing and Aaron Kurtzman had a big smile on his face when he turned to Hal Brognola. "We have the confirmation signal. They're down and in the right place. Even your CIA guy made it in one piece, and they'll be moving out on schedule."

Brognola glanced at the bank of clocks on the wall displaying the world's time zones. It was only nine at night in eastern Pakistan, giving the team more than enough time to move in, kill the missiles, pull back and find a place to hide before daylight. He had no doubts that this first phase would come off as planned. It was the movement across almost a thousand miles of less than hospitable territory to reach the secondary that worried him.

But as Striker liked to say, take the targets one at a time.

When he looked around for Barbara Price, he remembered that he had seen her leave half an hour earlier, and she'd not returned. "I'll let Barbara know," he said.

On the way out of the room, he stopped by Kurtzman's coffeepot and poured a cup. It was going to be one of those marathon sessions again, watching a real-time satellite shot of the region and monitoring the team's com-link transmissions. Regardless of what his doctor said, he couldn't do it without raising his caffeine level. Before he took a sip, though, he reached into his pocket, thumbed two Maalox antacid tablets off his roll and popped them in his mouth.

He didn't need them yet, but there was no point in asking for trouble.

The door to Price's office was open, and when Brognola stuck his head around the edge of the door, he saw that she was sitting in her chair bent over her desk with her head resting on her arms. She'd been working as hard as anyone for far too long, and he didn't begrudge her the rest. But that did not look like the most comfortable place in the world to nap.

"Barbara?" he called out.

When she didn't answer, he walked over to her. "Barbara?" Reaching out, he touched her shoulder and found it burning hot. When he pulled her upright and sat her back in her chair she moaned, but did not wake.

He was no MD, but checking her pulse, he found that it was racing. That and the fever meant that something serious was going on. Barbara Price was as healthy as a horse and didn't even get the winter bugs that swept through the Farm every few years or so. Then his eyes fell on the empty teriyaki stick wrappers in the trash can by her desk, and he felt a knot form in the pit of his stomach.

Punching the intercom, he called the security chief. "Chief, I need the medic and a stretcher up here in Price's office ASAP."

"Yes, sir."

The blacksuit medic arrived quickly, and two more of the security force followed him with a folding military stretcher.

The medic knelt beside the chair and quickly ran Price's vital signs. "She's running a temp of 104 degrees," he told Brognola. "Her pulse is 121, and I don't like her BP. I can't do a blood work up here, but I know she's got something serious. We need to get her out of here now."

"Do it."

While the medic keyed his radio and alerted Charlie Mott to fire up the chopper for the medevac, the two blacksuits with the stretcher moved in. The four men carefully took Price from her chair and laid her on the stretcher.

"And," Brognola said, bending to the trash can, "do you have a biohazard bag handy?"

The medic produced one from his kit, and Brognola put the teriyaki stick wrapper in it. "Send this with her. I think it's what made her sick."

As soon as the blacksuits left with the stretcher, Brognola hit the intercom on Price's desk. "Aaron," he said, "Barbara's sick. She's running a seriously high fever and her blood pressure's bad."

"You think it's the plague?"

Leave it to Kurtzman to get right to the point. But if it was, Brognola was the one who had given it to her. "The medic doesn't know, but I'm sending her to CDC Atlanta just in case."

"I'll call ahead and use the SOG priority."

"Do that," Brognola said, "and tell them that she'll be escorted by our blacksuits."

"Do you want me to inform Striker and Phoenix Force?"

Brognola thought for a moment. "Not now and not before we know what she has. Around here, though, we'll assume that it's the plague and we'll act accordingly. Until further notice we eat and drink only from prepared sources."

"You don't think that someone has attacked us here do you?"

"No, I don't," he said honestly. "But I can't take a chance on it. Not while we're in the middle of a mission like this."

"You got a point,"

"And," Brognola said, "wherever the hell Katzenelenbogen is, chase his ass down and tell him that I want him back here immediately."

Pakistan

THE STONY MAN TEAM made the hour-long march to its launch point without a hitch. With James and Hawkins taking security positions, the rest of the team lay on the top of a ridgeline and surveyed the target area below.

Since the camouflaged missile base was in the middle of nowhere, the Pakistanis apparently hadn't wanted to draw attention to the site by putting a security cordon around it. There was a small military compound several miles to the south, but there had been no local security patrols on the way in or even remote sensors. Depending on remoteness for security wasn't a bad tactic, but it had been misplaced this time. Rust eyed the motor pool five hundred yards from the main compound. Since the overall plan depended upon their securing a ride, the lack of a fence made it a perfect place to go hunting for a way to keep from wearing out their boot leather.

"I may not be much of a parachutist," he told McCarter, "but I've been hot-wiring cars since I was a kid and I'm a damned good driver. How about my going into that motor pool and trying to secure us some transportation while the rest of you do your thing?"

"I'll go with him," Grimaldi volunteered. "I'm also pretty good with a hot wire."

"Wait till we move out, then do it."

THE PAKISTANI IN THE DISPATCH OFFICE was taking a nap on the cot at the rear of the shack. Since Grimaldi wasn't carrying a silenced weapon, he drew the fighting knife from his harness and crossed the floor. A hand over the man's mouth and the blade across his neck sent him into an even deeper sleep.

"Clear," Grimaldi radioed to Rust.

The first thing the CIA man saw in the dispatch shack was a key rack by the door. "This may be a little easier than I thought it was going to be. These keys are all tagged with numbers, so all we have to do is pick out what we want to drive, read the numbers and find the keys.''

"I don't read the local language," Grimaldi said dryly.

"No sweat, I do."

Not too far from the dispatch office, two fairly new Land Rovers sat parked side by side. From their markings and sand camouflage paint, they appeared to be standard army issue, which meant they had a good chance of being in decent mechanical condition. There were newer, more powerful four-wheel drive vehicles in the world, but it was still hard to beat the original.

"How about these two?" Rust asked.

Grimaldi gave them a quick once-over. "They look good to me."

After mentally noting the numbers on their hoods, 23 and 76, Rust went back to the dispatch office, found the keys and pocketed them. Scooping up the rest of the keys, he shoved them into the other side pocket of his pants. "That should slow them a bit. Now if they want to chase us, they're going to have to do the hot-wiring instead of us."

"You're a sneaky little bugger."

Rust grinned in the dark. "It goes with being a Company man."

Grimaldi keyed the mike to his com link. "We've secured two Land Rovers," he said, "and they both have gunmounts. So, if you guys find a machine gun laying around, you might want to add it to the collection."

"Roger," McCarter sent back. "Make sure that you add a gas can or two."

"We're doing that right now."

The refueling point was also well organized. A stack of filled five gallon jerricans lay off to one side of the main storage tank ready to go. So as not to disarm themselves, the commandos each picked up a can in their off-hands and lugged them to the Land Rovers.

After the last gas cans had been loaded, Grimaldi went back to the refueling point. Pulling a quarter-pound block of C-4 plastique from his assault pack, he took the protective strip off the back to expose the adhesive and slapped it out of sight on the storage tank. After making sure that it was sticking tight, he flicked the detonator switch to remote. When it hit the fan, he'd blow the tank to add to the confusion. With luck, the burning gas would take out most of the remaining vehicles.

CHAPTER FIFTEEN

When the Stony Man assault team moved to within a hundred yards of the main site, they stopped again to recon the target area. Even under IR scan, they couldn't detect sentries. Once again, too much confidence was proving to be worse than too little.

"I know this is the right place," Rafael Encizo said. "But I can't believe they don't have guards posted."

"We have to luck out once in a while," Gary Manning replied.

As the last set of satellite photos the team had received at Diego Garcia had shown, two Red Dragon missiles were set upright on their launchers with two more laying on their sides as if they were being worked on. Only four launchers had been counted, so the other two missiles that had been delivered had to be stored in the concrete building next to the work area.

Seeing the two missiles on the work cradles with their nose cones removed, Manning had an idea. "The warheads are plutonium-fueled, right?" he asked.

"That's what Kurtzman said in the briefing,"

McCarter answered. ''Third-generation copies of a Russian design given to them by the Chinese.''

''Good. I have an idea that should save us a lot of exposure time down there.''

''What's that?''

''If we can get an explosive charge on one of those warheads,'' the demo expert explained, ''when it goes off, it'll cause the implosion blocks to detonate out of sequence and send the bomb into a nonnuclear explosion. Not only will that finish off that one missile, it'll spread the plutonium far enough to contaminate this whole area. It'll take years before it cools down enough to be cleaned up. That way, we'll only have to hit that one missile to take them all out.''

''There's no danger of it going critical?''

Manning shook his head. ''Not a chance. For it to do that, the implosion blocks have to go off in a precise sequence. If even one doesn't work properly, it won't go nuclear.''

McCarter looked over at Bolan. ''Striker?''

''We can do it that way,'' he agreed. ''But I want to rig at least two of them. We can't risk a demolitions failure.''

After one last scan, McCarter keyed his com link. ''Let's do it.''

In their night-black combat suits, the six Stony Man warriors were shadows moving through the darkness. Not having the compound brightly lighted was a plus for them as far as concealment went, but it also meant that they'd have to keep a sharp eye out for sentries who might also be keeping to the shadows.

Now that their transportation had been secured, Rust had nothing to do but wait, and the waiting was the worst part for him. As an experienced field operative, he was used to waiting, but not under these circumstances. All it would take for this to go bad would be for one of these guys to have insomnia and decide to stop by the motor pool to look for his lost lunch box, or something like that, and they'd be in deep trouble.

Grimaldi had ordered him to stay with the vehicles while he went to take a position at the back of the motor pool so he could better watch the approaches. If things went south for the team, he was to start his Land Rover and race down to pick them up on the fly. Grimaldi would be right behind him. Since it would be a hot pickup, he'd be driving with one hand and shooting with the other like something out of a Bonnie and Clyde movie.

Rust was so busy listening to the com link and trying to see what was happening at the launch site that he almost missed the Pakistani who came up behind him. Since the intruder had no idea that death was waiting in the motor pool, he wasn't even trying to be quiet. But trained men tend to walk carefully at night anyway. Rust didn't pick him up until he was almost on top of him. He didn't have a silenced weapon, and the man was too close for him to even whisper a warning over the com link. He was going to have to do this the hard way.

The assault harness he had been issued had come with a Marine Ka-bar fighting knife attached to the left shoulder strap. Carefully slinging his H&K over his shoulder, he drew the fighting knife and tried to remember the cold steel training he had received as a CIA recruit so long ago.

In his night-black combat suit, Rust was all but invisible in the shadows and the Pakistani didn't see him as he walked by. Before he went two more steps, Rust lunged for him.

His left hand shot out to cover the man's mouth and jerk his jaw to the side. The knife hand drove the blade into the side of his neck right under his ear. The thrust was angled to stab deeply, severing the jugular, the carotid and the trachea before exiting his throat.

It was just like he had been taught all those years ago by the Marine drill instructors. The knife went in and the guard went limp. He held the man to his chest as he shuddered and died, the smell of hot blood and his voided bladder sharp in the cool night air.

When the Pakistani stilled his movements, Rust quietly lowered the corpse to the ground and rolled it out of sight under a nearby truck. Then he took several deep breaths to control the shakes before contacting Grimaldi on the com link.

"Flyboy, this is Spook. We just had a visitor, but I took care of him."

"Roger, just keep your eyes open for more of them."

Rust had so much adrenaline racing through his system that he couldn't doze off if he were hit with a hammer. Reaching down, he took a handful of sand and rubbed it on the blood soaking the right sleeve of his jacket. It wouldn't get all of it, but it made it less sticky.

WITH BOLAN, McCarter, Encizo and Hawkins securing the area around the launchers, James assisted Manning with the demo work. The Canadian had thought that he would be able to place the charges directly on the warhead casings of the missiles laying on their sides. But when he got up to them, he saw that a complicated shock-absorbing frame surrounded the warhead itself.

"I've never seen a warhead mounted like this," he radioed to McCarter, "so it's going to take a little longer than I thought."

"Just do it."

Not wanting to take the time to remove the shock frame, Manning cut his demo blocks in two and worked them past the braces to reach the outer housing. After fitting two pounds of C-4 to the first warhead, he connected the blocks with a daisy chain of detonation cord and double remote control detonators.

"The first one's done," he reported.

"Activate the detonator," McCarter ordered.

Normally, Manning didn't like to work around active detonators. But if they were suddenly ambushed, he might not be able to get back to it and the weapon had to be destroyed. "Charge one is hot," he radioed.

Rigging the second missile went a bit faster, and he activated its detonator as well. "They're both ready," he reported. "But I want to slap secondary charges on the two missiles on the launchers. The last thing we need is for those two to cook off in the explosion and launch."

"Make it fast."

MAJOR ALI ZERI of the Pakistani army's secret nuclear weapons development unit wasn't at all happy about being on the road at that time of night. Even in this day and age it wasn't unknown for bandits to roam the high desert regions. But this trip couldn't be avoided, not if he wanted to keep his head on his shoulders. A problem had occurred at the secret Gandara missile site that only he could deal with, and it couldn't wait until morning. When he had explained to the generals of the junta why the Red Dragons weren't operational yet, he had been ordered to have at least two of the missiles refitted and ready to be launched in twenty-four hours at the latest.

The problem was that the Chinese missiles had been designed for nonnuclear warheads, and adapting them to carry a more deadly cargo hadn't been a straightforward conversion. Unlike high explosive warheads, nuclear weapons relied on sensitive electronic components to function. These had to be cushioned from the shock of the missile launch and the vibration of the solid fuel rocket engines.

A mistake had been made in the design of the warhead's shock-mounting system. The collar that mated it to the missile airframe wasn't strong enough to hold the weight of the nuclear casing and the shock frame. This mistake hadn't been discovered until three days ago when the first two missiles had been placed on the launchers and the collars failed.

In light of the military emergency, he had personally seen to the redesign of the mating collars. The first two of the complicated new parts were in the back of his truck, and they would get the generals off his back. His team at the research center was working to complete the other four to get all the missiles operational.

He would have arrived several hours earlier, but the helicopter carrying him and his technicians had an inflight emergency and had been forced to land at a base more than one hundred kilometers short of his destination. Armed with orders that gave him authority over anyone he needed to assist him, he had borrowed enough vehicles and escorts to make up his convoy. He was having trouble recognizing the terrain in the dark, but the driver assured him that they had only a few more kilometers to go.

GRIMALDI SPOTTED the lights of the approaching vehicles as a glow against the night sky behind the ridgeline.

"Striker," he called over the com link. "I think

we've got company coming. I have what I think are headlights coming up the road from the south.''

"We're almost done here," Bolan sent back. "Can you hold them off for a couple more minutes?''

"Can do.''

Hearing Grimaldi's call, Rust went to join him. He had never fought a delaying action before, but it looked like this was his week for trying new and different things. At least he was a pretty fair shot with an H&K, so he could give a good accounting of himself.

MAJOR ZERI WASN'T in the lead vehicle of his little convoy. That honor had been given to the infantry captain commanding the escort troops. Zeri's two trucks with his technicians and the mounting collars were safely in the middle. If anything did happen, it was up to the infantry to protect them.

As they crested the ridge and were approaching Gandara's motor pool, gunfire suddenly rang out. Someone was shooting at them!

The lead vehicle ran into a stream of fire and drove off the road, the driver dead. The other escort vehicles slammed to a halt, and the troops jumped down to take cover.

Zeri wasn't a hero, but it was obvious that an attempt was being made to attack the missiles. Signaling for his other truck to follow him, he pulled out of the convoy and backtracked until he was well out of the line of fire. Once clear, he turned to circle around to come in on the compound from the east.

EVEN UNDER THE BEST circumstances, two men ambushing an unknown number of troops at night was a tricky maneuver. At Grimaldi's suggestion, Rust had fired up his Land Rover and, driving with his lights out, flanked the Pakistanis' position. He'd fire a couple of bursts and drive off. After laying down the initial fire to make the enemy deploy, Grimaldi got in his Land Rover as well and the two of them opened fire.

The Pakistanis didn't group their vehicles and use them for cover. They had deployed in a line and weren't concentrating their fire. Nonetheless, Rust counted at least two dozen assault rifle muzzle-flashes in the dark, and that was a lot of firepower.

Fortunately, with it being dark, he didn't have to see how close the return fire was coming to him. Slapping a fresh magazine in the well of his H&K, he dropped the clutch and charged again, firing on the run.

"We're coming out on the west side," he heard McCarter call over the com link. "Break contact now and pick us up on the fly."

Rust was glad to hear that. Even though he was keeping on the move, the opposition had figured out that there was only one shooter in his vehicle and started concentrating their fire on him.

Ripping off the last of the magazine in his subgun, he cranked the wheel hard to get out of there. Before he could accelerate, he heard a round slap into the body of the truck and felt a blow to his right leg.

"Fuck!" He slammed on the gas and powered out of the turn as fast as he could go. The leg was numb and hopefully wasn't bleeding too badly, but he couldn't stop to check it now. Even if it killed him, he had to make the pickup.

Keeping the lights off, he raced across the desert, homing in on McCarter's com link chatter. When he spotted a strobe light, he headed for it and a quarter mile later slid to a halt.

"Hop in the back, lad," McCarter shouted to Rust as he and James piled into the Land Rover. "I'm taking the wheel." Among the many skills listed on his rap sheet, the ex-SAS commando was an experienced race-car driver, and moving across open country at high speeds was one of his specialties.

Rust gladly relinquished his seat and moved into the back for the ride.

IN THE SECOND Land Rover, Grimaldi was handling the driving chores. At Manning's order, he paused at the top of the ridge so the demo man would have line of sight for his radio-controlled detonators.

"Fire in the hole!" Manning gave the traditional blaster's call as he hit the switch on the transmitter.

At the missile base, four explosions sounded as one. Black smoke and dust billowed up, obscuring the launch site, and the two missiles on the launchers toppled to the ground.

"That's not much of an explosion for all this work," Grimaldi said. "I'm a little disappointed in you, Gary. You usually do better work than that."

"I didn't need much of a bang to do the damage

this time," Manning explained. "The plutonium will do it for me. As well as being great nuclear weapons material, it's one of the most toxic substances in the world. A couple of specks in the lungs is all it takes to kill you rather quickly. Most of those guys will be dead by morning, and the rest of them by tomorrow night."

"But if they decide to try to follow us, we'll still have a problem."

"Only for a couple of hours," Manning said confidently. "After that, they'll be too sick to drive. But that's what you get for messing around with that damned stuff."

"Nonetheless," Grimaldi said, grinning, "let me show you how a real explosion is supposed to look."

He pressed the firing key of his transmitter and the motor pool turned into a roaring, boiling fireball. "That's a proper explosion."

"Show-off."

MAJOR ZERI HAD BEEN far enough away when the demolitions went off not to be affected by them. In fact, he, too, had thought that they were rather small. He knew better than to go too close to the launch site, but he couldn't keep from it. He had to know how much damage had been done to the missiles. If he returned to the junta without knowing exactly what had happened, he'd be a dead man. Also, there was a chance that he could still fit the new mating collars to the missiles in the storage building and meet the dead-line.

With so much smoke and dust in the air, it blanked the headlight beams and he had to drive almost up to the launchers to assess the damage. It was only when he saw the smoldering, twisted wreckage of the warheads that he remembered one of the major drawbacks to working with plutonium. Like magnesium, it burned in the presence of oxygen.

Recoiling as if he had been hit in the face with a baseball bat, Zeri shouted for the driver to turn around. He knew, though, that it was already too late for him or for any of them. The smoke and dust he was breathing contained plutonium dust and one small speck was all it took. He would be dead within twenty-four hours.

CHAPTER SIXTEEN

San Diego, California

The next morning, Hermann Schwarz was waiting in the parking lot of Knight Electronics in the cab of one of the company's largest trucks. The day before, Zion had asked Blancanales if the Temple could use his rigs to make a freight pickup south of the border. Of course, Blancanales had been more than willing to do a service for the master and had tapped Schwarz to be the wheelman. How better to recon the enemy's locations than to pick up from one and make a delivery to another.

He was entertaining himself listening to the Temple of Zion morning radio broadcast when he spotted Blancanales walking out of the Knight Electronics building with another man at his side. From the looks of the guy, he had to be one of Zion's strong-arm boys. That would make his planned recon a little more difficult, but he'd play the cards he'd been given.

"Good morning, Mr. Corona," Schwarz sang out as soon as Blancanales got within voice range.

"Good morning, Fred," Blancanales answered. "Are we all ready to go?"

"Yes sir," Schwarz replied. "The truck's all gassed up, and I have the invoices and customs paperwork."

"Let's do it then."

Blancanales slid into the cab next to him and the gunman took the seat next to the door. The trip south down I-5 to the Mexican border went without incident. In fact, the Temple gunman sat completely silent throughout the entire trip. Blancanales also said nothing beyond responding to a couple of Schwarz's sarcastic comments on the traffic.

At the crowded Tijuana border crossing point, the Border Patrol waved the truck through without even looking in the back. No one in their right mind smuggled anything into Mexico except stolen cars. And the white trucks with the blue knight logos made frequent enough trips between the two countries that they were expected.

Once clear of the checkpoint, Blancanales asked Jacobs, "Where to?"

Following Jacobs's directions, Schwarz drove through town before turning off on National Route 2 and taking it a few miles to a newly constructed business park. Most of the buildings bore the logos of U.S. companies, reflecting the impact the North American Free Trade Agreement was having on both countries. The lure of cheap labor was creating a bonanza for both the American companies who moved south and the Mexican workers who filled the jobs. They drove past these new buildings, however, and headed into an older Mexican area.

"On the left," Jacobs said, pointing to a building that was marked as belonging to a beer distributor.

Schwarz maneuvered the big truck around the back and saw three rather large crates with several smaller ones waiting on the loading dock. The size of the fork-lift waiting to pick up the larger crates indicated that they were heavy.

"Let me give you a hand, guys," Schwarz said as he started to slide out from behind the wheel.

Jacobs shot a look at Blancanales, and almost imperceptibly, shook his head.

"That's all right, Fred," Blancanales answered. "The guys here can do it. I pay you to drive, not lift cargo."

"Whatever you say, Mr. Corona."

Being exiled to the truck's cab didn't mean that Schwarz couldn't do something useful. Palming the miniature camera that was built into his battered old Zippo lighter, he went to work. Using the truck's side mirrors, he got several shots of the crates being loaded into the back and of the guys loading them. What good they might be, he didn't know, but he couldn't just sit there and do nothing.

It took less than an hour before Jacobs and Blancanales returned. The Temple man had a clipboard with printed invoices on it and handed it to Schwarz. "This will get you through customs."

At the border crossing back into the United States,

Schwarz presented the customs agents with the invoices for his cargo. The agents barely glanced at them before stamping their approval, and he was waved through. Once more, no one bothered to look in the back of the truck.

"Where to, Mr. Corona?" Schwarz asked once they were back on I-5 heading north.

The thug turned to Blancanales. "Go into San Diego and take the Harbor Drive exit."

"Got it," Schwarz said.

When they arrived at their destination, another warehouse in an industrial district, Schwarz was again told to stay in the truck's cab while the cargo was unloaded. And again he used his camera to get what information he could from the side-view mirrors. This time, though, three forklifts made short work of the load and had it inside in fifteen minutes.

"What in the hell was that all about, Pol?" he asked when Blancanales returned.

"Damned if I know. All I know is that those crates were heavy, real heavy, and the markings on the outside had all been painted over."

"I got a few shots through the side mirrors of the handlers to add to our mug shots for this gig. Maybe Carl can come up with something from them."

WHEN BLANCANALES and Schwarz drove away, Immanuel Zion stepped out of the warehouse office. "Any problems?" he asked Jacobs.

The security chief shook his head. "Our information

was right on. Customs didn't even open the back of the truck.''

"Good. What's the status of our Phalanx technician?''

Jacobs smiled. ''He's still screwing his brains out, but he's ready to go to work whenever we need him.''

The thing that made using the stolen Phalanxes even remotely feasible was the appearance of an ex-Navy enlisted man who had been a weapons systems specialist on a destroyer. The sailor had gotten in trouble in the Navy, something to do with being drunk and disorderly, and had been discharged under less than honorable conditions. Like so many other lost souls, he had wandered into Zion's circus and, as soon as his particular expertise had become known, had been invited to become one of the Chosen.

Zion looked pleased. ''The contractor is due to start pouring the concrete today, so in two days we'll be able to start installing the guns. And as soon as they're operational, I want to start moving in the supplies. I want that place up and running as soon as possible.''

"Does that mean transferring the bullion as well?''

Like many others who feared a collapse, Zion had been stockpiling precious metals for some time now, much in the form of silver coinage. When civilization went to hell, banks would be among the first to go. And when that happened, paper currency would instantly become worthless. Silver and gold coins, however, had been used as money for over two and a half millennia.

"That's the first thing I want moved."

EVEN THOUGH BLANCANALES knew that Sarah Carter would be in his apartment when he came home, it was still a thrill to open the door and see her waiting for him. This wasn't the first time he'd had to work with an enemy operative dogging his heels, but it was certainly the most pleasant.

"How was your day?" she asked as she raised her face for a welcoming kiss.

"I finally got to do something useful for the master," Blancanales said, sounding properly enthusiastic. "I picked up some equipment for him in Mexico and brought it back."

Blancanales still had no idea what in the hell he had smuggled across the boarder for Zion. Whatever it was had to be bad news for peace and the public order. But he knew that a true follower would have been so overjoyed at having been chosen for such a task that he wouldn't think to ask the tough questions, so he couldn't either.

"I'm glad you were able to help when he called on you," she replied. "We all need to do what we can to help him."

Carter was tempted to warn him about getting too involved with the inner circle of the Temple, but she didn't dare. She couldn't risk losing the real sanctuary Zion was unknowingly providing her. A religious cult was the last place in the world that Dingo Jones would look for her, and as long as she stayed out of sight, she should be safe.

She hadn't lied to Zion when she had reported that she felt Arthur Corona was an honest man. He was and she knew it. But she also felt that there was more to him than appeared on the surface. Although he was walking the walk and talking the talk of a Seeker to perfection, he was subtlety different from the others who had joined Zion.

Male or female, most of the people who came to the Temple were either eaten up with emptiness and self-doubt or they were openly criminal. Arthur didn't have any of the traits she had learned the hard way were the mark of a criminal mentality. And she was certain that he was far too intelligent to have fallen for the Temple's bullshit. These thoughts, however, she would keep to herself.

Her assignment to be his helpmate was proving to be a pleasant task, and she felt that he sincerely liked her as well, and that was good. Since she had so little depth to her cover, she might be able to use Arthur as a backup if things went to hell with the Temple.

"Have you heard the Master speak of the sanctuary?" she asked.

Blancanales looked puzzled. "No. What is that?"

"It's the place where the Seekers will gather when the millennium comes. There we will wait for the truth, and then we'll go forth and enlighten the nation."

"Where is this place?"

"It's somewhere in the desert," she replied. "I've

heard that it was once a place of great evil, but that it has been purified and is being turned into a place of truth. When this work is completed, we Seekers will follow the master there to wait out the Apocalypse."

"Maybe my load was to help with that," he said.

"Maybe."

WASHINGTON, D.C., wasn't the only place in the United States where random cases of the mutated anthrax had started showing up. The government tried to keep a lid on this chilling information, but to no avail. The millennium plague had visited America, and it was headline news. From coast to coast, tens of thousands of Americans instantly became organic vegetarians. Some did it to keep from falling victim to the plague, but others did it just because it was a new trend and they didn't want to be left out.

Following the headlines, millennium plague detector kits started appearing in late-night TV infomercials. By the time the FDA could step in and shut them down, millions of the kits had been sold for as much as $199. But those who depended on these kits to shield them from the mysterious illness might as well have spent their money on holy relics or bubblegum. The detector kits, which had been repackaged from instant pregnancy kits, couldn't detect anything more than a certain human female hormone not likely to be found in any food stuff consumed by the public.

Pulling the kits off the market, though, simply added fuel to the Millennium Madness. Now the plague was a government conspiracy aimed at one particular group or other, usually an ethnic minority, depending on who was talking about it. Announcements by the CDC and FDA that the kits were completely useless didn't stop the rumors.

For a year now, the Millennium Madness had waxed and waned from day to day. A new panic would be invented, everyone would get on board for a few weeks and then it would fade. There was, though, an ever-growing hard-core segment of the population that took the pronouncements of doom seriously.

In southern California, where so many of the hard-core millennium freaks had gathered, the death toll continued to climb. San Diego wasn't the only California city that had a semipermanent camp of those waiting for the millennium, and not all of these refugees had gone to the sea. In Los Angeles, they went to the mountains. Yosemite National Forest had become the home to thousands of these refugees. So many were camped in the national park that the Park Service tried to close it, and that had been a mistake.

Like most Americans, the squatters in the park were armed and they were ready to defend their "rights." The first confrontation produced only seven bodies—three park rangers, a state police officer and two squatters. The second round went to the authorities, but public reaction to the TV coverage of the firefight caused the police forces to withdraw when they were ahead eighteen to four.

The President then got into the affair and declared

the park off-limits to state authorities. But not wanting to start a second civil war, he also pulled all federal agencies out as well. For the first time since the days of the Old West, anarchy was becoming a way of life.

IN HIS DEEP UNDERGROUND fortress, the Old Man of the Mountain followed the millennium developments on the most modern electronic equipment money could buy. He was working to bring a medieval life-style back to most of the earth, but that didn't mean that he wouldn't use the best of modern technology to make it come to pass. Every report of chaos, anarchy and death in the West brought a smile to his lips because he knew the effect it was having on the Muslim nations.

Modern communications made it as easy for a Middle Easterner to know what was happening in Europe and the United States, as it did for Americans to keep an eye on the Middle East. The use of the television media in the Gulf War had proved how powerful it was in shaping public opinion.

Admittedly, Saddam Hussein's amateurish attempts to use TV to sway opinion in the West hadn't worked well. In fact, they had backfired. Terrifying children, as he had done, was never a good ploy to use against the infidels. They foolishly valued children above almost anything except money.

The Old Man had watched the Gulf War carefully and had learned his lessons from it. Rather than produce propaganda, he just let the people witness the actual events as they occurred and then told them what what they had seen really meant. His imams were using television news to good effect. The millennium prophecies were explaining everything they saw, and they believed that the West was doomed as had been foretold.

CHAPTER SEVENTEEN

Pakistan

Now that they were on the road, Rust had time to think about his leg again. He had been shot before, and he wasn't going to panic this time, either. During his escape from Tehran in the aftermath of the embassy takeover, he had picked up a stray round that had drilled through his shoulder. It had been more than a week before he had received treatment for that one and he had lived, so he knew he could deal with whatever he had to this time.

This one didn't feel all that bad. The round had punched through the side of the Land Rover before drilling into his leg, so it had lost much of its force before the impact. Right now, it wasn't bleeding too much and the impact site was numb and that could be a good sign. He didn't want to ask the team to stop now to take care of it.

Calvin James caught him feeling his leg and turned in the passenger seat. "You pick up something back there?"

Rust was embarrassed, but he had to confess that he had been hit. "My leg stopped a round."

James climbed out of his seat into the rear of the vehicle. "Let's take a look at it."

Rust dropped his pants and held out his right leg. In the narrow beam of light from James's penlight, the entry wound didn't look too bad. It was oozing blood, but wasn't actively bleeding, which suggested that no major blood vessels had been cut. When he reached around to feel for the exit hole, Rust flinched and James knew the story. The bullet was still in his leg and he couldn't do anything about it until daybreak.

"I'm going to powder this and wrap it for now," he said. "I'll take the bullet out tomorrow when I have good light. I don't want to try it now because I might cause more damage than the slug did."

Rust grinned. "I guess I can wait till then."

"I can always try to do a major surgery on you in the back of a bouncing Land Rover driven by a mad Briton who thinks he's Sterling Moss."

"I'll pass, thank you."

"Thought you might."

When the sun rose over the rugged mountains of central Pakistan, it found the Stony Man warriors dug in to wait out the day. The Pakistani forces had no shortage of helicopter gunships, and being caught out in the open desert would bring a swift conclusion to their mission.

The two Land Rovers had been pulled into a draw and covered with a special plastic sheeting that was supposed to render them invisible to radar and magnetic imaging, as well as Mk-1 eyeballs. Under the camouflage, the commandos went about getting a meal and finding a place to sleep until the sun set and they could move out again.

Among ex-SEAL Calvin James's many talents, he was a trained combat medic. Phoenix Force did its level best to insure that it was always the other guy who took the hits, but accidents happened. The bullet in Rust's leg was a good example. And now that they were parked for the day, he could take care of the CIA man's wound.

"As they say," James stated with a grin as he prepared the stainless-steel instrument he would use to probe for the slug, "this is going to hurt you a lot more than it does me."

"I've heard that line before," Rust replied as he dropped his pants, "so just do it."

Fortunately, James was able to grab the base of the bullet on his first try and carefully withdrew it from the entrance wound. "Got it," he said proudly as it appeared. "Want a souvenir of your trip to scenic Pakistan?"

"Pass," Rust said. "I'll always have the scar to remind me."

After binding the wound again, James gave Rust a shot of a broad-spectrum antibiotic IM and handed him a vial of pills. "Take one of these every twelve hours or so, and you should be okay."

McCarter approached James. "How is it?" he asked.

"It's not that bad," James replied. "The slug lost most of its punch going through the side of the vehicle, so it glanced off his femur instead of smashing it. It's mostly just muscle damage. In two weeks, he'll be up and running on it."

"Can he walk on it now?"

James gave him a look that the Phoenix Force leader instantly understood. "If he wants to, he can."

"Then he'll just have to want to, won't he?"

Both of them knew that some men could take a small hit and be put out of action more from psychological factors than from the actual physical damage. On the other hand, some men could suffer very serious wounds and still fight because they refused to give in to it. How the CIA man would deal with it was yet to be seen.

McCarter went to where Rust was resting to assess the situation for himself. "How's the leg?"

"It's been better, but it's not too bad."

"In a normal military operation," McCarter explained, "we'd have some way to medevac you, J.R. But as you've figured out by now, we're not military and we're staying here until we get the job done. And that means that you're going to have to gut this one out. For a number of reasons, we can't leave you behind. I'm sure you understand."

Rust understood McCarter only too well. The only way he'd be left behind was if he were dead. Left alive, he'd be a risk for the team because if he was captured, he could be made to talk. This was standard covert operations procedure, but he had never had it applied to him. Before this, it had only been stories about some other poor bastard who'd been given the choice of gutting it out or snorting a round.

"I may not be up for a marathon—" Rust attempted a grin "—but, if it comes down to that, I'll still try to keep up with you. If I fall behind, though, do what you have to do."

McCarter had figured that as an experienced field agent Rust would know how the game was played, and he was glad that he didn't have to explain the cold, hard facts of life to him. He didn't think it would come down to that, but he liked having the rules understood up-front.

"I'll do what I can," he assured Rust, "to see that you don't have to fall on your sword."

"Much obliged."

Stony Man Farm, Virginia

HAL BROGNOLA READ THROUGH the report of the attack on the Red Dragon missiles and the team's escape from Gandara. It would have to be Rust who had taken a round. But if McCarter said that he was able to carry on, that was good enough for him. The CIA man had impressed him as a man who didn't give up easily.

"Do we need to report this plutonium contamination to anyone?" he asked Kurtzman.

"Not officially, but when this thing's in the can, I'll notify the CIA and they'll pass it on to the Atomic Energy Commission to do what they like with it. There's so much ground in China and the old Soviet Union that's uninhabitable for the next few thousand years that a few more acres in Pakistan won't really matter."

"Not unless you herd your goats through those hills," Brognola said dryly.

"Then you're screwed unless the Pakistanis fence the area off."

"When do they move out again?"

Kurtzman glanced up at the clock covering the Pakistan time zone. They'll be on the move in a little over six hours."

"How long do you think it's going to take them to reach that airfield?"

Kurtzman knew what Brognola was looking for, but he couldn't give it to him. They'd been over this part a couple of times before, but apparently he wanted to hear it once more so he could tell the Man again. The President wanted this to be over instantly so he could start putting pressure on Pakistan again. But that wasn't the way it was going down.

"If everything goes as planned," he said, "they're going to be out there for at least another two days and nights. Even when they reach Palimiro, they're going to have to recon the target and wait for night to attack."

He held up a cautioning finger. "And that's only if

luck's with them all the way and they don't run into anything unexpected.

"What are the satellites showing on the border?" Brognola changed subjects.

This was where the bad news came in. Every operation has its bad news-good news, but this one was racking up the bad news at a rapid pace.

"For one," Kurtzman said, "a full-scale deployment is almost complete on both sides of the border now. The Pakistanis got a jump on the Indians this time and have more people in place and ready to jump-off. The Indians, though, have a better road network and will be up to par in a day at the most."

"How about the border incident rate?"

"Surprisingly," Kurtzman replied, "it's lower than it was six months ago. It's almost as if both sides are wary of firing the first shot because they know that it's going to be the big one this time."

"That caution may not last long," Brognola said. "The new Indian prime minister has just—"

When the incoming message icon popped up on Kurtzman's monitor, he automatically clicked on it to see what it was. The sender's address was all he needed to see to instantly call it up on the screen. The note was short, and it confirmed that Price was infected with the anthrax known as the millennium plague. The second paragraph said that the pathogen had been transmitted by contaminated foodstuffs.

"You can call the team now," Brognola said calmly. "I want Striker to know about this."

Pakistan

THE NEWS THAT BARBARA PRICE had been stricken with the millennium plague hit the Stony Man team like a bomb.

Bolan walked out of the laager to think. This wasn't the first time that someone he cared for had been caught in the line of fire. His career as the Executioner had been born from the deaths of his parents and beloved sister at the hands of the Mafia. Later, the woman he loved, April Rose, had died in a KGB-sponsored assault on Stony Man Farm. Since that sad day, he had stayed clear of personal entanglements that might get in the way of his doing business. In his line of work, a man couldn't have the kind of concerns that came with a normal human love relationship shadowing his mind.

His connection with Barbara Price, though, was different than anything he had ever known before. Their relationship was really that of two business colleagues. He wouldn't go as far as to say that he didn't love her, but he wasn't "in love" with her. Nor, as far as he could tell, was she in love with him.

What they had was a mature friendship, yet both realized that the job always came first because it was more important. When the circumstances allowed, they spent time together. When they couldn't, though, that was all right as well. For the kind of people that they both were, that was the only thing that was possible.

That didn't mean, though, that he didn't intend to

see that someone paid the price for having hurt her. He would do the same for any of the men he worked with and it would be no different with her. Stony Man was his family, and taking care of family was how he had gotten into this business anyway. It had been a long time since Bolan had last wished that he was in a different line of work, one that didn't spill over onto those he considered his family. But he was in that line of work and it did, and he would deal with it when the time came as he always did.

"Striker?" McCarter said behind him.

"Yeah."

The Briton stepped to his side. "She's a strong woman," he said, "and you know that Hal will move heaven and earth to make sure that she has the best possible care available. She'll pull out of this."

"It's not just her," Bolan replied and McCarter knew what he meant. Both men fought and killed so others could live in peace, but that same peace always seemed to elude them.

"I know."

THE OLD MAN OF THE MOUNTAIN wasn't pleased when he was informed that the Pakistani nuclear missiles at Gandara had been knocked out by an unidentified commando force. They had figured large in his plans and without them, the nuclear war between India and Pakistan might not take place as he had intended. While most of the world looked upon the prospect of nuclear war with horror, the Old Man saw it as the salvation of Islam, the thing that would finally bring God's word to all the world.

The main reason that nuclear weapons hadn't been used since their debut in Hiroshima and Nagasaki was the mythology that had grown up about them. The cold war propaganda and antiwar activists had pumped tons of misinformation into the public's mind about the dangers of nuclear war, and most of it had stuck. Even when a single nuclear strike could have saved thousands of lives and billions of dollars, no politician had dared use them because of the propaganda.

The average Westerner didn't realize that both Hiroshima and Nagasaki weren't still glowing, radioactive holes in the ground. Neither city had been completely destroyed in the attacks, and there had never been a time since then that people hadn't lived there. In fact, the ruins had barely cooled before the Japanese had started clearing the debris and rebuilding.

To put it bluntly, the only thing that nuclear weapons brought to the battlefield that conventional explosives didn't was radiation, and most of it was very short-lived. It was true that one didn't want to be at ground zero of a nuclear warhead. But that would also be the case if the warhead was a ton of everyday conventional explosive. Just ask the Iraqi Republican Guards who'd had the misfortune to be targeted by two thousand smart bombs during the Gulf War. They, too, had been vaporized in the explosion.

In the nuclear exchange he had planned, the entire world would finally see that a nuclear war could be won, that these bombs were no different than any other, but were simply more powerful. Once the people of the Islamic world learned that nuclear weapons weren't the devil's work, they would see that they could be used for God's work. A well-armed Islamic world could use nuclear muscle to achieve their goals just as the West had used the threat of them to hold Islamic expansion in check.

From the destruction of Calcutta, New Delhi and Bombay, it would be a short step to nuking Tel Aviv, Washington or any other city of the infidels in order to spread the faith. It was true that Islamabad and Karachi might also fall, but that would show the faithful that the bombs weren't to be feared. They would see that they could survive the destruction and triumph in the end.

But even though this was a setback, the Old Man's plans might still come to pass. There was still the air-delivered weapons at the air force base in Palimiro. He would contact his agents in the Pakistani government and have them push for an immediate strike on India. These weapons weren't as powerful as the missile warheads had been, but they would do the job.

But if for some reason they, too, were taken out of action, he was determined that he wouldn't be foiled. He had taken a holy vow that the mushroom-shaped clouds would rise again. And if he had to detonate one in his arms while standing in the middle of an infidel city, he would.

CHAPTER EIGHTEEN

Pakistan

Rust had slept through the day surprisingly well and woke feeling rested. Being an old hand in the Middle East, he knew how to sleep in the heat. His leg was stiff, though, and he winced when he put his weight on it.

James caught the expression and walked over to him. "How's the leg?"

"It feels okay," Rust lied.

"Let's see it."

Rust unbuckled his belt and dropped his pants to expose the dressing. When James unwrapped the bandage, the wound looked clean. The flesh was still bruised from the impact, but it didn't show signs of infection. The massive doses of antibiotics seemed to be working. Nonetheless, he used an antibiotic ointment on the entry hole.

"It looks good," James said as he covered the wound with a thick gauze pad before wrapping it again.

"Right." Rust grinned. "If you've seen one bullet wound, you've seen them all."

HAWKINS WAS ON SECURITY at the top of the ridge as night fell. As close to the equator as they were, the dark came on suddenly. But with his night-vision goggles, he could see far enough in any direction to provide early warning of unwelcome visitors. He was starting to think that they couldn't be safer if they were on the dark side of the moon when he saw headlights approaching in the distance. Since they were well hidden, he watched for a while before calling it in.

Finally, when other headlights joined the first pair, he clicked in the com link. "David, Striker," he said. "You'd better get up here."

"What do you have?" Bolan asked.

"I've got a large truck, an eighteen-wheeler, with its lights on pulling into a draw about six hundred yards away. It's being met by what looks like a couple of civilian deuce and a halfs. They look like smugglers to me."

"On the way."

By the time Bolan and McCarter reached Hawkins's position, it was apparent that their visitors had no idea who they were sharing the desert with and they could be safely ignored. But as Bolan and McCarter dropped back down behind the crest of the hill, the Executioner said, "You know, we might be able to use that truck."

McCarter didn't have to ask what for. With their Land Rovers hidden inside the big truck, they could use the main highway a few miles away and cut a day off their trip as well as melt in with the rest of the civilian traffic.

"Let's do it."

Back at the Land Rovers, Bolan and McCarter briefed the others on the situation. Since this had to be a smuggling operation they were interrupting, it would be a simple move-in-and-leave-no-survivors scenario. They had all done it hundreds of times before.

"What do you want me to do?" Rust asked when he was left out of the attack plan.

"Can you drive with that leg?"

"Sure."

"I want you and Grimaldi to stay with the vehicles and monitor the com links. If we step in it, you come and get us again."

"Can do."

It took only a few minutes for Bolan and the Phoenix Force commandos to apply their black combat cosmetics and get into their assault harnesses. With the night-vision goggles to guide them, they melted into the night. McCarter, Encizo and Manning took one flank; Bolan, Hawkins and James the other. They were outnumbered more than two to one, but the smugglers would have no idea that anyone was sharing their part of the desert and they should be able to achieve complete surprise.

As they got closer, with the lights of the trucks blazing while the smugglers transferred their contraband cargo, the Stony Man commandos had to stop using their night-vision goggles. The strong light blanked out the optics, and they didn't need them now anyway. In the truck lights they could plainly see that the smugglers were all armed with AKs slung over their backs as they loaded what looked like heavy barrels up a ramp into the big truck.

Bolan and Encizo paired up this time, as did McCarter with James and Manning with Hawkins. Coming from three sides, the commandos approached silently to within forty yards of the trucks. On McCarter's radioed command, they opened fire.

In the initial burst of fire, six of the smugglers fell to the sand. Even caught in the kill zone, the others didn't try to flee. Dropping for cover wherever they could find it, they brought their AKs into action like veterans.

For several minutes, fire slashed across the sand with both sides being careful not to shoot up the trucks. With McCarter's and Manning's teams keeping them busy, Bolan and Encizo kept outside the ring of light and made their way around to the other side.

A pair of the smugglers had had the same idea, but they ran into Bolan before they could flank the commandos. Backlighted as they were by the headlights, the Executioner had a clear target. Triggering off two short bursts, he sent both men facedown in the sand.

The sound of firing on their flank sent the three surviving smugglers into a panic. Even though the muzzle-flashes told them that their mysterious attackers were few, they fought like demons. Thinking that their luck had run out, they tried to disengage and disappear into the desert. None of them made it more than a few yards.

As soon as the firing echoed away, the first thing the commandos did was kill the lights on the vehicles.

"What's that smell?" Hawkins asked, looking around.

Encizo pointed to the barrels laying on the sand. "Raw opium," he said. "Probably from Afghanistan. That's probably several million dollars leaking into the sand there."

"No wonder they were so well armed."

Manning checked the thick planks the smugglers had been using to roll the barrels into the big truck. "These look strong enough to use as ramps," he told Mc-Carter.

"We'll find out soon enough," the Briton said as he keyed his com link. "Spook, Flyboy," he radioed back to Rust and Grimaldi, "get the rest of our gear on the Land Rovers and drive them over here."

As Manning had predicted, the Land Rovers were able to drive right up inside the eighteen-wheeler's trailer. Even with the two vehicles inside, there was still plenty of room in the trailer for the men in the back. When they got tired of sitting in the Land Rovers, they could get out and walk around a bit to keep from getting stiff.

Before they left, the commandos shot holes in all the opium barrels. Drug busting wasn't in their mission statement this time, but they never passed up a chance to put a kink in the drug trade. Leaving the bodies and the other trucks where they sat, McCarter took the first shift in the cab of the eighteen-wheeler with Manning riding shotgun. Using his night-vision goggles, McCarter simply followed the truck's tracks back out of the desert to the paved road.

Stony Man Farm, Virginia

NOW THAT IT HAD BEEN CONFIRMED that Barbara Price had, in fact, been infected with the millennium plague, Aaron Kurtzman was determined to find a way to bring her back. To fill his mind with the background he would need to make the lightning-fast intuitive connections that served as his form of logic, he turned to the Merck Manual. First published in 1899, this little reference book was the medical bible of disease and pathology of the human species. If it could make a person sick, it was in Merck. In unemotional language, it told him the what and wherefore of anthrax and how it affected people.

From there, he went through cyberspace to the Center for Disease Control in Atlanta to learn their latest findings on the plague version of the disease. Unlike normal anthrax, this had several built-in modifications designed to defeat modern medicine. For one, while the anthrax bacteria was naturally resistant to heat and dryness, the plague version was almost armor-plated. Even strong UV and IR light had no affect on it at all.

The worst news was that the standard antibiotic therapy that took care of normal anthrax wasn't working on the plague version. None of the antibiotics available made the slightest dent in it.

Realizing how virulent this mutated bacteria was, Kurtzman felt that the man who had designed it would have had to develop an antidote or a killer enzyme at the same time that he had worked on the plague. Not to have a cure or protection on hand in case of an accidental infection would be tantamount to committing suicide. That meant that if he could find the man, he would find the cure and Barbara could be saved.

"I'm putting you in charge of the Pakistani operation until Katzenelenbogen gets back," Kurtzman said to Hunt Wethers. "I want you to keep the team out of trouble."

"What are you going to be doing?"

"I'm taking Akira, and we're going to go after the bastard who cooked up that damned plague. Until we can find the guy who did this, we won't be able to learn what he did to that bacteria so we can undo it."

"Can do."

Checking in with the various agencies working on the same problem, Kurtzman came up with new information immediately. The most interesting was the response from the Islamic nations with histories of state-sponsored terrorism. They were so afraid that they were going to be blamed that they had invited UN inspectors into their medical research facilities so they could prove that they weren't the ones responsible.

Iran, Iraq, Libya, Algeria, Egypt, the Emirates and even Syria had opened their doors and had been declared clean.

That could mean that the usual list of suspects were truly not guilty as they claimed. It could also mean that the lab that had produced the bug had been shut down and all traces of it had been made to disappear. Even with UN inspectors crawling all over the place, that wasn't a difficult task to accomplish. Particularly not when the bacteria could have been manufactured months ago and stored for future use.

Kurtzman concluded, however, that the man responsible for this latest Middle Eastern outrage was probably acting alone. Even in outlaw nations, there could be outlaws working for their own purposes. Since he was convinced that whoever was behind this was also responsible for the so-called Muslim millennium prophecies, he knew that the man's purpose was to destroy the West and wave the flag of Islam over the corpse.

Kurtzman's mind kept going back to Insmir Vedik, the Bosnian anthrax researcher who had disappeared from Sarajevo during the war. How, though, was he to find a man who had disappeared in a modern holocaust? Tens of thousands of Serbs, Croats and Bosnians had vanished as their enemies took vengeance for centuries-old wrongs. Many had been found already in unmarked graves and more were being found every month. Many more had fled the region in hopes of finding new lives. Others' shattered bodies filled hospitals all over Europe.

There were two places he hadn't looked for Vedik yet—the International Red Cross and the war crimes tribunal that was attempting to bring war criminals to trial. If this mystery man was behind this outrage, he might have shown his evil before.

Kurtzman immediately made a hit when he accessed the war crimes files. Dr. Insmir Vedik was mentioned several times as having butchered prisoners. In many cases, he had bled them dry to give the blood to wounded soldiers. In one case, he had purposefully infected a high-ranking officer with gangrene so he would suffer a painful death. Most often he simply had them killed.

In the investigations of these incidents, the reports all ended by saying that Vedik had last been seen in the company of Syrian volunteers who had supported the Bosnian army in the final months of the war. If that was the case, it gave him a place to look for him— Syria.

The Syrian president, Hafez al-Assad, was one of the true master players in the game called the Middle East. After a career of openly opposing Israel and supporting terrorists, he had been lying low. Now that he was the de facto ruler of Lebanon, Assad could use that shattered nation as a surrogate for anything he wanted to do while keeping his own hands clean. In fact, Beirut was starting to appear on the terrorist radar screen again, and that was as good a place as any to start looking for Vedik's tracks.

Slipping into cyberspace, Kurtzman started doing what he did best.

CHAPTER NINETEEN

San Diego, California

Now that Rosario Blancanales had made his mysterious cargo run from Mexico, Carl Lyons finally had something solid to work with. From the beginning, his instincts had told him that Immanuel Zion's operation was worth investigating. But even with Blancanales on the inside, until now he'd had nothing positive to back his gut feeling. While he still didn't have a smoking gun, at least he had a hard target to look at—the warehouse the delivery had been made to.

"You feel like making a run on the Temple tonight?" Lyons asked Hermann Schwarz early that evening as they finished eating their dinner in the hydrofoil. "I want to turn the heat up on those bastards."

"What do you mean?" Schwarz asked.

"What do you mean 'what do I mean?'" Lyons frowned. "I want to start working on those people so we can develop some openings. So far, we don't have diddly-squat to work with, only suspicions. I want to throw something at Mr. Zion and see how he reacts."

"What do you have in mind?" Schwarz grinned. "Leaving a pipe bomb in the collection box?" He was bored, too, and was itching to put his specialized talents to work. Beyond acting as Blancanales's truck driver and working the Internet, there'd been little to keep him busy lately.

"That's not a bad idea. But I was thinking of doing something more basic."

"Like breaking and entering?"

"Something like that. Now that we have a pretty good list of the major Temple players, we can start calling on them and see what they have in their closets and basements."

"That might be fun," Schwarz agreed. "We might even leave a few toys behind and see what that does."

"No booby traps," Lyons cautioned. "I just want to do the surveillance stuff at this point. We'll do the bust 'em and break 'em later after we've found out exactly who to put the screws to."

"Bummer," Schwarz said. "I was hoping to do something that makes a little noise."

"We'll get to that part later."

"Do you want me to let Pol know what we're up to?"

"Not yet," Lyons said. "With that damned woman hanging around his neck, we have to be extremely careful that we don't compromise his act. Jesus. You'd think he'd know better than to complicate the situation like that."

"It's not like he had much choice. When Zion put

her on him, he couldn't refuse without endangering his cover.''

"I know." Lyons shook his head. "I just wish that he was still doing this gig solo."

Schwarz grinned. "I doubt if he does."

Lyons ignored that remark and thumbed through his printout of home addresses for the high-ranking Temple faithful. "It's too bad that security chief guy lives at the temple. I'd love to roust that bastard."

"How about doing that Temple warehouse Pol and I made the delivery to?"

"That was my first thought," Lyons agreed. "We can hit it early and then drop in on one of the Temple big shots later on."

"I'd better make us another pot of coffee," Schwarz said. "We're going to need it. And while we're waiting for it to perk, let me tell you about that warehouse."

"You weren't kidding about this place," Lyons said as he and Schwarz surveyed the warehouse where the mysterious cargo from Mexico had been off-loaded.

"Like I told you," Schwarz said, "we've got our work cut out for us here. These modern structures are a real bitch to get into."

They had driven their van all the way around the warehouse looking for an easy way to get in, but with no result. The target was a squat concrete monolith situated in the middle of a huge parking lot. It had loading docks at the back and only two doors in front. There were no side doors, no windows except in the front offices and not even air vents high on the walls. It did, however, have a flat roof and a fire escape leading up to it.

"You want to try the roof?" Lyons asked.

"Since this is supposed to be a quiet recon, I guess that's our only option."

"What did you see for security when you were there?" Lyons asked.

"There were surveillance cameras covering the loading docks, but since we drove right in and out, I didn't get a chance to count how many or to look for anything else."

"You can take out the cameras, right?"

"No sweat, Ironman." Schwarz grinned. "I just happen to have Mother Schwarz's patented video pickup zapper right here in my kit bag."

The item he took out resembled a wire skeleton rifle stock with a video camera mounted on it. A shielded electrical cable ran from the unit to a bulky battery pack Schwarz clipped to his belt.

"Okay," he said, "I'm ready to put out the lights. But I can only get eight shots out of this thing without changing battery packs, and I don't have a spare with me. So, we'll have to pick our targets carefully."

Leaving their van parked well away from the warehouse, the two slipped around the landscaped berm to the parking lot on the north side of the building. Coming directly from the front or the rear would be counterproductive because those two approaches were sure to be well covered. Considering that car theft was one of San Diego's major industries, the parking lot would be watched as well, but hopefully not so closely.

The problem with eliminating video pickups was that they didn't emit any kind of signal like radar sets or motion sensors that could be detected from afar. With video cameras, you had to eyeball them to locate them and that meant seeing them before they saw you. Schwarz was cheating, though, by using a modified set of night-vision goggles to look for the faint heat given off by the remote control electric motors that swept the cameras from side to side.

"There we go," he muttered. "Up on that pole on the other side of the parking lot."

Lyons looked and saw a twenty-foot pole with what looked like four boxes mounted right under the light on top. "Can you hit it that far away?"

"Piece of cake. This thing is line of sight, so if I can see it I can hit it."

Schwarz's video zapper was nothing more complicated than a powerful red-dot laser night-sight. Granted, it was much more powerful, but it was just a red-light laser. The unit did have a regular low-power laser sight mounted on top to insure that the main beam was on target before it was fired.

Using his night-vision goggles, Schwarz tripped the sighting laser and brought the red dot into the middle of the video camera lens. When it was centered, he hit the firing button for the main laser. The unit hummed for a few seconds and went silent.

"That's it?" Lyons said. "The camera doesn't look damaged at all."

"It isn't damaged, no. The monitors inside just can't pick up anything from it. All the optics are burned out."

"So where's the next one of the damned things?"

"I'm looking, I'm looking."

THE GUARD on video monitor duty in the Temple warehouse looked up from his paperback novel when the screen from the north side parking lot camera flashed and went dark. He dutifully made a note in his log and went back to his book. This job was as boring as dirt. He had no idea what in the hell he and his fellow guards were supposed to be guarding. But the job paid well enough not to ask too many questions so he had no complaints beyond boredom.

He was so engrossed in his book that he missed the second video camera mounted on the same pole blinking out. The third, however, caught his eye because Schwarz had to fire his laser twice to hit it and the first try caused it to flare.

Seeing that he now had three cameras dead, the guard punched the phone button connecting him to the guard room where the walking patrol stayed between rounds.

"I've got something screwy going on with the security cameras," he reported. "How about taking a look at the breaker box to see if we're blowing circuits or something."

"Can't you check them from there?"

That was the other thing about this job that pissed him off. Most of the time the walk-around guards didn't do squat when they weren't making their rounds, but he had to stay alert at his station at all times.

"I already hit the reset buttons," he said, "and they didn't come back on, so put the cards down and go check the damned thing before I have to call it in. I don't feel like having Jacobs on my ass tonight.

"Okay, okay."

After checking the circuit breakers inside the building, the guard decided to take a look and see if someone was messing around outside. For a time, they'd had a problem with kids using the empty parking lot for late-night skateboarding, but busting a few heads had put an end to that. Maybe some of those kids hadn't gotten the word yet and needed another lesson.

LYONS AND SCHWARZ HAD CLEARED a pathway through the security cameras all the way to the north end of the loading docks. The fire escape was fixed to the rear of the building, so there would be no noise as there would have been with a pull-down type.

Lyons was stepping onto the bottom rung of the ladder when the door beside it opened and a guard stepped out onto the loading dock. When he saw Lyons, he reached for the pistol in the holster in his belt.

Before the man could draw his weapon, Schwarz had his silenced Beretta 93-R on target and sent a double tap of 9 mm hollowpoint rounds into his heart. The guard collapsed without a sound beyond the thud of his body hitting the dock.

"What in the hell is going on here?" Schwarz asked. "That guy didn't even give us a warning."

"We'll worry about that later," Lyons snapped. "Get this asshole under cover quick."

For what had started out to be a simple soft probe, the mission had suddenly gone hard.

THE GUARD SUPERVISOR was holding a hot hand and wanted to get back to the game. When the fourth player didn't come back immediately, he reached for his handheld radio. "Buck?" he radioed. "What in the hell are you doing out there, boy? Get your ass back in here and take it like a man."

When he received no answer, he got up from the table, buckled on his patrol belt and headed for the door.

"You want me to go with you?" one of the other cardplayers asked.

The supervisor stopped. "Yeah. And get your heavy stuff."

The second guard grabbed his M-16 assault rifle and ammo harness from the ready rack. While they usually made their patrols armed with only handguns, they had real firepower available if they needed it. Their orders were to prevent anyone from getting inside the warehouse at all costs. Jacobs promised he'd handle any problems if they had to get serious.

LYONS AND SCHWARZ WERE DRAGGING the dead guard off the dock when the door slammed open again and two men stepped out, one of them with an M-16 in his hands. Seeing Able Team commandos dragging his partner, the guard brought up the M-16 and triggered off a burst.

The shots went wild, but Lyons responded instantly. The 12-gauge SPAS slung over his shoulder leaped into his hands as if it were spring-loaded. He tracked and fired without even having to think about it.

The man with the M-16 took the load of double-aught buckshot in the chest and flew backward. The man he was with was flat on the dock, shouting into a handheld radio. Lyons bounced a load of buckshot off the concrete and was rewarded with a scream of pain.

The two commandos were trying to disengage, when the door flew open again and two more men stormed out. This time Schwarz used his silenced H&K MP-5 to good effect. In seconds, both gunners were down and the Able Team warriors were moving away from the warehouse as fast as they could. Waiting around for the SDPD would mean a stay in jail until Brognola could bail them out.

IMMANUEL ZION WAS ANYTHING but the picture of religious serenity when Jacobs told him about the attack at the warehouse. He didn't like being disrupted when he had just settled down with the treat of the evening, but she would wait. This was the most serious problem he had encountered so far in building his personal empire. An armed gang trying to break into his warehouse wasn't something he could put off.

"As best as I can tell," Jacobs reported, "there were only the two of them. There might have been more, but most of the video cameras were knocked out and we only have tapes of two men."

"I thought you told me that those were the best security cameras money could buy?"

"They were. But over half a dozen of them went down when those guys showed up and I think they shut them down somehow."

"You're sure that they didn't penetrate the secure room?" Zion asked. Most of the warehouse held innocuous supplies needed to keep the temple running. Only the secure facility really needed to be guarded. That was his arms room and bullion storage area.

"I'm positive of that. My men turned them back long before they could get in."

"And how many of them did you say were killed?"

"Two dead and three more wounded," Jacobs repeated. "When I had the wounded taken to the hospital, I reported them as having been shot in a car-hijacking attempt in the parking lot when the shift was changing. They've all been briefed to tell the same story, so there won't be a problem."

"And the bodies?"

"They've been taken care of."

"Good." The last thing Zion needed right now was to have the police investigating deaths around his warehouse.

"And," Jacobs continued, "with your permission, I want to start moving the weapons to the missile silo so they can be properly secured and, if at all possible, I want to start doing it tomorrow."

"Do you want to use Corona's trucks again?"

"No." Jacobs shook his head emphatically. "And that's something else we need to talk about. I'm wondering why the warehouse got hit right after he made that delivery for us. It could be a coincidence, but I don't like coincidences."

"You think he's bad?"

"I think he could be something other than what he's pretending to be. And that driver of his, I didn't like that smug little bastard at all."

"Do you want to make them disappear?"

"That might not be a bad idea," Jacobs said. "But what about the woman you gave him, the blonde?"

Zion thought for a long moment. Wasting something as nice as that was a real sin, but this was a case where he could afford to be a little sinful. There were plenty more where she came from.

"Her, too," he finally decided. "When she reported to us, she acted like she liked him a little too much. That's the problem with using women for that kind of work. They get all emotional."

"I can handle her." Jacobs couldn't keep the smile off his face. "It'll be a pleasure."

Zion knew what that look meant and didn't think that this was a time for that. "Just don't let it get in the way of your doing the job."

"You know me better than that."

Zion had to admit that was true. Jacobs had taken care of more than one woman who had become difficult enough to pose a danger to him. But never had one of them been involved with something this serious. Usually, they just freaked out and insisted on bearing his child or something like that.

"Just do it as soon as possible."

CHAPTER TWENTY

Stony Man Farm, Virginia

Yakov Katzenelenbogen swept into the computer room like an avenging angel, but he looked like a train wreck. His clothes were rumpled, his eyes were bloodshot and he badly needed a shower and a shave, in that order.

Aaron Kurtzman caught sight of him and turned in his wheelchair. "Someone needs to check the screen door," he said. "We've got all sorts of things getting in."

Katz walked directly to the coffeepot and, not even rummaging around for a clean cup, poured himself a shot in the first one that came to hand. He took a long drink before turning.

"If the Israelis ever learn to make a decent cup of coffee," he said, "it might be a nice place to live."

"Hunt," Kurtzman called across the room, "call the medics. Katz just said something nice about my coffee."

Cradling the cup in his good hand, the Farm's tactical operations officer walked over to the situation board and started to study it. "It looks like you guys have been humping the pooch in my absence." He shook his head. "How'd you manage to get this screwed up, anyway?"

"Maybe it had something to do with having our vaunted operations expert screwing around on the other side of the world. And, speaking of that, how the hell did you get back here so fast?"

A grimace passed across Katz's face. "You really don't want to know. But I can tell you that sitting in the backseat of an F-15 for hours on end looking at the back of a flight helmet with a Coca-Cola decal on it can get tedious. I'm never going to drink another Coke as long as I live."

"How'd the air-to-air refueling go?"

"That's something else I don't want to talk about. One of those tanker boom clowns kept trying to put the damned nozzle up my ass."

He drained his cup and put it on the nearest flat surface. "But I heard that you guys could use a hand, so I'm back. Hal briefed me on the chopper flight here, so let's start getting this mess sorted out."

He turned to Hunt Wethers. "Where are Mack and Phoenix Force right now?"

Wethers called up a map of Pakistan and marked their last reported location with a blinking icon. Now that the commandos had a better ride, they were making about the best time that was possible in a country that wasn't known for its freeways. "They're still a day away from the Palimiro airfield and there's nothing we can do but wait.''

''And what's Able doing?''

''They're still trying to work their cult temple, gun-smuggling lead in San Diego, but it's been slow.''

''Better them than me,'' Katz said. ''I hate working with crazies.''

''If you're working in California these days, you can't help but work with crazies. The whole place has gone completely nuts.''

When he'd been brought up to the minute, Katz turned to Kurtzman. ''How's Barbara?''

''She's stable. The CDC guys have found a combination of antibiotics and steroids that keep the bacteria in a nonreproductive state. But if they stop treatment, the patients relapse in less than a day or so and die.''

''What have you come up with on the bastard behind this?''

''Well, I was just getting ready to give you a call about that. It may be that the man we want is in Syria.''

''What's with the 'may be' part, Aaron? That's not like you.''

''It's the best I've been able to come up with so far,'' Kurtzman admitted. ''The guy I'm looking at is a Bosnian medical doctor named Insmir Vedik, and he was last seen in the company of the Syrian volunteers at the end of the Bosnian war. That's the closest I've been able to get to him.''

''But why would he want to go to Syria?''

"That's easy," Kurtzman said. "If members of the UN ever get their hands on him, he'll be facing a war crimes tribunal followed by a long stint in the slammer, a real long one. He's kind of the Joseph Mengele of Bosnia."

"Wonderful."

"That's why I was going to call and try to get you to tap into your Mossad contacts. They have more people in Syria than we do. In fact, the Company says that they don't have a single man on the ground in Damascus."

"I'm not surprised," the ex-Israeli commando said. "Put together a packet and I'll see what I can do."

"The packet's ready, but I'm still waiting on a photo. I've got the UN war crimes boys digging through what used to be the Medical University at Sarajevo trying to find one in a yearbook or something."

"I'll get the process started anyway."

"Thanks."

HAL BROGNOLA TOOK NO JOY when his suspicions about the source of the anthrax that had infected Barbara Price were proved to be true. In fact, it made him sick to his stomach. It had been, of course, the teriyaki stick wrapper he had retrieved from the trash can in her office that had proved what had stricken her.

After samples had been taken from the inside of the wrapper to test for anthrax contamination, it had been disinfected for forensic examination. It was found to have a small puncture hole in it, the kind of hole that could have been made by a hypodermic needle. With that kind of evidence in hand, he used his presidential authority to institute a full-court press to find out who was behind this crime.

Since the President had invoked the antiterrorist statutes when the first plague attack occurred in Oman, pulling people in for interrogation wasn't a problem for the federal authorities. To kick off the investigation, the Egyptian immigrant family that ran the deli Brognola had visited and all of their employees were brought in. While that was going on, two more teams worked on the New York manufacturer of the snack food and the local distributor who covered the Washington, D.C., area.

When the initial reports started coming in, Brognola called a meeting in the war room. "The D.C. area distributor for those teriyaki sticks has a missing employee," he announced. "And he happens to be a recent immigrant from Lebanon."

"Why am I not surprised?" Katz didn't smile.

Lebanon was on the road to recovery from her disastrous twenty-five-year civil war, but the Lebanese weren't yet the masters of their own affairs. With the Syrian occupying force the de facto rulers of the small nation, Beirut had once more become a central clearinghouse and launching point for Islamic terrorists.

"It gets better." Brognola looked over at Kurtzman. "This guy was born in Syria, and that keys in with that Bosnian doctor you were looking for who joined up with the Syrian volunteers in Bosnia."

"But I don't understand," Kurtzman frowned. "Why contaminate something as minor as teriyaki sticks instead of the New York city public water supply or something like that? That's not the way to get an epidemic started."

"Contaminating snack foods isn't an effective way to start an epidemic, no," Brognola agreed. "But it works to reinforce the myth of the millennium plague as a punishment from God. Along with Barbara, there's been a dozen other D.C.-area residents who were infected from eating contaminated smoked-beef products."

"I agree with Hal on that," Katz said. "This wasn't done to terrorize America as much as it was to show the Middle Eastern audience that God is still punishing us. This whole program is aimed at them, not us."

"And," Brognola said grimly, "it also shows that this wasn't an attack on the Farm as such. If I hadn't stopped off on the way to Andrews to get something to eat, Barbara wouldn't have been infected."

"You had no way of knowing the damned things had been contaminated," Katz said.

"That doesn't make it any better."

Brognola turned to Kurtzman. "Since the President has everyone from the FBI to the Public Health Service working on this one now, he doesn't want us to get involved beyond finding the source of these attacks. And he wants an update on how your search is going."

"Does he understand that this is like finding that

proverbial needle in a haystack or does he want me to use my Ouija board?''

"He understands," Brognola replied. "But he still wants a report."

He turned to Katz. "He also wants an update on the Phoenix operation."

"But of course."

Atlanta, Georgia

BARBARA PRICE WOKE to find herself in a hospital bed in a brightly lighted room. The last thing she remembered was walking into her office to check on something while the team was still winging its way to the drop zone in Pakistan. She automatically raised her right hand to look at the date on her watch, but it wasn't there. Both arms were, though, strapped down and hooked up with several kinds of medical monitors. Whatever had happened to her was apparently serious.

A man in a white lab coat and surgical mask caught the movement and turned to face her. "Miss Price?"

She tried to answer, but only croaked.

He took a paper cup from a tray and brought it to her. "Drink this before you try to talk."

Holding her head, he helped her drink. "Can I get you another one?" he asked as she downed the water.

"No," she managed to get out.

"To answer what would be your first question, you're in the CDC hospital in Atlanta and you have been infected with the so-called millennium plague."

"The others?" she asked, her voice raspy.

"You were brought here alone," the doctor replied. "A man from the Justice Department has been keeping tabs on you, but he hasn't asked about anyone else."

"Thank God." She let her head sink back down, and her eyes closed of their own accord.

Dr. Hendrickson checked the biomonitors hooked up to his patient and was satisfied. Even though the bacteria hadn't been cleansed from her body, it was in a state of dormancy now. She was making a recovery from the damage it had caused to her system and was out of immediate danger. The problem was that if they couldn't find a way to kill the bug, she would inevitably relapse and they wouldn't be able to stabilize her again.

He noted all of the monitor readings on her chart and left to make a couple of phone calls. It was late, but Hal Brognola had emphasized that he was to be called immediately if there was any change in her condition and had left twenty-four-hour numbers where he could be reached. Not for the first time, the doctor wondered exactly who she was.

Syria

DR. INSMIR VEDIK DIDN'T LIKE having so much time on his hands. Until a few months ago, he had worked twelve- and fourteen-hour days on the millennium plague project, preparing the material needed for the Old Man of the Mountain's plan. It had been brutally intense work, as the nature of working with deadly pathogens required such intensity. But he had thrived on it and missed it now that it was behind him.

He'd had only one assistant on the project, Rashid, a Jordanian medical student who had lost his family in an Israeli air raid on the Bekaa Valley. Vedik didn't hate Israelis the way Rashid did. He hated Serbs and Croatians instead. But shared grief gave them the same motivation to see vengeance on their enemies.

Now that both the pathogens and the protective enzymes had been prepared and stockpiled in quantity, there was little for him to do inside the mountain fortress. He ran a clinic for the Old Man's followers, but he rarely had more to do than treating a few cuts and bruises.

Vedik desperately wanted to take a vacation from the depths of the mountain. Now that there was nothing to keep him busy, he was starting to feel his confinement. Before he had worked himself to exhaustion each day and had slept the sleep of the dead each night. He'd had no time to even take notice of the claustrophobic nature of his environment. Now, he was dreaming again as he had done before the Old Man of the Mountain had recruited him.

The dreams disturbed his sleep and, as a Muslim, he couldn't use strong drink to ease him through them. All he had to help were drugs. While they weren't prohibited by the Koran, he knew what they were doing to his body, to say nothing of his intellect. He had to go somewhere where he could feel the sun on his face and breathe air that no one had breathed before.

The walls were closing in on him, and he feared for his sanity.

"My work is done here," he told his leader that morning. "I want to go back into the world."

The Old Man thought over the doctor's request. Those who joined the Old Man of the Mountain did so for eternity. Those who wished to resign from his service were allowed to, but they could never be allowed to go free. They were escorted out of the mountain fortress and their bodies buried in the desert. The barren vastness of north-eastern Syria held countless graves, and a few more wouldn't be noticed.

Vedik's main task had been completed, but the Old Man still wasn't ready to send the Bosnian to his reward. While the anthrax had done its work of frightening almost all of the Westerners out of Muslim lands, it still had its uses. As the Christian millennium approached, it might be necessary to have more outbreaks of the plague. For his plan to work, the Western nations had to be kept off balance and, if possible, thrown into chaos.

Nonetheless, the Old Man was a good leader and judge of men. The Bosnian doctor wasn't a holy warrior, and he couldn't be expected to have a warrior's iron in his heart. "I will send you to Beirut for a little vacation," he said. "I think you will like it more than Damascus."

Since the end of the Lebanese civil war, Beirut had been in a frenzy trying to recover. Hotels, office buildings and expensive apartments were going up as fast as they could be built. It would be years, though, before the city would once again be "the Paris of the Middle East," as it had been before, a playground where East and West could meet. And if the Old Man's plans came to fruition, it never would be.

There was no sense in ridding the Islamic nations of Westerners if all the faithful did was turn around and ape the decadent West. For Islam to truly triumph, the Muslim world would have to be purified and brought back to what it had been at its height. The Iranian imams had gone a long way toward making that a reality, as had the taliban in Afghanistan. But, even they hadn't gone far enough. Both the Iranian and Afghani leadership weren't following the Koran as closely as they should. To be a real Islamic leader, a man had to be more than just faithful to the law. It had to be his only concern.

When his plan reached fruition, the Koran wouldn't only be the law of the land in the Muslim world, it would be the law as much for the rich and powerful as it was for the poor and powerless. As his predecessors had done centuries ago, he would send his assassins out into the Middle East to insure that the rulers obeyed God's law. Those who didn't would simply be killed. If their successors didn't obey, they too would be killed and so on, until all those who professed to follow the Prophet truly did so. Only then would God's paradise come to earth.

Until then, though, cities like Beirut had their place. And if sending Dr. Vedik there for a week would soothe his mind, it was useful. It was also useful to him in that it was the center of his activities. To preserve the secrecy of his fortress, the Old Man used Beirut as a place to mount his operations from. The city had long been the headquarters of almost every Islamic freedom-fighter group in the Middle East. His warriors were known to the Syrians who now controlled the city, but they weren't molested.

Vedik bowed his head. "I cannot thank you enough," he said. "A week will be enough to refresh me and I will return then."

The Old Man didn't bother to mention that the Bosnian would be watched every minute that he was out of the mountain fortress. Until Islam was triumphant, he would never be left alone.

CHAPTER TWENTY-ONE

San Diego, California

Rosario Blancanales was wrapping up a quiet late evening at home when his doorbell rang. "Are you expecting someone, Arthur?" Sarah Carter looked up from her book.

"No." He frowned and glanced at his watch as he got up. If either Lyons or Schwarz had wanted to see him, they'd have called first.

"Mr. Jacobs!" Blancanales didn't have to fake surprise when he saw the burly Temple security chief standing there. "What brings you here?"

"We need to talk." Jacobs shouldered his way through the half-open door. Two more of the Temple troops followed him into the apartment.

Since he was sharing his living quarters in order to make his cover seamless, Brognola didn't have ready access to a weapon. His cover didn't include his being armed. In fact, the only piece on the premises, a 9 mm Beretta pistol, was safely hidden away. Unarmed as he was, he had no choice but to go along with whatever was going down here.

Carter knew that this wasn't a courtesy call. For Jacobs and his boys to come calling wasn't a good sign. It meant that Arthur was in trouble. And if he was, she was, too. That was just how Zion did things. It was so ironic that she had fled to the Temple to escape this kind of strong-arm crap, and it had followed her.

One thing, though. She wasn't going to go down without a fight. Dingo Jones might have been a world-class bastard in many ways, but he had taught her how to defend herself. As he had said, there was nothing more worthless than a woman who had to have a man fight her battles for her.

"Can I get you guys something to drink?" Blancanales asked as he headed for the kitchen.

As if on command, the three visitors pulled their weapons. "I think not," Jacobs said. "You're coming with us."

"Hey!" Blancanales started backing up. "What's going on?"

Carter got up and moved toward the intruders. All three of them automatically shifted their eyes to her, and that gave Blancanales his break. Snatching the full wine bottle from the countertop behind him, he pivoted and slammed it against the head of the gunman nearest to him. Unlike in the movies, the bottle didn't break, but the gunman's head did.

As the man slumped to the floor, Blancanales grabbed the guy's gun hand, slipped his trigger finger over his and started firing. With the gunman's body hanging limply, and taking his gun arm with it, it was awkward to aim the Glock. But awkward was better than nothing. Blancanales's second round took Jacobs high in the chest. With two down, Blancanales took the time to pry the Glock out of the first man's hand.

When he brought it up again, Carter was standing over the last guy, her foot swung back to kick him in the crotch a second time. Blancanales shifted his aim and drilled him through the head.

"It's okay now," Blancanales said as he reached out for her.

"But they're dead." She felt stupid saying that, but she wasn't used to having dead people lying on the floor.

"They came here to kill us," he reminded her. "I know it's a cliché, but it was either them or us. Come on now. We need to get out of here while we still can."

"Shouldn't we wait for the police or something?"

"It'll all be taken care of," he assured her. "But it'll be best if we aren't here when the authorities arrive. Grab your purse and any valuables you have here, and get a jacket. I'll replace the rest of your clothing later."

"Now that that's over," Blancanales said as soon as they were in his car and heading away from the apartment, "you might as well know that I'm not a businessman. I'm part of a special task force that's been working to try to stop shipments of military weapons from being smuggled into the country.''

Once more, Carter wasn't surprised. Arthur Corona had been a little too intelligent to have been swept up in the Temple of Zion hysteria.

"Are you a Fed or a cop?"

"Neither," he answered honestly. "My associates and I are civilians. But on this job, we're working with both federal and local agencies."

"You're a mercenary, then."

Blancanales smiled faintly. "I guess you could call us that."

Mercenaries could be either good or bad, but with Zion gunning for her, she had to go along for the ride. At least until she found out more about what was going on with her protector.

"Where are you taking me?"

"I want to report to my partners and find out how my cover was blown."

Carter was comfortable with that because she knew it was nothing she had done. In fact, all of her reports to Zion about him had been glowing.

SCHWARZ GLANCED at his security camera screen when it beeped at him. "Company's coming, Ironman. It's Pol, and it looks like he has that girl with him."

"For Christ's sake!" Lyons snapped. "That's all we need right now. Does it look like he's under duress?"

Schwarz chuckled. "We should all be so lucky to be under that kind of duress. Man, is she a looker."

Nonetheless, Lyons met them at the rail of the hydrofoil with his Colt Python in his hand. He hadn't lived as long as he had by taking chances.

Blancanales ignored the pistol as he ushered Carter onto the deck and led her into the boat's cabin. Seeing that his friend was in no way endangered, Lyons holstered the piece and followed her. After the introductions were made, Blancanales mixed her a drink while he took Lyons off to the side to explain what had happened in the apartment.

As Carter sipped her drink, Schwarz sat in front of his laptop and started tripping through cyberspace. He couldn't do it as quickly as Kurtzman did, but he had all the programs he needed to do a background check and it didn't take him very long.

"You're a very unusual person, Miss Carter," Schwarz said as he looked up from his monitor. "You don't exist anywhere except as a member of the Temple of Zion."

"What do you mean?"

"I mean you have no existence in cyberspace, no IRS records, no social-security number, no student loans, no phone bills, no credit cards, no bank accounts, no nada. Best of all, your driver's license is an initial issue, and it's only six months old."

She had heard that a person could be tracked by computers, but she had never thought that she could be unmasked by one as well. "You must have me mixed up with another Sarah Carter. I understand that it's a fairly common name."

"That it is," he agreed. "But none of the Sarah Carters I'm finding look anything like you. In fact, they don't even come close. So, do you want me to start running missing persons first or federal fugitives?"

Carter realized that the time had come for her to fish or cut bait. The man called Carl didn't have to wear his badass hat for her to know him for what he was— a hard man. She now saw that she had also been conned by Corona, or at least partially conned. Here with his friends, he, too, was showing competence she hadn't seen before. Gadgets didn't look or act like any keyboard cowboy she had ever seen before. He was more like some kind of cybersleuth.

Whoever these guys were, they were more than she wanted to deal with right now, and she didn't think that she'd be able to get away with much bullshit around them. If she wanted their help, she had to come clean with them.

"Gentlemen," she said, "as you have figured out by now, my real name isn't Sarah Carter. I'm kind of in my own personal version of a witness protection program, and I'd rather not have to tell you much more than that."

"Are you running from the law?" Lyons asked.

"No." She shook her head. "From kind of a boyfriend."

"What kind of a boyfriend?" Blancanales asked gently.

"A thug," she said simply. "And if he finds me,

he's going to take a week killing me and enjoy every minute of it.''

''What kind of a thug?''

''A wealthy one with enough money to buy damned near anything he wants.'' Her voice was bitter. ''First he bought me, then he bought the cops when I found out what he was like and tried to get away from him.''

''We know the type,'' Lyons growled. He hadn't liked her interfering with Blancanales's undercover job, but he had absolutely zero tolerance for men who abused women in any way.

''Let me explain something to you, Sarah,'' Blancanales said. ''We're in a position to help you more than you realize. In exchange for you telling us everything, and I mean everything, you know about Immanuel Zion and his so-called Temple operation, I'll personally see that your Sarah Carter identity becomes a reality that no one will be able to question. You'll be able to have a life, a job and more importantly, a history that no one will be able to find fault with. In other words, you'll be completely safe.''

She had heard this routine before in any number of made-for-TV movies. Each time some poor schmuck was promised a world of protection if he cooperated, but got popped in the first fifteen minutes.

When he saw that Carter wasn't buying it, Blancanales turned to Schwarz. ''Get hold of the Farm and have them put Hal and his ID card on the monitor.''

When he turned back to the woman, he was all business. ''I'm going to have a very senior Justice Department official come on-line so you can talk to him. In return, no matter what your decision is, I need to ask that you never mention this incident to anyone.''

Carter started to panic. The last thing she needed was to get mixed up with the FBI. ''But you said that you weren't a Fed.''

''We're not,'' he replied. ''But, as I told you, we're working with them. The man you're going to talk to will be able to do damned near anything you want if you will assist us in this matter.''

''Even if I'm wanted?''

''Particularly if you're wanted,'' he said. ''Just as long as it isn't for treason or for murder.''

''Okay,'' she said in a small voice. ''I guess I have to trust somebody.''

Reaching up to her nape, she dug into her thick mane of hair and brought out a small leather drawstring pouch with a hair clip sewn to it. ''To understand my situation, you need to know about this.''

Opening the pouch, she held it out to Schwarz. Inside lay a microchip the size of a quarter in a small plastic envelope. ''What's this?'' he asked.

''It's the prototype of a killer virus program that can completely destroy the international computer-banking network.''

The three Able Team commandos looked at each other in utter astonishment.

''Now I know who you are,'' Schwarz said in wonderment. ''You're the industrial spy that Ian 'Dingo' Jones of Rainbow Cybertech has posted a million-dollar reward for. He claims that you ripped off one of his secret projects. You changed your hair coloring and ditched the glasses, but it's you, isn't it?"

"What in the hell are you talking about, Gadgets?" Lyons growled.

"About seven or eight months ago, Dingo Jones fired up his own 'America's Most Wanted' web site featuring this woman." He paused and looked up at her. "Damn, I can't remember your name."

She sighed. "It's Anne, Anne Keegan."

"That's right. Anyway, Jones has been offering a million-dollar reward to anyone who could give him information leading to her capture and the recovery of his missing material, a prototype system for greatly improving satellite communication, as I recall."

He glanced down at the chip in his hand. "I guess this is it."

"It is, but it's not what he said it was," she hurried to say. "It's a killer chip designed to destroy the world's banking computers, starting with the United States."

"Why would a multimillionaire want to do something like that?" Lyons asked.

"Among other things," she explained, "Dingo controls a large part of the world's stocks of precious metals, as well as major mining contracts in Australia, South Africa and Asia. If the banks go, he'll be one of the wealthiest men on earth because he'll have all the gold and silver."

"This is interesting," Lyons said. "And we'll pass

it on to those who need to know about it. But right now we need to know about Immanuel Zion and what in the hell he's up to.''

"That's simple," she said. "He has this missile silo somewhere in the desert, and he's busy turning it into a heavily defended fortress for his Chosen.''

"What do you mean?"

"Well, he has some kind of Navy surplus air-defense system that he's going to install so no one will be able to attack him when the end of the world comes.''

Again the three Able Team men exchanged glances. This had turned out to be a very profitable evening, as well as one full of surprises.

"Are these weapons called Phalanxes?"

"I think that's the word I heard." She frowned. "But it means a group of Roman soldiers doesn't it?"

"Greek actually," Schwarz said. "But in this case, it's also the name of a weapons system."

"Lady," Lyons said, "no matter what your name is, you've just earned yourself the best protection this nation has to offer. No matter what you did or didn't do, this Dingo guy won't ever be a bother to you again. Nor," he added, "will the guy who calls himself Immanuel Zion. They're both going down hard.''

After hiding for so long, Anne-Sarah really wanted to believe that this was actually happening to her. All she had wanted was a chance to live her life without having to look over her shoulder all the time. But, coming from three guys living on a boat in San Diego made this more like a scene from a B-grade movie than what she would have expected from three knights on white horses.

"I sure hope so," she said, her voice weary. "I've been hiding for so long and I'm tired of being afraid."

"One way or the other," Lyons said, "you won't have to run anymore and you won't need to be afraid."

CHAPTER TWENTY-TWO

Pakistan

It was late afternoon of the Stony Man team's second day in Pakistan, and they had been on the road ever since capturing the eighteen-wheeler. It had been a grueling drive, but they were quickly closing in on the town of Palimiro and the nuclear-armed F-16 base. The Farm's last update said that they were still in time to prevent a holocaust, but that there could be no delay. Had they still been trying to make the trip during the hours of darkness in the Land Rovers, they would have been well behind the power curve. The clock was ticking faster with every passing hour.

It had taken a full day for the Pakistani military junta to react to the destruction of the Red Dragon missiles at Gandara. And now that they were finally taking action, they were doing a good job of locking the hen-house door after the chickens had been stolen. Heavy helicopter gunship traffic was spotted in the distance crisscrossing the desert, and several troop convoys passed them going the other way. Hidden as it was in the stream of civilian traffic, though, no one gave the Stony Man warriors' vehicle a second glance.

In the cab of the Volvo truck, Rafael Encizo was taking the daytime shift behind the wheel with J. R. Rust riding shotgun with him. At a casual glance, Encizo's Cuban coloring and Rust's permanent Middle Eastern tan made them the team's two members least likely to stand out as foreigners. Up close, however, Rust's light hair and eyes would give him away.

When McCarter pointed out that fact, Rust shrugged and said that he could pretend to be an Afghani. Many of them still carried the genes of Alexander's Greeks, the last foreigners to conquer the region, and there were thousands of them in Pakistan. His being the team's resident linguist settled the matter. If they got stopped, someone had to be able to say something in a local language

"It looks like there's some kind of roadblock up ahead," Rust said as the truck crested a hill and started down a long grade.

"I see it," Encizo grunted. A mile or so ahead, two armored personnel carriers and half a dozen trucks flanking both sides of the road had halted the civilian traffic. Clicking in his com link, he passed the word to Bolan and the others inside the truck's trailer.

"Striker wants to stop and recon," he told Rust.

"Fine with me. I need to take a leak anyway." Pulling the truck off the side of the road didn't immediately draw attention as it would have done in the States. They had seen almost as many vehicles on the side of the road as had been driving on it. A road trip in Pakistan was a casual affair rather than a race to reach a destination.

Encizo and Rust got out of the cab and went around to the back of the truck. When a break in traffic occurred, they opened the rear door to let McCarter and Bolan out. The two worked their way off the road up to where they could get a clear look at the roadblock, then returned.

"It looks like the troops at the roadblock are planning to be there for a while," Bolan reported to the commandos in the trailer. "They've got their tents up and their cook fires going. So, we'll wait till dark, off-load the Land Rovers and see if we can find a way to get around them. We don't need to crash a roadblock at this point in the game."

"Suits me," James said. "Riding in this damned trailer quit being fun several hours back."

AN HOUR AFTER DARK, the traffic had thinned enough for the team to drive their Land Rovers down the ramp without being seen. Since their gear was still loaded on the vehicles, all they had to do was top off the fuel tanks from their remaining jerricans and they were ready to go.

McCarter and Grimaldi led off, with Hawkins driving for Bolan. The GPS made it child's play for McCarter to navigate with the lights off on a moonless night, and the night-vision goggles made it possible for Grimaldi to drive without running into major boulders.

The smaller rocks and holes, however, made for a bumpy ride.

Two hours later, they were in the foothills north of Palimiro and McCarter halted. "According to the map and the GPS," he called back to Bolan on the com link, "we'll have a good line of sight from here come daybreak."

"Let's get some sleep then."

Once again, the two Land Rovers were concealed with the tarps and the Stony Man team members took turns standing guard while the others slept.

THE PAKISTANI AIR FORCE BASE at Palimiro wasn't built on empty ground as might have been expected. Back in the twenties, the small airstrip the British had first scraped out of the ground had been a mile or so away from what had then been a small village. But the town had grown since then and, as it had grown, the empty space had vanished. Since things like airplanes falling out of the sky were considered to be acts of God that couldn't be prevented, no one had even thought to keep a buffer zone between the military and the civilians. Now, houses and shops were hard up against the perimeter wire on all sides of the base.

"We're going to have our work cut out for us just trying to find our way into that bloody airfield," David McCarter muttered as he surveyed the town below them. "There's no way we can do it without driving past thousands of the locals, and I don't think that stopping for directions is going to be on."

"That's where you're going to need me," Rust spoke up. "Someone needs to go into town, scope the situation up close and map the route in. Riding in there, guns blazing, isn't going to cut it this time. You wouldn't make it half a mile."

McCarter hated to admit it, but there was a lot of truth in what the CIA man was saying. "Okay, lad, you and me. We'll go in and check the lay of the land."

"But you don't speak the language."

"Of course not." McCarter almost sounded offended. "But I do speak the second-most commonly used language in Pakistan, English. We will go in as Englishmen, petroleum engineers, and have a bit of a look-see. You will keep your mouth shut in that Urdu of yours and only listen to what you can pick up. We'll conveniently get ourselves lost and end up at the air base. We'll ask directions, that sort of thing, and have a good look around while we're doing it."

"You're stark raving mad!" Rust said in disbelief.

McCarter grinned. "Aren't I though."

"While you two are gone," Bolan said, "I'll get in touch with the Farm and see if they have an Intel update."

"Also," McCarter suggested, "see if the satellites have shown that the nukes are actually being kept here. I'd hate to bust in only to find that the cupboard is bare."

Jack Grimaldi had also been scoping the air base. Their way home depended on his finding an aircraft to fly them out after the assault, and he had hoped to spot a Bell UH-1 Huey parked somewhere down there. He knew the Pakistanis had been given hundreds of the machines over the years, and he was counting on at least one of them to still be operational. He'd cut his teeth on combat flying in Hueys and still felt more at home in them than anything else with wings or rotors.

"Check out the aircraft for me while you're at it," he told McCarter. "If you can find me a Huey, we'll be halfway home."

"You sure you don't want a 747?"

Stony Man Farm, Virginia

YAKOV KATZENELENBOGEN was happy to hear his old friend Mack Bolan on the satellite link. Since he had retired from commanding Phoenix Force, he missed being in the field, particularly when Bolan was on board for the mission. The two of them went back a long way, and he missed the easy camaraderie of working together on a mission.

Bolan's first question was what Katz had expected. "How's Barbara?"

"She's fine," Katz reassured him. "Hal's keeping close tabs on her, and she's being treated by the head of the millennium plague task force himself. We're getting two updates a day, and the hospital has orders to call us the minute anything changes."

That sat well with Bolan. Having Brognola looking after her was the next best thing to being there himself.

"What's the latest on the target?" Bolan asked.

"The NRO thinks that the weapons have already been transported to Palimiro. There was a heavily guarded convoy that went through town the day before yesterday that ended up at the air base. The satellite went out of range before we could see what this cargo was and where it was off-loaded. But we have a heavier troop count than before, and a security cordon has been thrown around one of the buildings, number fourteen on your map."

"That's proof enough for me."

"I'm not trying to rush you," Katz said, "but when do you think you'll be able to make your move? The Man's on our ass, and I have to tell him something."

"David and Rust are making a close-in recon of the air base and scouting our way in right now. Depending on what they bring back, we'll try to do it tonight. If they report difficulties, however, it's up in the air. He's going to have to understand that."

Katz couldn't argue with that. Eight men against a town of several hundred thousand and a base garrison of a couple more thousand wasn't a "ram-'em-and-slam-'em" situation. They would have to see the ground up close before they even tried to penetrate the target area.

"Tell David to be cautious," Katz warned. "The junta has been whipping the population into a war frenzy. They're broadcasting the Islamic millennium prophecies damned near all day long and telling them that God's really on their side this time. Foreigners aren't going to be too popular right now, particularly infidels.''

Bolan chuckled. ''When was the last time David did anything cautiously?''

''You have a point there.''

''I'll give you a call as soon as they get back and let you know what we can do then.''

''I'll be waiting.''

Atlanta, Georgia

THIS WAS THE PART of his job that Dr. Hendrickson hated the most—delivering bad news. The bad news this time wasn't as bad as it would be if Barbara Price was an Ebola victim, but it wasn't really good news, either. Even so, he owed it to her to tell her the truth.

Price was once again the stunning woman he had known that she was. One of the nurses had helped her get cleaned up and looking like something other than a terminal patient. Propped in a half-sitting position, her blond hair had been combed out and she was even wearing a trace of makeup. Not for the first time, he sincerely wished that she hadn't been infected.

''When do I get out of here?'' she asked as soon as he walked into her room.

''Well…'' he hesitated.

''When?'' Her eyes bored into his.

Hendrickson was a bit surprised at her directness. He hadn't had the pleasure of dealing with Barbara

Price when she wasn't sick and, therefore, he had no way of knowing that she wasn't just a pretty face.

"What seems to be the problem?" she asked when he didn't immediately answer.

"We…" he tried again. "We have been able to stabilize your condition, but we haven't cured you."

"What do you mean?"

"I mean that you still carry the anthrax infection. The problem is that we haven't been able to find a way to kill it yet. Right now it's in a dormant state, but it's still alive inside you."

She didn't even blink. "What does that mean long-term?"

"We don't know."

"What's your best guess?"

He took a deep breath. "In the short term, we should be able to keep you alive for six months or so. In this arrested state, the anthrax bacteria works very slowly. But this isn't normal anthrax. It has been given a viral gene that makes it impervious to anything we can do to it. As I'm sure that you know, viruses aren't affected by antibiotics, and even though anthrax is caused by a bacteria, with the added gene, this version acts like a real virus. The treatment we're giving you is only temporarily holding the anthrax at bay. It isn't killing it."

"In short, I'm going to die from this, right?"

He nodded slowly. "Unless we find a way to kill it, I'm afraid so."

He was surprised to see how calmly she took the news. The majority of the men he had given this talk to had shown shock or despair, and some had even cried. She was taking it without even as much as a change of expression. "I understand that you are in contact with Hal Brognola, right?"

"That's correct. I have been keeping him up-to-date on your status."

"I'd like you to give Hal a message for me."

"Certainly."

She looked him straight in the eyes. "Tell Hal that I want him to get me out of this goddamned place immediately."

"But I can't release you." He was shocked. "First off, if I stop treatment you'll relapse in short order and die. And, secondly, you're still in an infectious state. You can give the plague to others."

She raised herself a little higher against the head of the bed. "In that case, tell him that I want a communications suite installed here, and I want it ASAP."

If Hendrickson had wondered before who she was to rate a presidential adviser checking in on her, he was totally confused now. Who in the hell was she to be able to demand such things? "I'll see what I can do, but—"

"You will call Hal Brognola immediately and tell him what I told you. Got that?"

Faced with such an iron will in such a lovely package, Hendrickson said what any red-blooded American man would have said. "Yes, ma'am."

"Thank you." She seemed to deflate a little. "Now,

can I get something to eat around here other than baby food, or do I have to call out for a pizza?''

Hendrickson suppressed a smile. Feisty as well as beautiful. He liked that. ''I'll have something sent in at once.''

''Something with meat in it.''

''Certainly.''

''And, Doctor?''

''Yes?''

''If you do come up with something that needs to be tested before you start using it, test it on me. If it works, then I'll be able to get out of here that much quicker.''

He couldn't help but smile. ''I'll keep that in mind.''

Stony Man Farm, Virginia

''BARBARA'S UP AND EATING,'' Brognola reported. ''In fact, she had the doctor call and tell me that she wants a commo suite set up in her room.''

Kurtzman smiled. ''I'm surprised that she didn't ask to get out.''

''Apparently, she did. But Hendrickson put his foot down on that one.''

''Brave man.''

''He is curious about who the hell she works for to be giving orders like that, but I fielded that one.''

''Are you going to give her access?'' Kurtzman asked.

''I'll have a secure phone put in, but that's about it. I don't want her to have a computer terminal as long as she's in there. If she relapses, there's too many people who might be able to access it.''

''Good point.''

''But she's not going to like it.''

Kurtzman grinned. ''I'm glad she called you instead of me.''

CHAPTER TWENTY-THREE

Palimiro, Pakistan

McCarter and Rust drove their Land Rover into the town of Palimiro as if they were going to their own hometown. The CIA man was handling the driving chores while McCarter took mental notes of everything they passed. The town was typical of the new Pakistan. To say that it was congested was like saying that water was wet. Since urban planning wasn't a big priority in this part of the world, the crowding was less organized than it was in Hong Kong. The fastest way to get around in this was to walk.

"One thing's for damned sure," McCarter said as they sat in their third traffic jam of the past half hour. "If we want to get out of here fast, we're bloody well going to have to fly out. There's no way we'll be able to drive out through this mess."

"Not quickly at least," Rust agreed. Even after having spent so much time in the Middle East, he had to agree that the traffic in Palimiro was an extreme case. Apparently, the concept of using lanes of traffic hadn't reached Pakistan yet. The closer they got to the airfield, the worse it seemed to get. And since a good portion of that traffic was military, they couldn't get too aggressive about trying to force their way through it.

When they finally reached the road that ran along the air base's fence, they turned onto it and drove half a mile around the perimeter before stopping in front of a tea shop that gave them a good look at the base. Being caught making notes wasn't wise, so the two men sipped their tea and concentrated on remembering what they were looking at.

They were on their second cup when an old American M-151 jeep full of Pakistani troops with air police armbands drove by. When they spotted the two Westerners, the vehicle skidded to a halt, blocking their Land Rover as the troops bailed out.

"Foreigners are not allowed here!" the man with sergeant stripes on his armband snapped in English. "Let me see your passports!"

"I'm sorry, old chap," McCarter said, giving his native accent full rein as he stood. "I'm afraid that they're back at our hotel, you know. It simply doesn't do to muck about carrying something as valuable as one's passport in a..."

"Where are you staying?"

"I say, Perkins," McCarter said, turning to Rust as he also had gotten to his feet. "What is the name of that wretched hotel? The Grand Whatever, isn't it?"

He turned back to the sergeant. "Terribly sorry, old chap, but I seem to have for..."

The air policeman slammed the butt of his AK into McCarter's belly. The commando folded as was expected, but he came out of the crouch fighting. With the odds being what they were, Rust knew better than to jump in to try to help McCarter. All that would get him was shot. He knew that he had to keep his cool at all costs.

The only way that McCarter's fate would be learned was if he could successfully evade pursuit and make it back to the others. Striker wasn't going to be happy about this, but it wasn't his fault that British citizens were high on the official Pakistani hit list right now. From what he had picked up from the conversations he had overheard, the only thing worse would have been if they had admitted to being Americans. Then they would have simply been shot instead of taken into custody.

With all four of the APs concentrating on subduing McCarter, Rust backed out of the way into the shop, spun and dashed out the back.

ALTHOUGH HE HADN'T BEEN in that part of Pakistan before, the narrow backstreets of Palimiro weren't foreign to the CIA man. He had been in hundreds of streets just like them throughout the Middle East over the years. If he used his head, and got just a couple of breaks, he might be able to keep ahead of his pursuers. And, of course, if his leg held up. Until he had started running, he had almost forgotten that he had been shot recently.

Ducking into another tea shop, he ordered a tea in Urdu and then asked the owner the way to the nearest neighborhood latrine. As he had expected, the shop-keeper gestured out the back and when Rust hit the even more crowded alley, he reversed directions. He was now headed back toward the air base, but that was the last place the air police would expect him to go. The risk, though, was that the APs had put the word out to the locals that they were looking for an infidel.

Even under these circumstances, using a little simple tradecraft might make it easier to insure that he wasn't spotted. Passing a clothesline, he "borrowed" a *lungi*, the universal long tunic garment of the country. A block farther on, he added a turban to his disguise. His military boots were still a dead giveaway, but he didn't want to give them up for sandals. He did stop long enough take the laces out and scrub the leather with sand to make them look more worn.

He was making sure that the alley was clear when he spotted a bundle of firewood leaning against the walls of a shack. It wasn't much as far as firewood went, just a bundle of small twisted twigs, roots and branches, but it was what most poor Pakistanis cooked with. It was also a good accessory for his disguise.

Hoisting the bundle onto his right shoulder, he leaned his head into it as he started walking north out of Palimiro. The bundle wasn't very heavy, ten pounds at the most, but it was bulky and hid most of his face.

He walked slightly stooped as if his burden was much heavier than it really was. He also kept his pace slow as if he was weary. The throbbing in his leg made that a must. It would take him longer to get where he was going that way, but he couldn't afford to draw attention to himself.

After walking half a mile to the east, he took a bearing on the sun and turned north. Once he cleared the built-up area, he'd be able to recognize where he needed to go.

"WE HAVE A LOCAL approaching," Calvin James reported from his security position in front of the camp. "And he's approaching with his hands in the air."

"I'm coming up." T. J. Hawkins grabbed his MP-5 and started up the rocks.

Both men were surprised when they recognized J. R. Rust under the dust and the native dress. "Where's David?" James asked.

"He was grabbed," Rust panted. "You got a canteen on you?"

Hawkins handed the CIA man his canteen, and Rust drank deeply.

"What happened?" James asked.

"We were parked along the road running past the base when a security patrol came by. They saw us, and stopped to ask who we were and what we were doing. David tried to tell them that our passports were at the hotel, but they weren't buying it. When they put the grab on him, he put up a fight and I was able to duck out."

He shook his head. "I've been on the run since then."

"Let's go tell Striker the good news."

"WHAT ARE WE GOING to do about David?" Encizo asked Bolan after Rust recounted his tale again.

"We'll have to do something about getting him back."

"That one's on me." Rust immediately jumped in before anyone could speak up. "I was with him when he was grabbed, and I should be the one who tries to get him out of there.

"Remember," he added before anyone could turn down his offer, "I speak the language and I think I can get onto the base without having to blast my way in. From there, I can try to free him while you guys are taking care of business. That way, we'll all be back together before we move out."

"How do you think you can get in?" Bolan asked.

"I was thinking I'd try to pass myself off as a vendor," Rust replied. "When we were watching the place, I saw that vendors were being allowed onto the base without too much problem."

"What kind of vendors?"

"As near as I could tell, damned near everything you can think of. I saw food sellers, bottled gas deliveries, laundrymen, the usual sort of thing for a Middle Eastern military setup. They don't have the kind of quartermaster system we do, so they have to resupply from the local economy. I figure I'll hot-wire a local vehicle and try to talk my way in. Once in, I'll look for the jail.''

With McCarter gone, leadership of Phoenix Force fell to Rafael Encizo, but he deferred to Bolan on this one. ''What do you think, Striker?''

''We have to at least try,'' Bolan said seriously. ''If J.R. was able to keep from getting caught today, maybe he can get inside on his own. And it might be a good idea to spring David while we're rigging the delivery racks. That way if we run into trouble, we'll be a good diversion while he goes for the rescue.''

''What did you see for aircraft?'' Grimaldi asked. It was all fine and good to talk about who was going to spring McCarter from the local slammer. But if they didn't have a ride they could borrow, they all might as well join the Briton on the inside.

''I saw a couple of choppers on the order of the Hughes 500, small observation choppers. But there were only half a dozen larger machines. I saw one Huey, but I'm not sure that it's serviceable, and a couple of Russian Mi-8 Hips.''

Grimaldi grimaced. On a good day, the Mi-8 wasn't a bad bird, but it had its quirks and he wasn't that comfortable with it. ''What about smaller fixed-wing stuff?''

''There are a couple of Russian turbo-prop twins, but that's about it.''

The pilot shook his head slowly. He had a choice between two Russian designs, neither one of which he'd really want to fly on a sunny day after a week-long maintenance check.

"And on the topic of transportation," he said. "Since our man J.R. here walked home instead of driving, that puts us one Land Rover down. We're going to be a bit crowded on our way in."

"That'll just make us look more like the locals," Rust said. "Without a taxi service, everyone hitches a ride with anyone who will stop for them. We'll just look like Westerners who couldn't find a ride."

DAVID MCCARTER COULDN'T say that being captured was an entirely new experience for him, but it had been some time since the ex-SAS commando had screwed up this badly. After all the talk about Rust not being quite up for the mission, the CIA man had acted like a cold professional when their luck ran out.

He had seen that McCarter had been trapped and that trying to help him would only have resulted in him going into the bag as well. So, like the pro he was, he took the chance when it came and faded into the woodwork. The fact that Rust wasn't sharing the cell with him pointed to his having made good his escape. Either that, or he'd been gunned down trying to get away.

For planning purposes, though, McCarter would assume that Rust had made it back to the others and that they would try to spring him. This was going to complicate the operation more than he liked, and the smart thing would be for them to just write him off. But he knew that Striker and the lads wouldn't leave him behind.

Unfortunately, though, that would almost guarantee that they would take casualties. The seven of them, counting Grimaldi, weren't quite up to taking on the thousand or so Pakistani airmen he has seen on his way in. The air police contingent alone was at least two hundred strong. And as had seen proved by his being forced to take up a new residence, they were well armed and they knew their stuff.

But, on the off-chance that his assumptions about Rust weren't correct, he started looking over his cell inch by inch. Sometimes even the best-kept jail contained something a man might put to use.

After spending half an hour and finding exactly nothing to aid him in any way, McCarter laid on his narrow bunk to try to get a little shut-eye. Since he had been imprisoned before, he knew the value of resting when he could. The Pakistanis would come for him soon enough, and he would be glad that he was well rested.

He barely had a chance to close his eyes when he heard footsteps come down the hall and stop in front of his door. The Pakistanis could use a few tips on interrogation techniques. He hadn't been left alone long enough for his situation to start working on his mind. He was still fresh and not the best subject to talk to.

Apparently, they were in a big hurry to find out what his story was, and that wasn't a good sign. It could mean that they had already checked out his rather flimsy cover story and found that it didn't hold water. When the door opened, McCarter sincerely wished that he hadn't screwed up. Getting to his feet, he stood calmly for the second act of this farce.

AFTER THEIR PLANS WERE MADE, the Stony Man team checked over the gear and waited for the sun to go down. Bolan tried to reach the Farm to tell them of McCarter's capture. After trying twice without making contact, he called Manning over. "Take a look at this, will you? I'm not getting through."

"I don't think it's anything wrong with the radio," Manning said, trying it himself. "According to the readouts, it's transmitting. I'd say that one of the satellites has gone down."

"Shit," Hawkins stated.

"We go in anyway," Bolan said quietly. "And we're not leaving until we do the job we came to do and get David out as well."

No one had any argument with that.

James picked up his medic bag and sought out Rust. "You were limping," he said. "How's the leg?"

"It got me here, so it can't be too bad."

"Let me take a look at it anyway."

There was fresh blood on the inner bandage, but there was still no sign of infection. "You just strained it a little and broke it open, that's all," James said. "If you could stay off it for a week, it would be fine."

"Maybe I can start that program tomorrow morning."

"Let's hope so."

THE RIDE INTO TOWN was uneventful. Right after sundown, Grimaldi drove the packed Land Rover in a wide sweep around to the west to stay off the main roads, but they still reached the outskirts of Palimiro in an hour. Now that night had fallen, the traffic was much lighter than it had been earlier, but it was still heavy enough that the Land Rover didn't attract attention.

Finding a place to park out of sight, Rust got out and adjusted his *lungi*. His assault harness and silenced MP-5 were out of sight under the loose-fitting tunic and unless one looked too closely, their outlines were hidden. "I'm ready," he told Bolan.

"Good luck."

"Right," Rust said. "But remember, if I don't get back to you in an hour, it means that I'm out of it."

"IT'S ABOUT TIME that something went right," Rust muttered to himself when he saw the Toyota pickup truck sitting behind the laundry. Like many trucks in Pakistan, the Toyota had a locally manufactured canopy mounted over the bed that had been decorated with everything from mirrors to plastic beads. To Western eyes, it looked as gaudy as a circus wagon, but no Pakistani would give it even a second glance.

Better yet, the hand-painted sign on the door proclaimed the services of the Very Fast Laundry, and there were bundles of dirty clothing in the back. That made it perfect for what he had in mind because even a military base on full alert needed clean laundry.

Quietly opening the door, he saw that the key wasn't in the ignition. But before he started trying to hot-wire it, he reached up to the driver's-side sun visor and felt around. Sure enough, the keys were there. No matter where he went in the world, many people who didn't lock the doors of their vehicles left their keys behind the visors.

Slipping behind the wheel of the Toyota, he fired it up and, shifting into first gear, drove off as quietly as he could.

A hundred yards down the road, he keyed his com link. "I found a ride and I'm headed for the main gate."

"Give us fifteen minutes," Bolan advised. "We're still short of our objective."

"No sweat."

CHAPTER TWENTY-FOUR

Stony Man Farm, Virginia

Carl Lyons's request for a cleanup team to sweep Rosario Blancanales's San Diego apartment was handled as a routine matter. Since Hal Brognola had passed the request on to the people who did that kind of work, it was taken care of the same way as it would be for any federal covert agency. The bodies would be removed, the carpet would be exchanged and any bullet holes repaired. The makeover of the apartment combined with a little computer razzle dazzle would send "Arthur Corona" back into cyberspace where he had come from. And when you came from nowhere, you couldn't be tracked.

The only thing out of the ordinary that came out of that incident was the information about the microchip Anne Keegan had produced.

"What do you want us to do about this supposed banking-system killer chip that woman gave to Able Team?" Aaron Kurtzman asked Brognola.

"Put it on ice," the big Fed said. "We don't have

time to mess with it right now. If Striker and Phoenix can keep the Pakistanis from starting a nuclear war, we'll worry about it then.''

"But this thing has the potential for causing a hell of a lot more damage than a pissant nuclear war! We lose the banking system, and the entire civilized world grinds to an abrupt halt.''

"I don't have time to worry about the banking industry right now,'' Brognola growled. "I have to go to Washington and talk to the President about the Pakistani mission. The Britons have just informed him that one of their agents thinks that the junta has already ordered the nuclear strike and that it's being prepared right now.''

"But you still want Lyons to keep working on the West Coast weapons angle, right?''

"If he has anything to work, yes. If not, pull them back here for reassignment.''

San Diego, California

WHEN IMMANUEL ZION AWOKE that morning, he realized that he hadn't heard from Jacobs the night before on the outcome of his visit to Arthur Corona's apartment. Sometimes disposing of the bodies took time. But when Jacobs and his two men didn't report for duty on time a few hours later, Zion started calling around to try to locate his missing security chief.

When no one reported having seen him, Zion got extremely concerned.

Phoning the security section, he got Roger Berk, Jacobs's second in command, on the line and ordered him to report to his office.

"Have you heard from Jacobs yet?" Zion asked.

"No, sir," Berk replied. "But when we went to Corona's apartment, we found Jacobs's vehicle was still parked down the block."

"Did you go inside?"

"Not yet. We're waiting until the people in the other apartments go to work before we break in."

Zion had a gut feeling that the break-in team would find the place empty. Something had gone wrong. It was obvious now that bastard Corona was a plant. The problem was that he didn't know who he was working for. If he did, he might be able to turn this around before it got too out of hand. The Temple had many friends in many high places, but he had to know which one to tap.

"Leave that job to someone you trust," he said. "I need you to supervise something else for me. I want the shipment that went into the warehouse the day before yesterday to be moved to the silo immediately. And I want all the drivers to have radios with them so that no one gets lost on the way. Also, I want a chase vehicle following them with an armed team in case anyone tries to get in my road."

"That's no problem, sir. I'll put one of my men in each truck with a radio, and the chase vehicle will have one able to reach us here."

"Then," Zion continued, "as soon as the trucks are

moving, pull the files on both Corona and Sarah Carter, get their photos and stats copied and put the word out on the street that I'm offering a million dollars, no questions asked, to find them.''

"No problem.''

"Then, I want that information put out to all of the people we have in the various state and federal agencies. I want to know who this Corona guy is and what he was doing here.''

"That may take awhile,'' Berk said cautiously.

"I don't care if it takes till Armageddon,'' Zion said. "I want that bastard.''

"Yes, sir.''

When he was told that the truck convoy had left the warehouse with their cargo, Zion called his personal helicopter to the pad on the temple roof. Climbing into the passenger seat, he told the pilot where to find the convoy in the maze of highways leading out of San Diego. Paranoia went hand in hand with religious mania and, even with the radios and guards in each truck, he wasn't about to trust anyone with his Phalanxes.

Washington, D.C.

WHEN HAL BROGNOLA LEFT the White House this time, it seemed as if the world was about to come to an end and, even with Stony Man Farm's resources, there seemed to be damned little he could do about it. Among the watchers of the global scene, the consensus was that the world had maybe one day left, two at the most, before the nuclear genie escaped from the bottle. Like in a Western movie, it was high noon, the Indians and Pakistanis were standing in the street waiting for the other guy to blink. In this case, though, it was already known who would fire the first shot.

In return for a signed pledge of America's total support to India no matter what happened, the President had obtained a promise from their prime minister that they wouldn't be the first to use their nukes. That left the Phoenix Force option open. But it was starting to look like this was when the law of averages was finally going to catch up with the Sensitive Operations Group and Stony Man Farm.

He had to admit though, that even if everything turned to excrement this time, Stony Man had had a good run, and he knew that the President could rightfully be proud of them. Brognola had sent the SOG action teams into damned near every corner of the world to do what they could to stave off catastrophe. In one critical incident after another, they had overcome seemingly impossible odds with a winning combination of guts, firepower and pure luck. But not even the best in the world could win all the time. It was beginning to look like this would be the mission when they would not be able to come through in time, if they did at all.

But in the long run, a nuclear war in the Indian subcontinent might not be the worst of America's worries right now. Along with every other medical and intelligence agency in the Western world, Stony Man had run into a blank wall trying to get a handle on the source of the millennium plague. Even with the most powerful, sophisticated espionage system in the world, they couldn't find a man who really didn't want to be found. Computers and satellites could only find what was there to find, and he had to admit that it was easy enough to vanish in that part of the world.

Not for the first time, Brognola wondered at the wisdom of having cut back too heavily on what the intelligence community called HumInt—spies.

Men and women on the ground risking their lives to develop leads was still the most effective way to gather information needed to make effective plans. From ancient times, spies had worked wonders in determining the course of human history. Now, when they were needed more than ever, it was almost a lost art and no one seemed to care. There wasn't a single CIA spy in all of Syria.

Stony Man had come up with information indicating that the man who might be behind the plague might be in Syria. In a situation this serious, that was two too many "mights" and they still didn't have anything concrete to work with. This guy could be on the dark side of the moon for all they could find out about him. And in the absence of snatching this madman and picking his brain, all of the combined efforts of the Western world to combat this disease were coming to naught.

All that was known was that the plague version of the anthrax bacteria had a viral gene spliced to it, but not even the best minds at the CDC knew what it was or how to kill it. As the director of the CDC had told the President, without the knowledge that only the plague's maker had, there was no way to predict how many lives would be lost before someone stumbled onto a way to stop it.

And if nuclear war and an unbeatable plague weren't enough to deal with, the Millennium Madness hadn't abated. If anything, as the days counted down it had only gotten worse and was now spreading faster outside of the United States than it was in the land of anything goes and the home of countless fringe nut groups. Even if the Pakistanis backed down and some CDC scientist hit the jackpot overnight, the world still wasn't going to be safe for those who simply wanted to live their lives in peace. There was an ever-growing number of millennium whackos to deal with, and how did you stop mass psychosis? Even he was beginning to think that the end of the world was at hand.

More than the fate of the world, Brognola mourned what was happening to the Stony Man team. So much of his life had been devoted to them for so long that they had become more his family than the woman he was married to and their children. He and Bolan had created Stony Man and had carefully nursed it until it had become what it was today. Or rather what it had been until a week or so ago.

Barbara Price had been stricken with the plague and would die if a treatment wasn't found quickly. Even then, there was no way to tell how it would affect her in the long run. Along with not knowing how to kill it, CDC had no idea what it was capable of doing to the human body long-term.

Phoenix Force was poised to make one last superhuman effort, and they would probably go down in flames. Bolan was with Phoenix this time, and Brognola didn't know if he was glad or sad that this was the case. Striker had lived a charmed life for a long time and maybe his luck would continue to hold. He did know that having him on the scene might be the key to their having any kind of chance at all to pull off the raid. He also knew that this could be the time that the soldier fought his last battle.

If Phoenix went up in flames, Brognola didn't think that it would be resurrected. Regardless of the legend, even the immortal phoenix had to die some time. Maybe the millennium would ring in more than Armageddon.

Beirut, Lebanon

MIRA VLODAN STOPPED in the middle of the crowded sidewalk in Beirut. Her breath caught in her throat and it felt as if her blood had turned to ice. As she fought to catch her breath, she ducked behind a kiosk to hide from the man she had spotted. The man calmly sipping his tea at the sidewalk café on the Corniche, the city's most fashionable avenue, was the Bosnian beast, Dr. Insmir Vedik, the man who had almost destroyed her when Bosnian Muslim forces overran the small Croatian town of Zendec.

Vlodan had been a nurse in a Croatian army field hospital in the town when the defensive line collapsed and the Bosnian troops advanced too quickly for the hospital to be evacuated. Some of the staff fled for their lives, but she, several other nurses and one doctor had remained behind to continue caring for their patients. Her hospital had treated the wounded of all three sides, military and civilian, equally. When the latest madness in the Balkans was finally over, Serbs, Bosnians and Croatians would have to learn to live together again, and treating those in need was a small step toward reaching that goal.

The man sitting at the café had entered the hospital accompanied by two dozen troops. From the insignia on his uniform, she saw that he was a medical doctor and relaxed a little. After the doctor reported to this officer, the man turned to his troops and ordered them to take the nurses outside for their pleasure. The Croatian doctor protested and was gunned down on the spot. Then, the butcher walked down the row of beds shooting all the patients in the head.

The fact that the nurses had been given to the troops for their amusement wasn't what outraged her the most. Ethnic rape had long been a part of war in the Balkans, and all sides practiced it as a matter of routine. She had treated many victims of military gang rapes and knew the reality of it. The killing of the medical staff, as well as the patients, however, had been a new horror for her.

At the end of that terrible day, she had been claimed

by a young Bosnian army captain. Why he had wanted her after she had been raped, she didn't know, but she was grateful to have been rescued.

At dawn of the second day, Mira Vlodan awoke to the sound of the artillery and tank guns of a Croatian counterattack. Her captor quickly called for his Russian-made GAZ jeep and had her wrists bound before putting her in the back of the vehicle. They were fleeing down a back road when the vehicle hit a buried mine.

It detonated under the passenger side of the GAZ and killed the officer outright before flipping the vehicle onto its side. The driver was caught under the GAZ when it came to rest, but she had been thrown clear. It had taken her several hours of wandering before she encountered a Croatian patrol. After telling her story to the army authorities, she had gone back to nursing casualties in Croatian hospitals.

When the Dayton Peace Accords went into effect, Vlodan left Bosnia. She had no family to hold her there and no good memories. Unlike most refugees from that unhappy land, with her medical training she quickly found work at a French medical charity working within Beirut's Christian and Druze communities.

She had no idea what Vedik was doing in Beirut. The last she had heard about him, he was being hunted for war crimes. In fact, she had testified before the International War Crimes Tribunal as to the fate of the hospital in Zendec. As she had learned, she had been very lucky to have escaped with her life. Most of Vedik's victims hadn't lived to testify against him.

Though her instincts were to run over and attack Vedik with her fists, she knew better than to let him see her. The hard eyes of the two men at the table with him told her that they were professional bodyguards. They would shoot her down like a dog in the street before she could even touch him. The war might be over in Lebanon, but the need for bodyguards wasn't.

She had to do something, though. A man like him couldn't be allowed to roam free as if he were a human and not a beast in human disguise. Then she thought of the World Health Organization staff at the UN building and decided to tell them about Vedik. They would be able to contact the War Crimes Administration and have him arrested and put on trial. Being careful to not be seen, Vlodan went back the way she had come and hailed the first cab that drove by.

Mira Vlodan wasn't unknown to the personnel of the WHO's Beirut office. She had often represented her organization at meetings. Knowing that she could only stand to tell the story one time, she waited until she was seen by one of the higher-ranking officers. The man sat expressionless as she told of that day of horror in Croatia.

"Insmir Vedik, you say his name is?"

"Yes." She nodded. "He was on the staff at the Sarajevo Medical University before the war started. I know that he is wanted by the war crimes tribunal because I testified before them about what he did in Croatia.''

She dropped her head to hide the tears. ''He is a beast,'' she sobbed. ''A bloody murderer, and he must be brought to justice.''

The UN officer was Swiss, and he considered female emotional outbursts to be counterproductive to promoting peace in the world. In fact, he felt that if women played less of a role in diplomacy and international affairs, the world wouldn't be such a mess. Nonetheless, if, and it was a big if, this wasn't a case where the imagination of a troubled woman was playing tricks with her mind, he was required to report her sighting. If a wanted war crimes suspect had been seen in his jurisdiction, he was required to report it. First, though, he would check with certain people before he did anything about this Vedik.

Though he was Swiss, the UN official wasn't as neutral as the international organization's charter would have had him be. He had a large family in Bern, and the UN pay scale didn't adequately cover his expenses, at least not adequately enough for his tastes. One of the best things about being posted in Beirut was the opportunity the city offered for the sale of information. Being Swiss, he was neutral in that he sold information to anyone who could pay for it, but his best customers were always the Islamic factions and the Syrians. It might be well worth his time to let them know about this development.

"Rest assured," he said officiously. "I will personally take care of this."

"Thank you," she said gratefully, wiping away her tears.

"It is nothing," he said. "I am just doing my job."

CHAPTER TWENTY-FIVE

Beirut, Lebanon

The UN official at the World Health Organization office didn't know it, of course, but one of the men he often sold information to was a deep cover agent for the Old Man of the Mountain. Unlike his predecessors, the Old Man knew that he needed more than a cadre of highly trained assassins if he was to be successful. He needed to know what was happening in every corner of the Middle East. His agents were well placed and well equipped to pass on any information as soon as they heard it.

When the Old Man learned that Insmir Vedik had been spotted in Beirut and his presence had been reported to the UN, his orders were direct: kill whoever had made the report as well as whoever he had reported to. When he was told that it was a woman who had spotted the Bosnian doctor, he didn't change his orders. She was to be killed immediately.

Stony Man Farm, Virginia

"GIVE ME SOME GOOD NEWS, people," Hal Brognola growled as he walked in and took his place at the table in Stony Man Farm's war room.

"Well," Yakov Katzenelenbogen stated, "Carl and the guys have come up with some of the Phalanx shipboard defense systems that went missing from the Coronado Navy yard."

When Brognola didn't interrupt to ask the appropriate question, Katz resumed. "They'd fallen into the hands of a major cult leader and they've been emplaced around a surplus Titan III missile silo in eastern California."

"Tell them good work, and send the troops in."

"I'd love to," Katz said, "but we've run into a little snag on the federal level this time. There's something called the *Religious Freedom Act* that says that if..."

"I know what it says," Brognola replied. "Get to the bottom line."

Kurtzman knew how Brognola was feeling, but these things had to be discussed by the numbers to insure that nothing got left out.

"The bottom line is that the authorities can't move against them because they are a church, and we do not have proof positive that the weapons are there. If we can get a photo or something like that, it will be a different story, but until then, the site's off-limits."

"That's the good news?"

Katz met his eyes squarely. "That's the best news we have."

Brognola closed his eyes as if in pain. "What's the rest of it?"

"Phoenix has gone into a communications blackout."

Now Brognola exploded. "How the hell did that happen? I have to be able to tell the President the instant anything goes down over there, and I can't do that if I can't talk to Phoenix!"

"You might want to pass your concerns on to the people who are in charge of the SatCom network," Aaron Kurtzman replied calmly. "They screwed the pooch on this one big-time. No one told them to maintain status for the duration of this emergency, and they tried to load a software update to the particular satellite that services that part of the world. It upchucked the program, and it's going to take at least twelve hours to bring it back on-line."

Brognola's face went pale. "Jesus, Mary and Joseph," he said quietly.

"We're trying to find an alternate routing right now," Kurtzman continued. "But the problem is that none of the available commercial satellites are equipped to handle the frequencies we use, and that's to say nothing of the skip-phase scramblers. So, even if we're able to restore communications that way, it'll all be in the clear. Any kid with a crystal set will be able to listen in."

"While the world goes up in a nuclear cloud," Brognola said.

He looked over at Katz. "Damage control?"

The Israeli shrugged. "There's not a hell of a lot we can do for Phoenix. We have a full spectrum NRO Keyhole-12 bird keeping watch on the airfield at Palimiro. But with commo to Phoenix out, all we'll be able to do is watch. If they're successful, we should be able to spot that from the air. And we'll also be able to see when it turns to shit."

Brognola glanced down to a fax on the table in front of him. "If that happens, the Navy has a Boomer parked offshore ready to launch in response to a Pakistani strike, the U.S.S. *Alabama*. Her Tridents are targeted at both Palimiro and the missile launch site Phoenix already neutralized."

"Will they launch when the F-16s fly?" Katz asked.

Brognola shook his head. "No, they have to wait until the actual detonation in India."

"Then, if Phoenix has to abort, they should be able to get out of the area before it turns into hell on earth."

"They might," Brognola said, not believing his own words and knowing that Katz didn't either. Both men knew that Phoenix Force wouldn't abort this mission, not when nuclear weapons were involved. Bolan and McCarter would take it all the way as they had done so many times before.

California

IMMANUEL ZION WATCHED the monitor screens in the Titan III silo Thirty-eight Alpha Hotel's central control room as the first of his Phalanx antiaircraft weapons was lowered into place on its mount. A team of electrical contractors had worked overtime to restore power to the miles of fiber-optic cables and wires that were the nerves of this complex. With all those nerves, there had to be a brain to control them and that's where Zion was standing.

The civilian computers that had been installed to replace the ones the government contractors had taken with them were far more powerful than the originals had been. The pace of computer technology was so rapid that the military couldn't keep up with it. By the time a military procurement contract could go through the laborious approval process, the computer industry would have made them obsolete. The computers Zion had installed were the best that money could buy, and he was quite confident that they would never become outdated. The Apocalypse would see to that.

Though the Phalanx weapons system had been built for shipboard use, they were the descendants of a series of air-defense weapons mounted on armored vehicles, which themselves were conversions of the aircraft 20 mm Vulcan cannon of Vietnam War fame. The silo's defense system had been designed to use an as yet unbuilt, upgraded version of the Phalanx as the last line of air defense for the site. While there were differences between the Navy guns Zion had acquired and the planned Air Force missile site defense version, they were similar enough that the Phalanxes could be fitted at the site with only a little modification.

Like any firearm, the Phalanxes were useful only as

long as they had ammunition. And at 3,000 rounds a minute, they went through quite a bit of it rather quickly. Though it was based on the 20 mm Vulcan cannon, the Phalanx was intended to fire depleted uranium or tungsten ammunition. Both of those metals were significantly heavier than steel and imparted more kinetic energy on the target on impact, an important factor when trying to knock out missiles streaking for a warship at supersonic speeds.

The problem was that the special Phalanx ammunition was almost unobtainable at any price. Standard 20 mm Vulcan ammo, however, was widely available on both the legitimate and black arms markets of the world. Several nations manufactured it for the Vulcan cannons mounted in their aircraft. Since Zion didn't think he would be facing a missile attack, the standard armor-piercing, explosive and incendiary ammunition would work nicely against police helicopters, and he had managed to purchase several tons of it.

As soon as the first Phalanx mount was securely bolted down, Zion called for the weapons tech. "How long will it take to get that thing operational?"

"The book says eight man-hours," the newly anointed Seeker said proudly. "But I've gotten them on-line in less than six before."

"Do it in four this time," Zion ordered. "I want to have it up before I leave this afternoon."

"I'll try my best, sir," the tech replied as he bounded away to get to work.

For the first time all day, Zion had time to spare to

miss not having Jacobs beside him. For most things, Berk would do okay as his replacement, but he didn't have the physical presence of his predecessor. If Jacobs were here, the burly mercenary would make sure that weapons tech worked as fast as humanly possible simply by looking at him.

But while he was waiting, Zion had other things he could do. For one, he could see how the hunt for Arthur Corona and Sarah Carter was going.

CARL LYONS, Rosario Blancanales, Hermann Schwarz and Anne Keegan lay in the sand on a hill a mile away from Titan III Silo Thirty-eight AH in the middle of the California desert.

Last night when Lyons asked her if she knew how to get to Immanuel Zion's sanctuary, she admitted that she didn't, only that she knew it was somewhere east of San Diego. Schwarz contacted the Farm and was able to get the site's location and a map of the area faxed to them. Driving their second vehicle, a four-wheel-drive Dodge Ram extended-cab pickup, off the main roads, they had been able to come up behind the site without being seen.

The guard post at the gate in the double-cyclone fence surrounding the site was manned by men in black uniforms. A steady stream of trucks was going through the gate and pulling up to the huge steel doors of the service entry. There, other men drove forklifts that were off-loading the trucks. The presence of a gaudy gold-and-white Jet Ranger chopper with a Temple of

Zion logo on the side indicated that the big man himself was supervising whatever was going on.

"Our man Zion's being a busy boy today," Blancanales stated. "I wonder what he's got going on down there?"

"Maybe he's stocking up for the millennium party," Lyons said as he videotaped the action. They were too far away to clearly see what was being unloaded, but the Farm would be able to enhance the tape and read the markings on the boxes and crates.

"That place looks funny to me," Schwarz said.

"How's that?" Lyons asked.

"Well, I'm really not what you could call an expert on Air Force ballistic missile silos, but I didn't think that they had integrated ground-and-air defense systems."

"What in the hell are you talking about?"

"Well," Schwarz said, aiming his field glasses at an odd-shaped concrete structure with a nonreflective dome on top. In an open triangle around it were three tan-painted steel domes that looked like mushrooms without stems. "Take a gander at azimuth three-five-six." He read off the numbers of the display in his vision field. "Range nine-three-seven."

"What about it?" Lyons asked as he ranged in his own binoculars.

"In the center of that cluster it looks to me like he has a hardened radar array that you could use for a sky watch. Then, farther out there are ground stations that look like sensors spaced out every twenty yards or so right inside the fence.''

Blancanales turned to Keegan. ''Are you sure you heard that Zion had a Phalanx?''

''Like I said last night, I remember because of the name even if I got its meaning wrong.''

''I think he's got three of the damned things,'' Schwarz commented as he watched one of the mushroom-shaped objects around the radar raise out of the ground a couple of yards and stop. ''And he may have one of them up and running already.''

''Is there any way to gimmick those damned things?'' Lyons asked.

''I don't think so,'' Schwarz said. ''At least not easily. The problem is that they're designed to withstand military electronic countermeasures, of course. Their radars are directly linked to their fire controls and when they pick up a target, if it's not squawking the right IFF signal, it blasts it out of the sky. It's as simple as one, two, three.''

''Can't the IFF signals be transmitted by police or other agency choppers?''

''They can,'' Schwarz admitted. ''But the Phalanx can also be set up to shoot at anything that flies over, IFF or not, and you know that's what Zion's done with them. For the scenario that he's working with, anything that flies over will be an enemy aircraft.''

''Is there any way that you can go on-line and screw up their computers?''

''No.'' Schwarz shook his head. ''They're self-contained, and there's no way I can access them unless I can get inside and use one of their terminals.''

"From the number of guards around there," Blancanales said, "I'd say that's a no-go."

Schwarz let his eyes drift over to the gold-and-white chopper parked in the middle of the silo. "There may be something I can do from a distance."

"What's that?"

"Well, if our man Zion always uses that chopper to come out here, that might be his weak point. I think I can get to him in the air."

"How's that?"

"I need to find a kitchen appliance repair place and pick up a couple of microwave transmitters. Then I need to find a small satellite TV dish antenna."

"You're going to beam them sitcoms?"

"Something like that."

Stony Man Farm, Virginia

WITH COMMUNICATIONS to Phoenix Force out of order, there was little for the Stony Man crew to do except watch the images the Keyhole satellite was transmitting to the NRO in Washington. Aaron Kurtzman had the optical, the IR and the radar images up on separate screens going from one to the other patiently looking for the signs of unusual activity at the Palimiro airbase.

Yakov Katzenelenbogen wasn't as patient as Kurtzman. Sweating out a mission was high on his list of least favorite things to do. So to keep from growing stir-crazy, he went back to trying to make contact with some of his friends in the Middle East. It was early evening there, and a good time to catch them at home.

For the round of inquiries, he was using the phone. Satellite relay made calling Beirut easier than calling Washington, D.C., most of the time. The first man he called was the leader of one of the smaller Druze groups in the city. Being neither Christian nor mainstream Muslim always made them the weakest of the sects and they always needed friends.

Getting straight to the point, though, wasn't part of the culture. Even with people he had known for years, he had to talk about their family, their business, politics and the weather before he could finally broach his subject.

"I am sorry I was not able to come to the phone immediately, my friend," the Druze said. "We had a tragedy strike our community today. Things have been so quiet lately, we have let our guard down. Maybe too much."

"What happened?"

"We lost a nurse from the French medical team that has been working in our neighborhood. Even with all the money that's been coming into the city over the past couple of years, as always, the Druze have been left out and this team has been running our clinic. Anyway, she was a sad woman, a Croatian refugee, but she was a wonderful nurse." He paused. "We will miss her."

"What happened to her?"

"She was assassinated."

"What do you mean?"

"I mean a Mercedes drove up to our little clinic and four gunmen in ski masks, I think they are called, jumped out. They asked for her by name and when they found her, they simply shot her in the head without a word and left. No one else was harmed and they gave no explanation."

"Do you know who the gunmen were?"

"I could only guess from the accents, maybe Syrians."

"Why would she have been a target?"

"I do not know except that when she came back to the clinic this afternoon, she was very upset. She told my wife that she had been to the UN building where she had reported seeing a wanted Bosnian war criminal on the streets of Beirut. Apparently, she had had some connection to the man in Bosnia and knew that the UN was looking for him."

The Baltic conflict had been a modern holocaust and there were many wanted war criminals on the loose, but the only war criminal Katz was interested in was Dr. Insmir Vedik. "Do you know if she mentioned this guy's name?"

"Let me ask my wife."

Katz heard a faint conversation in the background and the sounds of music from a radio. If he'd have patched the call through Kurtzman's computers, he could have listened in to the conversation clearly. But friendship had its limits.

"She doesn't remember a name," the Druze said when he got back on the line. "But she is sure that Nurse Mira said he was a doctor."

"I owe you one, old friend."

"You owe me more than one." The Druze chuckled. "But you can pay me the next time you come through this godforsaken town."

"That may be sooner than you think."

Katz smiled grimly as he walked over to where Kurtzman was still watching the monitors. "I have a line on our man Vedik. He was seen in Beirut today."

CHAPTER TWENTY-SIX

Palimiro, Pakistan

Like at all established military bases the world over, the Pakistani air force base at Palimiro had a main gate with sentries in a guard shack and a moveable barrier to control traffic. Unfortunately for J. R. Rust, there was also a guard barracks next to the gate. If he blew his entry, he'd be up to his neck in angry enemy gunners.

The main thing Rust had going for him was that while it was said that the Pakistanis spoke more than fifty languages, he knew two of them. He was conversant in Urdu, the official language, and Pashtu, a language used along the Afghan border region to the northeast. Pretending to be from a faraway place, however, might be useful in a growing city like Palimiro. People were drawn to it from all over the country and lower-paid workers, like vendors, were usually newly arrived migrants.

When Rust stopped the Toyota pickup in front of the lowered barrier at the guard shack, two sentries in pressed khaki uniforms and blue berets stepped out. One of them walked up to the cab of the gaudy truck while the other one went around to the back.

"Name?" the first guard asked in Urdu as he glanced at the laundry sign on the truck's door.

"Mohammad Khan," the CIA man answered, using a common name from the region where the Pashtu language was spoken.

"What is a Pashtun doing in Balochistan?" the guard asked while writing down the name and time on his clipboard.

Rust shrugged expressively. "God's will."

Since that was the universal Muslim way of making a long story short, it was accepted without question. Going into a long-winded, Western-style cover story would have been out of character for a rustic mountain man and would have aroused the guard's suspicions.

"Nothing back here," the second guard called out from the rear of the truck.

"Pass," the first guard told Rust. "But take care of your business quickly. You have to be gone by twenty-two hours. That's ten o'clock."

"As God wills it."

Firing up the Toyota pickup, Rust ground the gears convincingly as he let out the clutch. The guards laughed and said something in a language he didn't understand, probably a comment on the inability of a nomadic Pashtun to master anything more complicated than a goat.

Having worked with the Pashtun before, Rust fully

agreed with them on that. But playing a country hick who had moved to the city was a perfect cover. Everyone would expect him to be clumsy and to speak the official language with an accent.

As soon as he was well away from the gate, he keyed his com link to report. "I'm on the base and starting the search."

"Roger," Bolan replied. "We're in place and ready to move at your signal."

Driving slowly, Rust went through the built-up area looking for the base lockup. He knew that the air police wouldn't have handed McCarter over to civilian authorities. He was their catch, so they had to be keeping him around here somewhere.

BOLAN AND THE Phoenix Force commandos had chosen a spot on the far side of the perimeter for their entry where the fence faced a cluster of shacks. Judging from the pickup trucks and delivery vans parked in the area, it had to be a neighborhood where working men spent their evenings. It was easy to park the Land Rover so it wouldn't be noticed. If something went wrong this night, they might still need it.

When they left their vehicle, each commando carried a small bag and waited until they were hidden in the dark near the fence before they donned their night combat clothing and assault harnesses. After checking everything, they helped one another cover their faces and hands with combat cosmetics and settled to wait for Rust to find his target.

As they waited, a pair of Pakistani F-16 Falcons taxied to the end of the runway. Running up their turbines, the pilots lit their afterburners, came off the brakes and thundered down the runway. As the fighters flashed by, the commandos were able to clearly see their underwing ordnance loads.

"They're packing Sidewinders and their normal drop tanks," Grimaldi reported. "No nukes that I could see, so they're just a routine patrol. We're still in time."

"We'll know it if they're packing the nukes," Bolan said. "Every inch of this place will be wall-to-wall with troops and vehicles."

AFTER DRIVING around the base for fifteen minutes, Rust finally located a small building with the Pakistani air police insignia and the Urdu word for "confinement" on a sign in front. It wasn't a big lockup, so hopefully it wouldn't have a large staff. If luck was with him, there wouldn't be more than a couple of guys on duty manning the radio and making sure the prisoners didn't get too rowdy.

Parking the truck behind the buildings, he stepped out and looked around. When he was sure that no one was watching, he keyed his com link. "I've found the jail," he radioed to Bolan.

"Roger, we're making our entry now."

BREAKING INTO THE AIR BASE was as easy as cutting a hole in the cyclone wire perimeter fence. No foot patrols had been spotted and Manning hadn't detected any sensors or warning devices, so James didn't have to be shy about using his wire cutters. A three-foot-tall cut was made and the flap pulled back to make a door the commandos could crawl through unimpeded.

After everyone had wriggled through, James pulled the wire back in place, and, using black tape, taped the ends of the cut together. Anyone walking the fence in daylight would see what he had done, but by that time, they'd better be far from this place and on their way home.

The building that had been identified as the storage place for the nuclear bomb racks was located a hundred yards behind one of the maintenance hangars. Fortunately, it was nowhere near the building that was being used as the nuclear arsenal storage facility. Why the two buildings weren't closer together, as would have been expected, wasn't clear. But sometimes the gods of war smiled on Phoenix Force at the most unexpected times.

WHEN THE TEAM STARTED OUT for its objective, Jack Grimaldi broke off to find an airplane to take them home. Reaching the flight line, it didn't take him long to discover that there wasn't a lot to choose from. A quick look told him that the single Huey Rust had reported was definitely nonoperational. The turbine cowling was off and laying on the ground, which meant that someone was working on it.

Prior to the breakup of the Soviet Union, there

would have been other Hueys on the flight line. But since Pakistan and the United States had been on the outs for several years, buying Russian aircraft had been easier than trying to bypass the American arms embargo to buy parts for the U.S. products in the inventory. So, with the Bell machine out, that left second best—Russian Mi-8 Hip choppers and a couple of Anatov twin turboprops to choose from.

Grimaldi was primarily a rotary-wing driver, but that didn't mean that he wouldn't step into the cockpit of a fixed wing if circumstances called for it. First though, he wanted to check out the choppers. He was walking past the lineup of Hips when he spotted the unmistakably brutal shape of an Mi-24 Hind gunship hulking in the dark and skidded to a halt.

One of the reasons he hadn't wanted to jump into the first Hip he saw was that they weren't armed. Neither were the Anatovs, for that matter. And when they bid this place goodbye, there was a distinct possibility that the Pakistanis would put a couple of their F-16s into the air looking for payback. Having something beyond their individual weapons to discourage the fighters would be helpful.

Finding the Hind solved that problem. The aircraft had been the workhorse of the Afghan war where it had earned the nickname Flying Tank. In its day, it had been the most heavily armored helicopter in the world and one of the most heavily armed, as well. Even today, the M-24 was a formidable opponent and difficult to shoot down.

Best of all, though, was that unlike most dedicated gunship choppers, the Hind had room enough inside to carry eight fully equipped troops. Considering that the Stony Man commandos would be traveling light when they left this place, there would be ample room.

When he got closer to the Hind, even in the dark, he could see that the normally matte-finish desert camouflage paint had been waxed to a high gloss. He didn't know much about the Pakistani air force, but in any air arm he was familiar with, a wax job on an operational aircraft meant that it was the squadron commander's toy, his private ride. To back up that supposition, he saw that the gunship's stub wings weren't wearing their missile pylons. Like the wax job, taking off the pylons cut the drag and made the ship a lot faster.

He was pleased, though, to see that the turret under the Hind's nose was still fitted with its quad-barrel 12.7 mm Gatling gun. If he remembered correctly, the weapon was capable of spitting out more than 800 rounds per minute and the Russian 12.7 mm ammunition packed a little more punch then the U.S. equivalent, the M-2 .50-caliber round.

Reaching above the turret, he tripped the latches for the ammo storage compartment and opened the door. He had halfway expected it to be empty, but was pleased to see that fortune was again with him. The feed box was loaded with link-belt ammunition all the way to the top. Having that much firepower on hand might make their way out of the air base a little more feasible.

Opening the door to the pilot's cockpit, he climbed in and used his penlight to familiarize himself with the controls. Since English was the unofficial second official language of the Pakistani armed forces, he wasn't too surprised to see that all the instruments had been retagged, so he could read them. Finding the master electrical switch, he snapped it on. The ammeter on the instrument showed a full charge on the batteries, and the fuel tanks were full, as well. The Hind was ready to go the full operational range, which for a one-way flight should be about eight hundred miles.

The pilot had a big grin on his face as he keyed his com link. "Striker," he said, "I've found our ride home, a Russian Hind gunship. It's fully fueled and the 12.7 in the turret is armed. Give me a minute or two to go over the controls, and I'll be ready to go whenever you are."

"Roger," Bolan replied. "But hang on before you crank it up."

"Will do."

Now THAT their transportation out of Pakistan had been secured, the Stony Man warriors were free to start taking care of business. It had been a long journey, and they were ready to get the job wrapped up so they could go home. The fact that the delivery racks were being stored away from the weapons themselves greatly increased their chances of successfully completing that job. The NRO recon photos showed that most of the base's troops were tied up guarding the nukes.

The lights in the maintenance hangars were burning brightly as they made their approach. For the mechanics to be working this late meant that they had something cooking, and from all accounts they were making a nuclear stew. But since they were so busy, they weren't likely to notice the men in night-black who slipped around the hangar to the small building behind it.

Bolan, Encizo and Hawkins took up security positions around the building while Manning and James went for the entry. A large brass padlock was all that secured the door, and James made short work of it with his titanium mini pry bar.

Manning went in first and closed the door behind him before clicking on his flashlight to see if they were in the right place. The light immediately revealed shelves, each holding a six-foot-long aluminum pylon. "They're here," he radioed to Bolan after making a quick count. "And it looks like they're all accounted for."

"Roger."

"They don't look that dangerous to me," James said as he joined Manning inside and opened his demo pack. "Most jet fighters I've seen carry pylons like those."

"Not like these," Manning assured him. "They're

special, and without them the Pakistanis might as well throw their bombs for all the good it'll do them.''

One of the biggest problems with the Pakistani nuclear weapons program was that it had been conducted in great haste, as well as secrecy. Since they were a relatively small country, they would have been defenseless if the world's great powers had decided to put them out of business. Because of that, they'd been forced to cut corners whenever possible.

The plans they'd copied were for a Russian missile warhead, but at that time, they'd had no missiles able to carry it. Therefore, they had modified the warhead design to create a free-fall bomb. While the internals of the two devices were similar in that they both contained plutonium, that's where the similarity ended.

For all of their destructive power, nuclear weapons were complicated, sensitive devices, particularly their detonation controls. For a free-fall weapon to detonate at the proper altitude required that the detonation system "know" several things before it could function. It needed to know its altitude at the time of being dropped, its airspeed, the ambient air temperature and barometric pressure. When used in a missile, the rocket's internal instrumentation provided that information to the warhead. Away from the missile, though, the weapon didn't have access to the data, and that's what made the delivery racks so important.

The racks contained the instrumentation the bomb's detonation system needed to access right before release. Without that information, the bombs were little more than one-thousand-pound, streamlined rocks falling from the sky. It was true that when they hit, they might break open the containment vessel inside and spread radioactivity. But they wouldn't go into nuclear detonation. Therefore, once the delivery racks were destroyed, the bombs would effectively be neutralized. In time, they could be refitted with some other kind of detonation system, but not in time for the war that was threatening to break out.

Manning knew that the key to making this work was to either destroy the racks completely or to destroy the same parts of each rack so the parts couldn't be cannibalized from one to repair another. Since the front end of the racks contained the instrumentation hookup points, it made sense to place the explosives there.

With James assisting him, Manning quickly went from the first delivery rack to the next rigging them for destruction. Each one got two, one-quarter-pound blocks of RDX, one on each side of the instrumentation package, connected with a loop of det cord and a remote control detonator. A further length of det cord went from one rack to the next in a daisy chain that would insure that if even one of the detonators functioned, they all would go off together. It was overkill, but they had to guarantee that each and every one of the sixteen delivery racks were destroyed.

With the stakes as high as they were, Manning checked each charge and detonator again before sending James out to join the others guarding the building. The last charge he set, he had to do alone.

On the way out of the building, Manning placed a one-quarter-pound charge on the inside of the door-frame and connected a length of det cord running to the first charge in the daisy chain. To complete the booby trap, he ran a knee-high trip wire to the other side of the door connected to a slack-tight detonator with an antidisturbance switch. If anything happened to them and they weren't able to set off the charges with the remote signal, the first man through the door would do the job for them. Even if the Pakistanis spotted the trip wire and tried to disarm the charge, the antidisturbance fuse should go off anyway.

"Let's go," he said as he carefully closed the door behind him and reset the lock.

"Flyboy," Bolan radioed to Grimaldi, "this is Striker. We're on our way out now. Stand by to crank it up."

"Roger."

CHAPTER TWENTY-SEVEN

Palimiro, Pakistan

Bolan's call to Jack Grimaldi was also Rust's call to action. Stepping out of the pickup, he took the silenced MP-5 out from under his *lungi* and slung it over his shoulder out of sight behind his back. Keeping in the shadows, he walked to the front of the jail and watched through the window for a few moments.

As he had hoped, it looked like there were only three people in the front office. The man behind the desk with the sergeant stripes on his armband had to be the duty sergeant, and the two privates would be his runners.

After satisfying himself that only those three men were in the building, Rust swung his silenced subgun around and walked up to the door. Taking a deep breath, he booted the door and stepped into the room.

The sergeant seated at the desk got to his feet as if he were spring-loaded. As his hand clawed for the pistol in the holster on his duty belt, Rust hosed him down. The MP-5 SD made almost no noise as it spit

9 mm hollowpoint slugs. The only sound was the sergeant grunting as the slugs hit home and the thud of his body falling face-first on the desk.

The two privates weren't sure what was going on, and their hesitation was fatal. Rust spun on them, the H&K spitting silent death. Both men went down before they realized what was happening.

Rust dropped the half-empty magazine and rammed a fresh one in place before he went to check his kills. The three air policemen were dead, though, and didn't require additional attention. Now, he could find McCarter.

A big key ring hung from a hook behind the duty sergeant's desk. Stepping over the corpse, he snatched the ring and headed down to the hallway leading to the back room. The cells turned out to be separate rooms with thick wooden doors with grilled windows at the top. The first two cells he looked into were empty, as was the third. The fourth, however, held a man in khaki laying on a cot with his face turned to the wall.

"David?"

McCarter opened his eyes and sat up. Even in the dim light, the Briton looked like he had done three rounds in a heavyweight ring with his hands tied behind him.

"Jesus, man!" Rust exclaimed as he tried the first key on the ring. "What in the hell happened to you?"

"A nasty sergeant didn't believe that I was an oil field engineer. In fact, he got rather rude about it."

"A big guy with a scar on his face?"

"Yeah, why?"

"He tried to get rude with me, too, and I left him on the floor."

"You're okay for a Company man." McCarter grinned as he got to his feet.

"I have my moments," Rust said as he keyed the lock and swung open the door. "But we'd better save the kudos for later. Can you move okay?"

"It looks worse than it is. Let's get out of here.

"You do good work, lad," McCarter commented when they reached the front desk and he saw the three Pakistani air policemen laying in their blood. "I didn't hear a bloody thing."

"That's the code of the Company. Don't give the sucker an even break."

"Works for me."

McCarter snatched an M-16 and a bandoleer of ammunition from the rifle rack by the door of the jail.

"I've got a truck parked out back," Rust said as he steered McCarter in the right direction. "Striker has the charges set and Jack has found us a Russian gunship to fly home in. We're ready to leave this place."

"He always has to show off, doesn't he?"

"Who?"

"Our ace pilot," McCarter said. "He had to find a gunship to drive home. I was hoping for something a little more comfortable."

Sliding behind the wheel of his pickup, Rust keyed

the com link. "Striker," he radioed, "the Brit is out and we're en route to Flyboy's location."

"Roger," Bolan answered. "Report when you link up."

The raid on the Red Dragon missiles at Gandara had gone off with a minimum of fuss and so far, this operation was following suit. With Rust having sprung McCarter, Bolan and Phoenix Force could withdraw to the chopper immediately instead of standing by in case they were needed at the jail. They were making their way back past the maintenance hangar when the wail of an alert siren sounded.

Fortune was a fickle bitch at best, and she had just turned her face away from the Stony Man warriors.

RUST HAD JUST PULLED UP behind the Hind and was stepping out when the siren went off. "Oh shit!" McCarter muttered as he ran for the chopper.

Grimaldi recognized him and yelled down from the cockpit. "David, take the front cockpit! I need you on the gun."

"But I don't read Russian!"

"Everything's been labeled in English!"

McCarter clamored into the weapons systems officer's seat and snapped the seatbelt harness in place. As Grimaldi had said, the placards were in English and, when he hit the master switch to the turret, the windscreen in front of his face lighted up with the HUD display and sights. The firing controls themselves were a single rotating stick with a trigger switch on the top, pretty standard stuff.

Rolling the stick from side to side, he saw the gun turret follow his movement. This wasn't as high tech as the "look and shoot" helmet-to-gun system on an Apache, but he didn't mind a little hands-on work tonight.

"I'm ready to rock and roll," he called back to Grimaldi.

While McCarter was getting on the gun, Rust had clamored into the troop compartment and was ready to add the firepower of his H&K if needed.

Since Grimaldi had already preflighted the Hind, all he had to do was hit the fuel pump switch, arm the igniters and switch on the right-hand turbine starter. With an electric whine, the big five-bladed rotor started to turn. In less than a complete rotation, the Izotov turbine fired off, filling the air with the reek of burning kerosene.

As soon as the tach showed fifty percent, Grimaldi hit the starter switch for the left-hand turbine, which ignited almost immediately. When both turbines had spooled up, he jammed the throttles against the stop, watched the rotor tach and waited for the blades to come up to speed.

Even over the roar of the turbines and the sound of the blades cutting through the air, Grimaldi still heard the alert siren wailing. Since he had a gunner on board now, maybe it was time to put his new gunship to work.

"Striker," he radioed, "I'm going to lift off in a hover and see if I can clear the garbage out of the way for you."

"Roger," Bolan responded. "But watch out for the gun jeeps. There's half a dozen of them, and they're armed with machine guns."

"Hang on guys," the pilot called out. "We're going to bust up the party."

Pulling up on the collective, Grimaldi fed pitch to the five-bladed rotor and brought the Hind into a ground effect hover. A light hand on the cyclic maneuvered the heavy machine out of its parking spot onto the tarmac and, kicking in a little tail rotor, he nosed it in the direction of the firing.

THE SECURITY MIGHT HAVE BEEN lax at the air base, but when the alarm went off, the Pakistanis responded quickly. Along with the vehicle-mounted ready-reaction force, it looked like every man on the base had turned out with a weapon in his hand. Most of them didn't know who or what to shoot at, but they were shooting anyway. Their undirected fire was causing more damage to the base than anything the Stony Man team was doing. That element of confusion, though, might actually help the commandos get away. If they could keep in the shadows, they might be able to make it to the Hind unseen.

When someone hosed down a moving fuel truck, it immediately caught on fire and the driver bailed out. Driverless, it crashed into a building storing sortie reload ammunition for the fighters. The burning fuel quickly started cooking off 20 mm ammunition.

The burning fuel also threw enough light that the five Stony Man warriors were outlined against the night sky, and they were spotted. Caught in the open, there was no place to hide, so the commandos formed a circle and started taking on all comers.

Just then, Grimaldi brought the Hind in and set down on the tarmac as close as he could. "Go! Go! Go!" he called out over the com link.

No sooner had the commandos turned to run than two Land Rovers came roaring out of the darkness, the machine guns mounted behind the drivers spitting fire.

When the Land Rovers swept in after the team, McCarter centered the first truck in his HUD and gave the trigger a quick squeeze. He was being economical with his ammunition because at 800 rounds per minute, a half-second burst from the four-barrel gun was more than enough to destroy a thin-skinned vehicle. The Land Rover careened out of control and overturned.

Seeing his partner go down, the gunner in the second vehicle raked the front of the Hind with his RPD machine gun, but the 7.62 mm rounds bounced off the Hind's armor like BB pellets. Another quick burst of the 12.7 mm gun turned both the driver and the gunner into bloody ruin. A stray tracer found the gas tank, and the gun jeep burst into flame.

Since his weapon had proved to be such a good tool for tearing things up, McCarter spun the turret to line up on the flight line. The first F-16 that came into his sights got a short burst, and again the tracers did their job as it burst into flame. Two trucks parked next to a hangar got the same treatment.

In the troop compartment, Rust stood in the open door firing bursts over the heads of the running commandos. Scattered small-arms fire was hitting all around him, but most of it was bouncing off the Hind's armor. An occasional round screamed through the open door and imbedded itself in the troop seats inside.

Hawkins reached the chopper first and knelt on the ground, joining Rust in putting out suppressive fire. James soon joined him, with Manning on his heels. The two stood on each side of the door, covering Bolan and Encizo as they dashed the last few meters to the Hind.

When Encizo slipped and went down to his knees, James grabbed him by the assault harness, boosted him into the chopper and followed him inside.

"We're in!" Bolan called up from the troop compartment. "Go! Go! Go!"

Holding the grip throttle up against the stop, Grimaldi fed pitch to the blades with the collective and nosed the cyclic forward. Since the Hind had wheeled landing gear instead of skids, it could take off like a conventional aircraft and build forward speed quickly.

As Grimaldi started his takeoff run, Manning took out his remote control for the detonators and switched it on. When the LED showed red, he hit the firing button three times.

The small building behind the first maintenance hangar erupted with a flash and a roar. The individual charges had been small, but together they were impressive, and since it was a wooden structure, it started to burn immediately. The explosion added to the confusion, and the Pakistani troops slackened their fire at the Hind and started to look for a second attacking force.

When Grimaldi's airspeed indicator showed about eighty miles an hour, the pilot pulled up on the collective and the big five-bladed rotor hauled the gunship into the air like a stretched rubberband rebounding. A flick of a switch retracted the landing gear and, keeping the nose down with the cyclic, he balanced his rate of climb against the need to gain speed.

Though it was considerably heavier, the Hind was quite a bit faster than an old Huey. He should be able to reach two hundred miles an hour without too much difficulty. And while that wasn't much speed to put up against a supersonic fighter, anytime you were in a dog fight, every mile an hour counted.

After taking off to the east, Grimaldi banked the Hind gunship to the southwest and dropped low over the barren land. Rotary-winged aircraft flew fastest where the air was densest, so not only was he trying to stay out of sight down low, he would be getting the best out of his heavy Russian machine. The coastline was about a hundred and fifty miles away, and with the big Izotov turbines spinning out well over four thousand shaft horsepower, that should translate into about forty-five minutes flight time.

In the troop compartment, the Stony Man warriors could take a seat, but no one was relaxing. That would have to wait until they were clear of Pakistani airspace and safe on friendly soil.

Hawkins and James each took a side window of the chopper and stood air guard, watching to make sure that the sky behind them stayed clear.

Stony Man Farm, Virginia

"I'VE GOT ACTION at Palimiro," Aaron Kurtzman called across the computer room. "The building that supposedly holds the delivery racks is going up in flames."

"Are you sure that's the one?" Hal Brognola asked.

"Of course I'm sure. I've been watching the damned thing on the screen nonstop for three hours now."

"How about the nuclear storage area?"

Kurtzman ran through all of the sensor and optical imaging before answering. "It seems to be untouched, but there's a lot of activity around it."

Brognola relaxed. One of the most critical elements in this mission was to disable Pakistan's nuclear delivery systems, but to leave the weapons themselves intact. Or at least some of them. Although the Pakistanis were clearly the aggressors this time around, it could just as well have been the Indians and probably would be the next time. Completely disarming Pakistan would only invite an Indian attack at some time in the future. Until such time as both nations could have their nukes taken away from them at the same time, they both had to remain armed.

"I'll tell the President that he can call off the Boomer and tell the NSC to go home."

"Aren't you going to wait until the guys get free?"

"Since we're out of contact with them, how will we know?"

"Damned if I know," Kurtzman admitted. "But we need to notify the Carrier Task Force and tell them to be on the lookout for a Pakistani aircraft acting funny."

"I'll do that under White House authority," Brognola said. "It'll carry more weight that way."

"Just do it quickly. They may be on the way out now."

CHAPTER TWENTY-EIGHT

San Diego, California

Immanuel Zion was pleasantly surprised, but instantly suspicious when his receptionist buzzed his office to tell him that Sarah Carter was calling collect, insisting that she talk to him personally. "Take the call."

"Master," she said, "it's Sarah. I need your help."

"Sarah," he said, keeping his voice light. "Where are you?"

"I'm at a little place called Nelson's Junction on Highway 62." Her voice was breathless, and he could picture her talking on a pay phone at a gas station.

"I was very worried about you, Sarah." Zion let his voice slip into that silky, "butter-wouldn't-melt-in-his-mouth" Southern dialect he found so helpful in dealing with women. "I was afraid that you had been taken from us."

"I was." Keegan let her voice break. "After that man shot Jacobs and the men you'd sent to get me, he kidnapped me and took me into the desert. He made me help him get rid of the bodies and then he was going to shoot me, too.''

''What happened?'' he asked, not knowing if he was buying her story or not. ''How did you get away from him?''

''I begged for my life and promised that I would catch the first bus that came by and never return to California. He gave me five hundred dollars, and I'm waiting for the bus right now.''

Likely story, Zion thought. The truth was probably that she had screwed his brains out and the money was a payoff.

''Don't run from us, Sarah,'' he said. ''Come home. Come back to the Temple and no one will ever hurt you again, I promise you that.''

''But I can't come back to San Diego,'' she said, hovering on the verge of hysteria. ''He'll find me. He told me that he'll always be able to find me no matter where I go and that if he ever sees me again, he'll kill me.

''I'd like to come back,'' she sobbed. ''But I'm afraid. Can you come and get me?''

''I can send one of my men to get you.''

''But I won't know them,'' she wailed. ''Now that Buck's dead, I don't know anyone I can trust other than you.''

Even if she was telling the truth, there was no way that he was going to go to some piss-water hole-in-the-road in the California desert to retrieve her, not even with an armed escort. But before he could start explaining why she had to come to him, she solved the problem.

"Maybe I could go to the sanctuary," she said. "I know it's safe. And I could wait for you there."

If she was trying to lure him into a trap, she had made a mistake in suggesting that solution. But she had no way of knowing that he had one of the Phalanxes up and running and the second one was coming on-line today. Anyone who tried anything funny close to the sanctuary would end up spattered all over the desert.

"Do you know where it is?"

"Only that it's somewhere close to here."

"Where did you say you were?" Zion asked.

"Nelson's Junction. It's on Highway 62 close to the Nevada border."

Zion consulted the map on the wall behind his desk. "Okay," he said. "Get someone to take you to US 95 and go north. About ten miles from the junction, there's a sign reading Golden State Mining by a paved road. Take that road, and it's about four miles."

"US 95," she said. "Golden State Mining. I've got that."

"Have the guard at the gate call me when you arrive, and I'll be there within the hour."

"Thank you, Master, thank you."

CARTER TURNED to Rosario Blancanales with a grim smile on her face. "He bought it. He wants me to catch a ride to his sanctuary and he'll come and get me there."

"That was perfect." Blancanales smiled. "You should get an Oscar for that performance. I'll be the guy you catch a ride with and, after I drop you off, I'll stay close by in case you need to abort."

"I can give you a small radio you can use to call for help," Gadgets Schwarz said. "All you'll have to do is push the button and we'll be there."

"Okay," she said. "I guess I'm ready."

As HIS CHOPPER approached the sanctuary, Immanuel Zion radioed the guard post again to make sure that Sarah Carter was still waiting for him. He half expected that she had disappeared again in the hour since the guard had called to say that she had arrived. Even though she had come to him as she had said she would, Zion still wasn't convinced that there wasn't something funny about her story.

No matter who Arthur Corona really was and how talented Carter was in bed, letting her go just didn't add up in his mind. Not when Corona had apparently murdered Jacobs and the two guards. A man like that wouldn't want to leave behind a witness.

Something funny was going on, and he was going to enjoy finding out what it was. Once he had Sarah back within the temple's walls, he'd learn everything he needed to know and he would enjoy every last minute of it. In fact, he was looking forward to it.

WHEN THE CHOPPER came into view from the ridgeline overlooking the silo, Schwarz checked the battery pack to his homemade device one last time.

"That thing had better work, Gadgets," Lyons said. "Rosario doesn't have enough firepower with him to hold off all those guards down there."

Blancanales had taken their van to deliver Keegan to the silo's front gate and was waiting out of sight in case he needed to rescue her. He was armed and the van had a certain amount of Kevlar armor in the doors and side panels. But he was only one, and there were dozens of Zion's guards down there and they were all packing.

"It'll work," he said as he hoisted the device up onto his shoulder and peered through the sight.

After consulting with the Farm about the Phalanx's fire controls, he had put together a package containing three different microwave transmitters, the main laser from his video camera zapper and a small TV dish antenna converted to a transmitter. Since radar was simply microwaves, his gadget would send microwave beams to the chopper and they would reflect off it as if they had originated from it. The Phalanx fire-control radars would see the incoming chopper as an attacking aircraft and lock on to it.

The principle of using radar to confuse radar had been used by chronic speeders for years to illegally neutralize traffic radars. It was illegal in that modifying a microwave transmitter required an FCC licence. Schwarz, however, was under no such restraints.

Fixing the chopper in his sights, he fired up his homemade electronics countermeasures device. When he started picking up a return, he switched on the laser.

In the fire control room deep inside the missile silo, the threat board came to life as soon as the chopper came in view of the Phalanx's radar. According to the fire control computer, the approaching aircraft wasn't transmitting the proper IFF. On top of that, it was transmitting some kind of electronic countermeasures radar as well as a laser targeting beam. The targeting beam wasn't tightly focused, but it was of a hostile nature and exceeded the parameters expected of a friendly aircraft.

Analyzing all of that information in a few microseconds, the computer decided that the target was hostile and flashed a message to the weapon. Once the Phalanx's fire control made the decision, it locked on to Zion's chopper.

The six-barreled gun spun on its mount and, after tracking its target for a microsecond, fired. A deep, ripping roar echoed across the desert as the cannon fired a five-second burst. In that short time, 250 20 mm tungsten armor-piercing rounds slashed into the white-and-gold helicopter.

Since the machine wasn't armored, it was like shooting at a paper bag. The rounds passed from one side of the chopper clean through to the other, regardless of what filled the space in between. Zion, his pilot, his new security chief, two guards, the spinning turbine, the fuel tanks and all the other parts that made up the helicopter were shredded.

From the ground, it looked like the chopper abruptly stopped and came apart in midair. An instant later, vaporized fuel came in contact with the turbine's red-hot burner cans and detonated. The fireball blossomed in the sky like a red-and-black flower, and the shreds of what had been the chopper and its passengers rained onto the desert.

Schwarz lowered his gadget and smiled grimly. "We now have proof that the Temple of Zion has stolen military weapons on their premises."

"We also have further evidence scattered all over the desert," Lyons added as he clicked off the video camera.

"If someone can get to it before the animals do," Schwarz commented. "It doesn't look like there are too many big pieces left to collect."

In the aftermath of the explosion, people were pouring out of the silo to look at the column of smoke from the burning jet fuel rising over the desert. No one even noticed when Blancanales drove up to the main gate and opened the door for Anne Keegan.

WHEN ABLE TEAM got back to their boat at the marina, the story of Immanuel Zion's unfortunate "accident" was on the evening news. On the way back, they had stopped at the first San Diego TV station they could find to drop it off.

The coverage showed that state police tactical units

as well as SWAT teams from both the ATF and the FBI were on the scene at the Titan III silo and they were taking no chances. But regardless of the rhetoric the followers of the late Zion had listened to for so long, they weren't up to going head-to-head with hard-eyed, Kevlar-wearing cops packing assault weapons.

Armageddon had come to the Temple of Zion a little early, and it hadn't been what the Seekers of Truth had been led to believe it would be. With their leader scattered over the California desert, they were like sheep without a shepherd and they meekly allowed themselves to be taken into custody. Most of them would be quickly released for lack of evidence, but they had no way of knowing that. They just knew that their way of life had come to an abrupt end and they would have to face the millennium alone.

Lyons's video of the Phalanx blowing the chopper out of the sky was played over and over as the news anchors recounted the rise to power of the cult leader. It was about as tasteless a display as it could possibly be, but it fit right in with the apocalyptic mood of the nation.

AFTER EATING A QUICK DINNER scrounged from the hydrofoil's stores, Blancanales went out on the rear deck. Keegan was standing against the rail and staring out to sea. She turned at his footsteps, and he saw the questions in her eyes.

He walked up to her and put his arm around her shoulders. ''I know that you're kind of at loose ends right now, Anne," he said, "so I have an idea. What do you think about going to Virginia with us to talk with our boss about your old boyfriend Dingo Jones? We're going to do what we can to make sure that he doesn't even try to put his plans into action and you could really help us with that."

When she hesitated, he hurriedly added. "Even if you don't, though, our deal is still on. Like I promised, you'll get a new history that no one will be able to break and we'll relocate you and find you a decent job. But I just thought that you might like to help us put that guy out of circulation permanently. That way you'll never have to look over your shoulder again."

"Like you put Zion away?" she asked. The ripping, roar of the Phalanx as it blasted Zion's chopper out of the air was a sound she would never forget.

"That depends on him," Blancanales said honestly. "Zion didn't have to buy stolen military weapons and plan to hold off the world from his fortress in the desert. In this country, it's not a crime to be a sleazebag and set up a phony religion in a make-believe temple. If people want to be sucked into that sort of thing, that's their problem. But a religion, any religion, can't be allowed to become a front for illegal activities.

"It's a crime to be in possession of stolen military weapons with the intent to use them against American citizens. Even if the world does come to an end, as long as there's a government, it's still a federal crime. And I think that before the authorities are done with the Temple of Zion, we're going to learn that a lot more crimes were done at his order, crimes like murder. So don't waste too much time feeling sorry for him."

"I don't," she said. "It's just that since I got involved with you and your friends, I've seen several people die, and it's not like it is in the movies."

"I understand that," he replied. "It isn't like the movies at all. But you have to remember that the people who died were either trying to kill us or were committing serious crimes. These weren't innocent people by any standard."

He shrugged. "You know the old saying, 'do the crime, do the time.' In this case, though, the time they're doing is eternity, but that was their own choosing."

He got to his feet. "Anyway, I just thought I'd ask. We'll be wrapping up here and pulling out tomorrow morning. When we get back to our headquarters, though, we're going to start looking into Dingo Jones's activities. And while we don't know yet if he has been stashing weapons away, the chances are good that he's into more than just destroying the banking industry. A man who would plan to do something like that is crazy enough to want to set himself up as a dictator and that means he'll need guns."

She knew that he was right. Dingo did want to become at least the emperor of the world, if not a complete dictator. And as she knew too well, he wasn't above using violence to get whatever he wanted, including her. His company had been built on the graves

of those who hadn't wanted to go along with his plans.
None of the deaths had been tagged as murders. But
she knew that in at least one case, the accident that
had claimed the life of the owner of a facility that
Jones had wanted to acquire, had been set up.

"I'll go with you," she said. "But I want a promise
that I'll be free to go whenever I want to."

"I'll personally see to that."

WHEN LYONS RETURNED from settling the bill for the
hydrofoil stay at the moorage, Blancanales took him
aside. "Anne's coming back to the Farm with us."

"Says who?" Lyons asked.

"I've talked to Hal, and he wants to interview her
about this Dingo Jones guy and his plans to take over
the banking industry. He's going to be our next assignment."

"Wonderful."

"What seems to be the problem here, Carl?" Blancanales asked. He was starting to get a little annoyed
at Lyons's touchiness every time Keegan's name was
mentioned.

"You know that I don't like to work with outsiders," Lyons growled.

"If it wasn't for this 'outsider,' as you put it, we'd
still be sitting around here counting our fingers and
toes waiting for something to happen. We could have
done this by ourselves, but by the time we'd have developed enough information to put it all together, Zion
would have completed arming that damned fortress of

his and someone could have gotten hurt trying to bust into there.

"And don't forget if that computer chip she gave us turns out to be what she says it is, we're going to need her information about that Dingo guy. Otherwise, we'll have to screw around for weeks before we get enough on our own to go after him and he might be able to do a lot of damage in that time."

"Okay, okay," Lyons capitulated. "She can come with us."

"I'm not suggesting that we give her a key to the executive washroom or anything like that, but I think we need her right now."

Lyons reached out and clapped his hand on Blancanales's shoulder. "Just be careful, Pol," he said seriously. "She's not our usual type of informant."

"I know."

When Blancanales walked back out on deck, Schwarz came out of the ship's radio room. "He's headed for trouble, isn't he?"

Lyons shook his head. "Better men than him have gone on the rocks over much worse-looking women."

"There is that," Schwarz said. "But I guess if you're going to crash and burn, it might as well be over someone who looks like that."

"Bite your tongue, Gadgets."

CHAPTER TWENTY-NINE

Over Pakistan

"I've got two fast movers lifting off behind us," T. J. Hawkins reported.

Jack Grimaldi pushed forward on the cyclic to bring the speeding gunship even closer to the ground. He couldn't remember if the F-16s had been upgraded to look down-shoot down radar. But even if they had, putting his Hind's belly in the dirt was the best way not to be seen. Flying that low severely limited his maneuverability, but hopefully he wouldn't need to try to get out of the path of a missile if the enemy couldn't see him.

"They're splitting up," Hawkins reported. "One of the guys is going south, and the other one... Oh shit! He's turning our way."

"Let me know if it looks like he's spotted us."

"You got that right."

"Jack," McCarter called back, "what's an IRCM jammer? I have a switch up here with that marking on it."

"That's an infrared countermeasures jammer," Grimaldi replied. "Turn it on, and it'll help break a heat-seeking missile lock."

"It's up and running."

"I think he's spotted us, guys." Hawkins's voice was calm. "He's coming up behind us fast."

"Roger, hang on back there."

Though a jet fighter going up against a helicopter wasn't quite a fair fight, it wasn't completely impossible for the chopper to win. There had been the time a Cobra gunship had taken on an MiG-17 in Cambodia and won, and a similar incident had taken place over the Bekaa Valley during the 1972 war. If McCarter could get the turret gun on target against their faster opponent, they had a chance.

If not, they'd end up a bright splash of crumpled metal and burning fuel in the desert. At least, though, it'd be fairly quick.

To give them something to do more than anything else, Bolan had the Phoenix Force commandos open the firing port windows in the sides of the bird and prepare to add their firepower to the fight. If the jet missed them on the first pass, he'd be flashing by them too fast to aim at, but putting fire in his flight path could make him leery of getting in too close.

"Watch for a missile-launch flare," Grimaldi called out over the com link.

Hawkins didn't have time to reply before he saw the flare of a Sidewinder motor igniting as it dropped off the F-16's launch rail. "Fox one! Fox one!" he called out. "Coming in from starboard."

"Count it down!" Grimaldi called back, his feet poised on the rudder pedals and his hand gripping the cyclic.

"Get ready, get ready, get ready... Now!"

With his feet ready on the rudder pedals, Grimaldi slammed the cyclic stick hard over to the left. The Hind didn't have a rigid rotor system, but it should be good for at least a sixty-degree bank. That would blank the heat of the turbine exhausts and present the armored belly to the missile.

When the Hind rolled over onto her side, the missile's warhead lost its lock, and it flashed by harmlessly. A dozen yards past the nose of the chopper, its proximity fuse detonated.

Grimaldi felt a blow to the collective and knew that one of the rotors had taken a hit from the shrapnel. But when there was no vibration, he knew it had been minor.

"Keep an eye on him," he called back as he rolled the chopper level again. "The bastard has two of those things."

The F-16 had gone into a sharply banked turn after firing its first missile and was coming around to try it again. "He's inbound on the port side this time," James called out.

"Stand by," Grimaldi warned.

When James called out "Fox one, Fox one," Grimaldi had a new trick up his sleeve. Dumping his collective to flatten the spinning rotor blades, he kicked down on the right pedal controlling the tail rotor. With it feathered so it wouldn't counteract the massive torque from the screaming turbines, the Hind simply spun on its axis, presenting its nose to the missile.

With the exhausts pointed away from the Sidewinder and the IRCM jammer confusing the warhead, the missile again lost its lock and flew past them.

But even with both missiles gone, the F-16 wasn't out of the fight yet and bored in for the kill. The Falcon was armed with an M-61 20 mm Vulcan cannon. As Grimaldi well knew, the Vulcan was a fine weapon, probably the best 20 mm in the business. Not for the first time, he cursed the guy who first came up with the idea of selling U.S. aircraft to non-Western nations.

But unlike the heat-seeking Sidewinders, the Vulcan had to be aimed by the pilot, which turned this into a duel between two flyers. It wasn't anyone's idea of a fair fight, though. The F-16 had the 20 mm gun and he was armed with only a 12.7 mm, which was like a man with a pocketknife going up against a man armed with a sword. But even that could turn out right if the knife fighter was good enough.

"David," he called up to his gunner for this flight, "make sure that you give him enough lead. I'll get in as close as I can to cut down on the deflection angle, but you've got to lead him."

"I'll lead the bastard, all right." McCarter tightened his grip on the turret controls. "I'll lead him all the way to hell."

Grimaldi didn't have fire-control radar for the front turret, but he knew the envelope the F-16 had to work with. The jet had gone subsonic to try to stay with the slow-moving helicopter and that was its weakness. No matter what the jet did, he could always turn inside it.

When Grimaldi saw the brief muzzle-flash of the F-16's Vulcan, he snapped the Hind out of the line of fire and the cannon shells passed. As the jet closed on them, McCarter started hosing down the air in front of it. His HUD targeting display wasn't designed for air-to-air combat, so he had switched it off and was eyeballing it.

The 12.7 mm gun was firing a mix of high explosive, armor-piercing, and tracer rounds so McCarter could see where his fire was going. The turret had a limited traverse, but Grimaldi was banking the Hind to give him a better lead.

"Son of a bitch!" McCarter snapped as the F-16 flew away unharmed.

"Give him more lead!" Grimaldi advised.

This time, the Pakistani pilot came in closer before trying it again. This time when the Vulcan's muzzle flamed, Grimaldi dumped his collective, causing the Hind to fall out of the sky as the rounds passed overhead.

McCarter had his firing control all the way over and held down the trigger spraying a steel storm into the F-16's path. Again the jet was fast, but not fast enough. McCarter saw a 12.7 mm tracer march up the side of the Falcon and disappear into the aft fuselage. An instant later, fire started shooting out of the jet exhaust. A second after that, the jet's canopy exploded as the pilot pulled the plug on his bang seat to get out of the dying fighter.

The Briton resisted sending a burst into the parachute and flicked off his master switch. He was done working for now and not a moment too soon. The ammo counter showed that he was down to his last twenty rounds.

"Thank you, Jesus," Hawkins called from the troop compartment.

"You're welcome."

LESS THAN HALF AN HOUR later, Grimaldi crossed the coastline and climbed to five hundred feet above the Indian Ocean. That was high enough to stay out of the drink, but low enough that high-flying radar would have trouble spotting him. Now they would find out if they were going to have a safe place to land or if they would have to swim home. Switching the Hind's radio to Guard Channel, he hit the Push To Talk switch on his cyclic control stick.

"Mayday, Mayday, any U.S. warship. This is Operational Code Word Blue Mountain, I say again, Code Word Blue Mountain requesting emergency assistance. Over," Grimaldi called using Phoenix Force's ultra-high-priority code for the mission. Any U.S. forces hearing Blue Mountain would know that they were friendly and were to be given every possible assistance.

"Code Word Blue Mountain," a welcome voice

came over his headset, "this is Task Force Vigilant. State your emergency, over."

"This is Blue Mountain. I'm flying a Russian Hind gunship. I say again, Hind helicopter wearing Pakistani markings. My weapons are safe and my pylons are empty. Request permission to land on any chopper-capable U.S. warship. Over."

"Roger, copy, Blue Mountain. Maintain station until we can check you out. Over."

"Vigilant, I suggest that you make it quick," Grimaldi radioed back. "I am almost bingo fuel. Over."

"Copy bingo fuel, stand by. Out."

"Fast movers approaching," McCarter called out from the front cockpit.

"I got them," Grimaldi replied. "They look like ours, Tomcats."

For the two fighters to have arrived that quickly, they had to be the *Eisenhower*'s MiG Cap that had been directed to check out the strange intruder. That meant they were within a hundred miles or so from the carrier.

While one of the F-14s stayed high, the other swept his wings forward as he slowed and swooped down on the chopper. Though flying below the speed of sound, the Tomcat was still traveling twice as fast as the gunship. He was on them in a flash, passing close enough to buffet the chopper with its jet wash.

"Double Nuts," Grimaldi called to the Tomcat with the 00 marking of the Carrier Air Group Commander on its nose, "this is the Hind driver. How about giving me a break down here, old buddy. Another pass like that and I'll be in the drink.''

''Sorry about that, Hind. I had to check your pylons.''

''Roger that, Double Nuts. But even a blind blue suiter could have seen that they aren't even mounted.''

The Tomcat pilot chuckled. ''Roger, Hind. You're clear to proceed. Take a heading of zero-two-eight. We'll escort you in.''

''Bearing zero-two-eight, roger,'' Grimaldi confirmed as he gently banked the Hind to the north. Any aggressive moves would earn him a missile up the ass, so this was no time to play games. Overhead, the two Tomcats circled as slowly as they could with one always in firing position in case he did something stupid.

The Hind's fuel gauge was looking a little lean when the comforting shape of the *Eisenhower* finally came into view on the horizon. At the same time, the carrier's CIC came back on the radio. ''Hind, this is Task Force CIC. Bear two-three-seven and approach from the stern, over.''

''This is Hind, roger. Turning to two-three-seven and making my approach now. Out.''

As they got closer, McCarter could see the carrier's Phalanx mounts turning to track them, and he was careful to keep both of his hands visible through the canopy in case anyone was watching them through binoculars. This was no time to die in a hail of titanium 20 mm shells.

Grimaldi greased the Hind to a feather-soft landing

as if he were carrying a cargo of raw eggs. One of his trademark, fancy balls-out landings wasn't in order today. As soon as the wheels were down, he killed the fuel feed to the turbines and the big five-bladed rotor started winding down. "We're home, guys," he called over his shoulder.

"And Mother has come to greet us," McCarter said as he looked out the gunner's canopy.

Two squads of Marines in Kevlar vests and helmets with M-16s in their hands marched out to surround the chopper. When Bolan saw their reception committee, he reached to undo his assault harness.

"We need to leave our hardware in here," he said. "And step out slowly. Don't make any sudden moves until I can establish our bona fides."

"Home sweet home and we don't even get a cake?" James grinned.

"I don't care what's on the menu," Hawkins said. "Just as long as they don't try to feed us MREs."

As soon as the Stony Man warriors were lined up on the flight deck, a pair of Marines came forward to search them. They stood stock-still and allowed themselves to be patted down. It was a drill they were all familiar with. Anyone showing up at an American base in an enemy aircraft was bound to be treated suspiciously.

"There are small arms, ammunition and communications gear in the chopper, Sergeant," Bolan warned the Marine NCO. "I need them secured."

"Yes, sir," the sergeant replied, motioning for two more of his men to check the Hind.

When the personal searches were completed, the sergeant turned to a Marine major. "They're clean, sir."

"Take them to the detention deck."

Before the sergeant could reply, Bolan stepped forward. "Major, I am Colonel Rance Pollock, United States Army, and I request that my men be given suitable quarters while I talk to the task force commander. And, if possible, they could use a meal."

The Marine officer hadn't expected this and brought a radio to his mouth. After a short conversation, he turned back to Bolan. "If you will come with me, sir, the captain will meet you."

"And my men?"

"They will be quartered with my Marines," the major answered.

AS THE REST OF THE TEAM were being hosted by the Marines in their temporary quarters, Bolan and McCarter were deep inside the ship in a secure communications room with the ship's captain. Normally, Stony Man didn't like to involve their military support in their activities anymore than was absolutely necessary, but this was an exception. The *Eisenhower*'s task force was in the Indian Ocean to provide America's answer to the threat of nuclear war, and the task force commander needed to know what was going on. Also, they needed to use his secure communications to talk to the Farm.

"The Keyhole birds are showing that you did a good job," Hal Brognola reported. "We're just starting to get the photos in now and it looks thorough. The President's passing the information on to the Indian prime minister in the hope that it will get him to back down, as well. If not, there's always the joint chiefs' option, and you're sitting on a big part of it right now.

"The big news," he continued, "is that we may finally have a lead on the guy who started the millennium plague. Kurtzman has suspected a Bosnian Muslim, a Dr. Insmir Vedik, for some time now. But he's not been able to find out where he went after the Baltic conflict slowed down. The last thing we knew was that Vedik had been seen with a Syrian volunteer unit. To make a long story short, one of Katz's contacts in Lebanon reported that Vedik was sighted in Beirut a few days ago."

"Was it a positive ID?"

"Apparently so. In fact, the woman who saw him, a Croatian nurse working for a French medical team, was later killed in what looks like a purposeful hit to silence her."

"That sounds firm enough."

"It does. And the President wants you to look into it. I know that you guys have earned a stand-down, but this is something we need to check out before the trail gets too cold."

"If you'll have the President grease the skids, we'll saddle up immediately."

"I was hoping you'd say that."

"On another topic, how's Barbara?" Bolan asked.

"She's still okay. But she had a bit of a relapse. Nothing too serious, but the problem is that she's not free of the disease. None of the plague patients are. With all of them, the treatment is only holding the disease at bay, and the treatment isn't much better than the disease. If a complication arises and they have to stop treatment, the anthrax goes active again and kills them in a matter of a day or so."

"That sounds to me like we need to find this Vedik guy and get this sorted out."

"That's why I want you in Israel ASAP," Brognola said. "Katz will meet you there and give you the cover to get you into Beirut. Also, if you need to keep Rust on board, that's been cleared as well."

"We'll get there as fast as we can," Bolan said. "And Hal?"

"Yes?"

"Tell Barbara that we're on him."

"Will do."

CHAPTER THIRTY

The U.S.S. Eisenhower

Bolan turned to the ship's captain, who had been trying hard not to overhear his guest's classified conversation. "We need to get to Israel as soon as possible," he said. "Can you help us with that?"

The captain thought for a moment. "I may have to hand you off to the blue suiters midway through," he said. "But I can have a COD fly you to Diego Garcia and let the Air Force take you from there. Will that be satisfactory?"

"We don't care who's driving the bus, just as long as we get there."

The twin turboprop C-2A COD wasn't named for a fish, the acronym stood for Carry On Delivery. The CODs served as a carrier task force's aerial delivery trucks. Everything from mail to replacements to emergency supplies were flown from land bases or even other ships and delivered to the carrier.

"I'll see that you go first class, too," the captain promised. "I'll have the officers' mess put together an inflight meal service for you."

AFTER A HOT SHOWER and a meal, J. R. Rust laid on a borrowed bunk in the Marine quarters to wait for whatever was coming next. A Navy corpsman had checked the wound in his leg and had pronounced it to be healing well. It was still a little tender, but nothing that should hamper him too much.

The CIA man was still assessing what he had just been through. Even with all the field work he had done for the Company, none of it had compared to what he had experienced during the past few days. He had been given a rare look inside a part of the government that few people even knew existed. Every nation had its secret organizations, but Phoenix Force and the Stony Man Farm team were beyond secret. Had he not gone to Pakistan with them himself, he wouldn't have believed that such a group existed outside of a TV show.

More important, he had been part of a group of men that had changed history before it had had a chance to happen, and they treated it as merely another job. All the world would ever know about the mission was that India and Pakistan had backed down from a serious confrontation. Ho hum, a sentence or two in the evening news and CNN would give it an entire two and a half minutes.

Even though he had been in on the operation from the very beginning, he was having trouble believing it himself. It made him wonder how many other times Striker and Phoenix Force had intervened to make the world a safer place to live, but he was almost afraid to ask.

When Bolan and McCarter walked into the room the team had been given, Rust saw that something was up and he joined the other commandos. When Bolan briefed them on the change in plans, no one complained about the mission having been extended. There were a few logistical questions, but that was it.

"What about me?" Rust asked as the meeting broke up. "Am I in on this one, too?"

"That's up to you," Bolan replied. "I can send you back if you want, or you can come with us."

"You're going to Beirut, right?"

Bolan nodded.

"I'm familiar with the place and I speak a couple of the most common languages spoken there. I think I might be useful."

"I was hoping you'd say that."

AS THE REST of the team slept on the flight across the Indian Ocean, Mack Bolan watched the dark sea pass by below him, and his thoughts went to Barbara Price and the millennium plague.

In many ways, stopping a nuclear war in India had been of less importance than tracking down the man who had loosed the plague on the world. The war with Pakistan could have killed millions, but if the plague wasn't stopped it could kill tens of millions before it burned itself out as the other plagues of history had done before.

Bolan understood war as perhaps no other man on earth did. He knew all the reasons, both good and bad, that made men kill one another, and he knew in great detail how it was done. He could not, however, even begin to understand the mind of a man who would turn a disease into a weapon.

If the world was going to come to an end this millennium, it would be a man-made plague that would do it, not any nuclear weapon that had ever been designed.

Bioweapons had always been the greatest threat that modern science presented to the survival of humanity, not nuclear weapons. No matter how devastating, even the biggest nuke only affected the people in the immediate vicinity of the blast. A mutated disease, though, could eradicate every human from the face of the planet. And it was more difficult to guard against a microbe than it was to prevent a missile from being launched.

Even so, as long as there were men behind the microbes, Mack Bolan would find them and make them pay for their crimes. That was what the Executioner did best.

* * * * *

The heart-stopping action concludes with
ZERO HOUR
Book II of FALL OF THE WEST,
available in November.

James Axler

OUTLANDERS™

ARMAGEDDON AXIS

What was supposed to be the seat of power after the nuclear holocaust, a vast installation inside Mount Rushmore—is a new powerbase of destruction. Kane and his fellow exiles venture to the hot spot, where they face an old enemy conspiring to start the second wave of Armageddon.

GOUT11

An old enemy poses a new threat....

JAMES AXLER

DEATH LANDS

Gaia's Demise

Ryan Cawdor's old nemesis, Dr. Silas Jamaisvous, is behind a deadly new weapon that uses electromagnetic pulses to control the weather and the gateways, and even disrupts human thinking processes.

As these waves doom psi-sensitive Krysty, Ryan challenges Jamaisvous to a daring showdown for America's survival....

Book 2 in the Baronies Trilogy, three books that chronicle the strange attempts to unify the East Coast baronies—a bid for power in the midst of anarchy....